Peace

KERRY SERIES BOOK 3

CAROL CANNON

Cover by Perry Elisabeth Design | perryelisabethdesign.com
Interior Formatting by Crystal L Barnes | booksbybarnes.com

"Peace I leave with you;
my peace I give you.
I do not give to you
as the world gives.
Do not let your hearts
be troubled and
do not be afraid."

John 14:27 (NIV)

*I dedicate this book to my daughters, my son,
my granddaughters, and my grandsons.*

*I thank God every day
for the many ways in which
you have blessed my life.*

I couldn't love you more!

I want to thank you for choosing to read my book *Peace*, the third book in my Kerry Series. I chose to name this book "peace" because that's what I want in my life. It's not that I believe that my life could ever be without chaos and discord. The peace I seek is the peace that God offers each of us. That's the peace that Dixie finds in her life after it's been turned upside down. My prayer for you is that you will find God's peace in your life.

Carol Cannon

List of Characters by Family				
Fearsome Foursome	Layne Bryson Clairmont Weaver	Nona Jane Foxx-Harris	Dixie Rae Randolph Bradley	Betty Jo (Elizabeth Jolene) Chapman Breedlow
Husband	Mark	Bill (William) (Divorced)	Alex (Alexander)	Don (Donald)
Child	Nathan Heather (wife) Grayson (son)	Grace Adrian Bannerman (husband)	Hailey Josh Merrill (husband) Kaiden (daughter) Alexa (daughter) Rae (daughter)	Ethan Chloe (wife) Kelli (daughter) Matthew (son) Chase (son)
Child	Blair Zeke Coby (husband) Rachel (daughter), Madison (daughter)		Jason	Lily Matt Morton (divorced) Kendall (daughter)
Child	Aaron Jenny (fiancé)			

Chapter One

*D*ixie wiped the flour from her hands onto her apron before brushing the stray hair out of her eyes. She had just finished mixing a batch of bread dough. Some people might think it was strange to be making bread at three o'clock in the morning, but it had become a regular part of Dixie's night life. She'd been awakened yet again by worries that invaded her dreams. Once she was awake, she'd found it impossible to fall back asleep. Her mother had called it "busy brain," when random thoughts begin to swirl around in your mind and returning to a restful night's sleep becomes impossible.

Dixie had tossed and turned trying to escape the nagging thoughts and had finally given up on trying to go back to sleep, deciding her time would be better spent making her special cinnamon and raisin bread for her family, especially her granddaughters. She depended upon the distraction of mixing, kneading, braiding, and baking her special bread to help her find a little peace of mind.

Baking bread had become her "thing" since she'd broken her hand in three places when the chair she was standing on to put up the last strip of wallpaper in her first apartment had flipped. She'd reached out with her hand to stop her fall, which hadn't worked out the way she'd thought it would. As part of her physical therapy to strengthen the muscles in her hand, the therapist had suggested she might try kneading bread. Dixie discovered that she enjoyed the whole process of preparing homemade bread. Over the years, she developed a variety of her own secret recipes for homemade bread that she'd only shared with two people– her sister and daughter.

The batch she was making now, cinnamon and raisin bread, was her three granddaughters'–Kaiden, age 9; Alexa, age 7; and Rae, age 3– favorite. They called it "Nonnie Bread." "Nonnie" was the name that Kaiden had given her when she found it hard to say "Nana." Even though Dixie had tried at first to get Kaiden to say "Nana," she now loved her special "Nonnie" name. She would take them a warm loaf as soon as it came out of the oven, so they could have a special treat for breakfast.

As Dixie kneaded the dough, her mind left behind the pleasant thoughts of her granddaughters and returned to the worries that had robbed her of another restful night's sleep.

What is going on with Jason?

For the past couple of weeks, Dixie had noticed that Jason seemed anxious. He hadn't been his usual, easy-going, lovable self. What concerned Dixie was that he wasn't willing to talk to her or Hailey about what was going on with him. In the past, whenever he was bothered by anything, either they'd talk it out or he'd go to his big sister. This time he'd done neither.

Dixie smiled remembering how Jason was the child that she'd been told by her doctor would be impossible to conceive after the difficult birth of their first child. Hailey was nine years old when Dixie and Alex dropped her off at her Aunt Scarlett's while they enjoyed a relaxing weekend at St. Simon's Island. It had only been a few weeks after that weekend when flu-like symptoms sent Dixie to the doctor hoping to get some relief. It was during that appointment that she'd learned that the improbability of having another child was now most probable.

Alex had been ecstatic when Dixie shared her news that there would be another child. To say that Dixie had been upset at the prospect of having another child would have been an understatement. Dixie had been devastated. A baby hadn't been what she'd envisioned she would be dealing with as she headed into her forties. Dixie's mother had proclaimed it to be a true miracle from God. Dixie hadn't been sure about that, but the minute she held her newborn son in her arms for the very first time, she'd fallen hopelessly in love. Those big blue eyes of his had looked back at her as if he had always known she was going to be his mother. She couldn't put into words what his look had meant to her, but from that moment on, Jason had her heart.

Jason had not only captured Dixie's heart, but he also had his big sister's heart. The day they brought Jason home, Hailey claimed him as hers. She was beyond thrilled to have a brother and wanted to take him with her wherever she went. Dixie had half-heartedly set up a nursery for their second child using the crib that Alex had made for Hailey, but each time she put Jason down in the crib he cried until Dixie picked him up. She'd rock him, then gently lay him back in the crib, but before she'd gotten to the door he'd be crying. The doctor's advice had been to allow the baby to cry. He assured her that within a few minutes Jason would cry himself to sleep. Dixie had tried to follow the doctor's advice for several nights, but after an hour of listening to Jason's nonstop crying, she'd give in and pick him up. His constant crying had left her exhausted and frustrated.

One night after Dixie had put Jason to bed in his crib, he'd started up with his usual crying. She'd gone to Hailey's room to kiss her good night. She was concerned when she found Hailey's bed empty. After she and Alex looked everywhere they could think she might be, they checked the baby's room. There was Hailey with her arms wrapped around her baby brother, both sound asleep. Jason slept through the night with Hailey next to him. After Alex reinforced the crib making sure it would hold both a ten-year-old and a baby, that's where Hailey insisted on sleeping each night for the next year. Dixie believed Jason's crib was where Hailey's love of caring for children had begun.

Dixie gave a deep sigh as she thought about Jason, who was back in that same room which had once held his crib. She wished she could return to those simpler times when problems were so easily solved. Now he was thirty years old and not a baby, which made things a great deal more complicated. Jason was as smart and as talented as his big sister but had never been as determined as her. From the time Hailey was ten years old, she'd told anyone who would listen that she was going to be a "baby doctor," and that's exactly what she'd become. When Jason was ten he'd told everyone who would listen that he was going to be Raphael, one of the Teenage Mutant Ninja Turtles. That pretty much summed up the difference between the two siblings.

Jason wasn't the only concern that was keeping Dixie away from a good night's sleep. She was also worried about her relationship with Alex, her husband of forty-six years. Alex was a patient man, but since Jason had moved back home it had become obvious that he was losing his patience with the whole situation. He'd always claimed that Dixie spoiled their son. He thought she was wrong when she helped Jason out by loaning him money for whatever he needed until he could get back on his feet. Dixie didn't see it that way. She felt she was being a supportive parent. But now there was no doubt that the way she was handling this situation with Jason was causing a rift in her marriage. Dixie wasn't sure what she could do to make it better, but she recognized that something needed to be done and the sooner the better.

Dixie was taking the bread out of the oven when she heard the door to Alex's bedroom open. She glanced up at the clock. She couldn't believe it was six o'clock already. She knew that Alex would be pleased to have freshly baked cinnamon and raisin bread for breakfast.

Alex walked into the kitchen that was filled with the aromas of cinnamon and freshly baked bread. "That is one of the best smells in all of this world." He stopped as he took in the scene before him and added, "Oh, Dixie, have you been up half the night baking again?"

Dixie sheepishly smiled up at him as he came over to plant a kiss on her forehead and squeeze her shoulders. "I know it's crazy, but I just couldn't go back to sleep after I had another one of those awful dreams."

"Another one?" Alex turned her around, so he could look in her face. "You can't keep this up, Dixie."

Dixie hurriedly got up to make Alex a cup of coffee. "I know, but you don't need to worry. I'll have this all under control soon. How 'bout you slice off a couple pieces of bread while I get your coffee."

They'd gotten a pod coffeemaker as a Christmas gift from Hailey. Dixie loved how quickly she could make a perfect cup of coffee every time. Alex's day always started out with having his morning coffee, but Dixie was only an occasional coffee drinker. This morning she got down two cups knowing that she'd need that shot of caffeine to make it through the day.

As Alex cut into the warm loaf, he asked, "Did you have that same dream where you're driving the school bus with Kaiden, Alexa, and Rae on board and the bridge collapses into the river a hundred feet below?"

Dixie brought the two cups of steaming coffee over to the island and set one down in front of Alex. "No." She shuddered. "This one was more disturbing than scary."

"There's a difference?"

Dixie took a moment to reflect on the dream that had roused her out of a deep sleep. "I think so. Even though much of the dream was jumbled and confusing, it left me with an unsettled feeling, like something bad is about to happen."

Alex gave a short laugh. "Don't tell me you believe your dreams are telling the future?"

Dixie shook her head. "I hope not. There's been enough bad around here lately. I'm not sure I can handle anymore."

They sat in silence for several minutes drinking their coffee and remembering all the bad that had gone on in the past year and a half. Their good friends Layne and Mark had gone through a bad time with an accident that left Mark in a coma hovering between life and death for several days. To make matters even worse, it was Don, the husband of another close friend, Betty Jo, who'd caused that accident. Thankfully, Mark had fully recovered. Because of the accident, Don had discovered he was a diabetic, and now had his diabetes under control. Then, just when life seemed to be returning to normal, their friend Nona's life was almost destroyed by her soon-to-be-ex-husband's girlfriend. Around that same time, Jason quit another job and moved home. That's why Dixie was tired of bad things happening and was hoping for only good things coming their way.

Alex reached over to give Dixie's knee a squeeze. "Well, your homemade cinnamon and raisin bread sure isn't a bad thing."

He stood up, putting the final bite of bread in his mouth, and took his coffee cup to the sink. "I need to get going. I'm supposed to meet Josh at the jobsite at seven."

"Would you do me a favor on your way to work?" Dixie asked as she wrapped up a fresh loaf of her cinnamon raisin bread. "Would you drop this off at Hailey's for the girls to have with their breakfast?"

Alex took the bread. "Sure, but you do know you're spoiling those girls, right?"

"I know, but that's the best part of being a grandmother."

Alex laughed and gave Dixie a kiss on the top of her head before heading out the door.

Dixie watched Alex leave, thinking how thankful she was that their son-in-law Josh worked with Alex. Lately, Alex had given more of the responsibilities of the management of Bradley Contracting Company over to Josh. Alex was getting older and wanted to slow down. Knowing that Josh would be there to take over the company that Alex had built up into a successful business was a good feeling. Her heart felt a twinge of regret when she recalled how Alex's dream at one time had been to hand over his business to his only son, but, sadly, Jason had never taken much of an interest in the business. Dixie knew that Jason was a disappointment to Alex, but didn't know what she could do to change that.

When Jason quit this last job, Alex asked him to come to work for him until he found another job. Jason had turned down his father's offer, giving a detailed explanation of how he couldn't go on job interviews if he was committed to going to work every day. However, those job interviews that Jason was sure he'd be going on never seemed to materialize. Dixie knew that Alex was getting frustrated with Jason's situation. She knew it bothered him that Jason was still in bed when he left for work each morning. In a phone conversation that she'd once overheard between Alex and Josh, Alex had remarked that he suspected the only thing his son was committed to was avoiding work.

Dixie picked up her cup and drank the last of her coffee. As she stared into the empty cup, she wished she knew what she could do to make everything better for her family. She set the cup in the sink and began to clean up. It was Tuesday and she needed to get ready for her weekly Skinny Dippers weight-loss meeting. She was looking forward to spending time with her friends.

Once Dixie finished cleaning up the kitchen, it didn't take her long to get ready for her Skinny Dippers meeting. She had one of those flawless complexions that needed very little makeup, only a little blush and dab of mascara on her pale eyelashes. She never needed to spend much time styling her hair. She could just brush, finger-fluff, and go. She had always been one of those attractive women that other people noticed with her thick auburn hair, emerald-green eyes, and perfect white teeth. Her figure had also garnered her a great deal of attention when she was younger. However, as she'd gotten older, it had become more difficult to keep the pounds off her small five-foot two-inch frame. She was in a perpetual battle with her weight because she loved cooking and eating exceptionally good food. That's why she needed her Skinny Dippers meetings.

As usual, Dixie was ten minutes early to the meeting. When she was a child, her mother had purposefully made them late for everything. She had delighted in making an entrance with her two polished daughters in tow. Dixie had loathed those late entrances and made a promise to herself that when she was grown she'd always be early.

Dixie climbed the back stairs of the Dream Bean Coffee Shop up to the room where the Skinny Dippers met. Doreen and Patti, the two leaders for their meeting today, were rushing around getting the room ready for the weigh-ins and motivational lecture that always followed. When it was her turn Dixie took off her shoes and stepped up onto the scales. She'd tried to avoid sweets all week and hoped the effort had been worth it. She'd already decided that if she didn't lose any weight after making such a grand sacrifice, she was going to order two cinnamon twists and hot chocolate with whipped cream downstairs at the coffee shop after the meeting. She stepped off the scales holding her breath as she waited for Doreen to write down her weight on her card. Doreen looked up at Dixie and smiled as she handed back her card.

Dixie let out her breath as she studied the numbers Doreen had recorded on her card. She wanted to jump up and down and shout, but restrained herself. She put on her shoes and walked over to take a seat on the third row. She looked down at her card one more time to make sure she'd read it correctly. She'd lost 2 pounds! That's the most she'd ever lost in one week. She was so proud of herself that she was considering ordering two chocolate-covered donuts as her reward for a week of sacrifice.

"So, how'd you do?" Layne asked as she sat down next to Dixie.

Dixie jumped at the sound of Layne's voice.

Layne laughed, reaching out to steady Dixie, "I didn't mean to scare you!"

"Sorry, I was off in another world."

"Well, now that you're back in this one, did your plan of cutting out sweets to lose weight work in your favor?"

"It did!"

"Did what?" Betty Jo asked as she sat down on the other side of Dixie.

"I lost weight. Which is good and bad."

Betty Jo looked at her confused. "How can losing weight be bad?"

"Because that means that giving up sweets, one of my life's greatest pleasures," Dixie explained, "works if you want to lose weight,"

Betty Jo shook her head. "I see what you mean. That is bad."

"What's bad?" Nona asked as she hurriedly took her seat on the other side of Layne.

As usual, Nona was late. Patti was just starting what was considered the motivational part of the meeting.

"I'll tell you all about it after the meeting," Layne whispered as she turned her attention to Patti.

Dixie, Layne, Betty Jo, and Nona rarely found this part of the meeting inspirational, but they politely listened as Patti explained the ways in which they could avoid the pitfalls of not following a healthy diet. When the meeting was over, the four friends headed down the back stairs to the Dream Bean Coffee Shop, which had the best blueberry muffins and chocolate donuts in the South. The location of the Skinny Dippers meeting had been the main reason the four women joined this particular weight loss group over six years ago. After weighing in, they felt they deserved a little indulgence following a tiresome week of denial.

The four best friends settled into their regular places in their regular booth. Layne's husband Mark referred to them as the "Fearsome Foursome." In the past couple of years, with Mark's near-death accident and Nona being stalked by the obsessed, crazy girlfriend of her soon-to-be-ex-husband, they'd proved that as a foursome, they were fearsome.

By the time the waitress arrived at their table to take their order, Dixie had made the decision that she was going to reward her weight loss with one chocolate-covered donut. Two would be overkill, but one was just right. Thinking of ordering a donut made Dixie think about cake, which made her think about the engagement party she was hosting along with Betty Jo and Nona for Layne's son Aaron and his fiancée Saturday night.

After they'd each given their order, Dixie said, "I think we're pretty well set for the engagement party, but we need to finalize a few things before the big event. Are we still on for our medicure on Friday followed by lunch at The Grill?" "Medicure" was what the women called it when they treated themselves to a pedicure and manicure—because afterwards, they felt better about life. Thus, the name "medicure."

Layne placed her hand on top of Dixie's. "Aaron is sure hoping you're making your special Chocolate Ice Storm Cake for the party. Just thinking about that cake makes my mouth water."

Dixie laughed. "If that's the cake Aaron wants, that's the cake I'll make."

Layne smiled at her, "I can't thank you enough for hosting this party for Aaron and Jenny. They are so excited about it. I think Jenny has driven Aaron crazy deciding what she's going to wear."

Dixie patted Layne's hand. "I'm sure that whatever she wears, she'll be beautiful."

Betty Jo leaned forward in her chair. "Well, I can't wait! I've been looking forward to it since we set the date for the party. Don said to tell you he'd bring the flowers over around ten Saturday morning if that's okay."

"That's perfect," Dixie said. "By the way, do you know if Lily is bringing anyone special with her? I told her she was welcome to bring someone, but I haven't heard for sure if she was coming solo or not."

Lily was Betty Jo's daughter. Dixie had been secretly hoping that Jason and Lily would get together. After all, they'd been such good friends at one time. Maybe tomorrow night would give them the opportunity to rekindle their friendship or maybe become even more than friends.

"She's coming solo," Betty Jo said, sounding embarrassed. "I'm sorry she didn't let you know. She does know better than—"

"Oops!" Layne interrupted. "That's totally my fault, Betty Jo."

Turning to Dixie, she went on to explain. "Lily and I were talking the other day and she told me to let you know she was coming alone. I totally forgot to mention it to you."

Dixie waved her hand. "It's no problem at all. I'm just thrilled she's coming."

Then turning to Nona, Dixie raised an eyebrow and with a sly smile asked, "So, who's your plus-one going to be for this get-together?"

Dixie had been wondering if Nona would bring Bill, her ex-husband who wanted Nona back in his life, or Monty, her divorce lawyer who seemed to Dixie to be much more than that to Nona. Dixie saw the blush rise on Nona's cheeks when she looked around to see that they were all staring at her waiting for her response.

"Monty."

They all sighed with relief. Even though they'd been friends with Bill at one time, none of them had liked the way he'd left Nona for another woman. Then that woman had tried to destroy Nona's life. Thankfully, she'd been unsuccessful, but not from lack of trying.

Layne seemed to be the only one who had the nerve to express what Dixie had been thinking. "Thank God!"

"So, how is it going with Monty?" Betty Jo asked.

Nona grinned at her. "He sure isn't the conceited jerk I thought he was. Underneath that arrogant facade of his is a funny, considerate, nice man."

"Not to mention knock-your-socks-off attractive," Betty Jo added.

"Well, there is that too," Nona agreed

Changing the subject, Dixie asked Nona. "How's it going with Mr. James?" When Mr. James, Nona's father, had been diagnosed with Alzheimer's, she'd sold her house and moved in with him. It'd been a huge adjustment for Nona. All eyes looked once again to Nona, waiting for her answer.

Nona put a smile on her face. "Good, really good."

"'Really good' huh?" Dixie asked looking directly at her.

Nona's smile left her face. "Okay, the truth is it's not so good. It's tough every single day watching my strong, intelligent father disappear before my eyes."

Dixie turned to give Nona a hug. "I'm so sorry."

Layne and Betty Jo reached out and took Nona's hands.

"I hate that you're having to go through this, Nona." Layne patted her hand. "Is there anything we can do?"

Nona gave them a grateful look. "You're doing it right now. Just being here with y'all is the best thing for me."

At that moment, their waitress arrived at the table with their food. Dixie's mouth was watering as the waitress set the warm donut with chocolate icing running down the sides and pooling on the plate in front of her. She couldn't wait for the others to be served. She picked it up, closed her eyes, and took her first bite. It was everything she'd hoped it would be.

"I guess you really have been missing those sweets." Smiling, Layne watched Dixie devour her donut.

Dixie wiped her mouth with her napkin before answering. "You just don't know how much I needed this donut. I've been up since three o'clock this morning."

Betty Jo reached out for Dixie's hand. "Oh, Dixie, not another bad dream."

Dixie nodded. "I guess I'm worrying so much during the day that those worries become my nightmares at night." She wrapped her arms around herself as she remembered her dream. "Y'all, this one was so vivid and just plain creepy!"

Layne, Nona, and Betty Jo looked at one another. Nona put her arm around Dixie and asked in a gentle voice, "Do you think it would help to tell us about it?"

Dixie hesitated. "It might, but are you sure y'all want to hear about it?"

"It's okay, Dixie. I think after all we've been through lately, we can handle it," Layne reassured her.

Dixie took a deep breath and began in a hushed tone, "I dreamed that Alex, Hailey, Jason, and I were at the lake. It was one of those perfect, beautiful summer days, but it was back when the kids were little. Hailey was about thirteen and Jason was three. We were all down at the dock and the kids were running and playing when suddenly Jason just ran off the end of dock into the water. He sank like a stone. For some reason, I was the only one who'd noticed that he'd gone into the water."

Dixie paused, wondering why she'd been the only one to notice Jason going into the lake. She put the thought out of her mind and continued.

"I dived in after him, swimming straight down to try to catch up with him. I remember him looking up at me, frantically reaching up to me, opening his mouth trying to scream. I could see bubbles coming from his mouth drifting up towards me. I kept swimming downward as fast as I could, trying to grab his hand to pull him up. I remember thinking that if we went any deeper, I wouldn't be able to make it back up to the surface."

Dixie vividly remembered this part of the dream when she knew she couldn't go back up to the surface for air but made the decision to keep going down deeper and deeper.

"I didn't care through, because I knew I couldn't let Jason die alone. I kept swimming down, but he was sinking away from me faster than I could swim toward him. I remember watching and feeling helpless as he slipped further and further away from me, the image of him growing blurrier and blurrier in the murky water."

Dixie looked up at her friends who had been intently listening. "And that's when I woke up."

No one spoke for several minutes. It was as if each of them had lived the dream along with Dixie.

Finally, Betty Jo broke the silence. "Well, I can sure see why that dream would have made it hard to fall back to sleep!"

"I felt like I was going down in that lake with you, Dixie!" Layne added breathlessly, putting her hand to her heart.

Nona looked at Dixie and asked with concern, "What's going on with Jason? What has you so worried that you would dream up such an awful nightmare?"

Dixie thought about her question before answering, "That's just it. I can't figure out why I dreamed that. Nothing has changed with Jason."

"You're sure nothing else has happened that's made you amp up your worrying?" Betty Jo asked.

Dixie shook her head. "The only thing I can think of is the situation with Jason is not getting better. It's not worse, but it's not any better, and that does worry me."

"Well then, we're going to have to double up on our prayers for Jason," Betty Jo declared with confidence.

Layne agreed. "We can sure do that."

Dixie smiled, thankful once again for the blessing of her friends' love and support.

Chapter Two

As Nona drove back to her father's house, her home now, she couldn't stop thinking about Dixie's dream. It was obvious to her that somewhere deep inside, Dixie was worried that everything that was going on with Jason would eventually kill them both. That was a disturbing thought to Nona because she knew firsthand how worrying about your child could drive you to having nightmares. Nona had her share of worries about why Grace, her only child, refused to speak to her.

Nona had worried about their relationship continuously for months, even when she was sleeping. Then one day she'd concluded that worrying about it was useless. What she knew for certain was that all her worrying hadn't helped their relationship the least bit. She was now at the point where, if she started worrying about whether Grace would ever be a part of her life again, she'd take her fears and worries and imagine herself physically placing them in God's hand. Since she'd started doing that, her worries had stopped. She made a mental note to talk to Dixie about doing the same thing with Jason.

Nona parked her car just outside the back door and went into the house through the kitchen. After setting her father's prescription meds on the table, she went in search of him.

"Daddy," she called out as she walked down the hall toward her father's study where she was sure she'd find him, "I'm back from my meeting." She was surprised to find the door to his study closed.

She tapped on the door as she opened it. "Daddy?"

To her surprise, Nona found the room empty. She checked the other rooms, all the while hoping that her father hadn't left the house again. The last time he'd left on his own, he'd gotten confused and lost his way. It was hours before they'd found him. When she didn't find him in the front living room, fear began to take over her mind. She was just walking out of the room to get her cell phone to call for help when she caught the sound of voices drifting in from the front porch.

When she opened the front door, she was relieved to find her father peacefully rocking back and forth in one of the white wicker rocking chairs on the porch. She rushed to him.

"Daddy, I was getting worried when I couldn't find you in the house." She hugged his neck. "What are you doing out here?"

He smiled up at her as he pointed to his left. "I'm visiting with William. It's such a nice day that we decided to sit out here on the porch to partake of this fine weather."

Nona looked to where her father was pointing. There in the other white wicker rocker sat her ex-husband, Bill, looking for all the world as if he belonged there. For a moment, Nona was speechless. When she finally found her words, she realized by her father's smile and the way he was looking at Bill that he didn't remember that Bill was her ex-husband, and not her present husband.

Swallowing the words she really wanted to say, and not wanting to upset her father, she managed to say through gritted teeth, "Hey, Bill. You didn't mention that you were coming over here today to see Daddy."

Bill stopped rocking and looked up at Nona, giving her a wink. "Well, darlin', you know how much I enjoy talking to Mr. James. I found myself in the area and just couldn't resist stopping by to say 'hey' to your daddy."

"Glad you did, William! Glad you did," her father boomed out, "but

I believe I've extended myself beyond my capabilities for conversation on this fine morning. I'll take my leave if you would be gracious enough to assist in prying my feeble body from this rocker."

He began to ease himself to a standing position.

Both Bill and Nona hurried over to help. When her father was out of the rocker, he stood for a minute to get his balance. Nona helped him into the house. Bill started to follow them in, but one look from Nona let him know he wasn't welcome.

Nona settled her father in his bed. He'd started taking a short nap in the mornings a few weeks ago. When he took a morning nap, he seemed to be less muddled in the evening, which seemed to be the hardest time of day for him when dealing with his Alzheimer's. When she was satisfied that her father was comfortable, she returned to the porch to confront Bill.

"Why didn't you do the kind thing and get in your car and drive far away from me?" Nona hissed, not wanting to wake her father.

"I have to admit that I did consider doing that very thing for just a moment." Bill smirked. "But I didn't want to miss out on this lovely conversation we're having."

"What are you really doing here, Bill?" Nona demanded.

"I came by hoping you'd be home." Bill reached out for her. "I thought we could talk,"

Nona stepped back, wrapping her arms around herself. Exasperated, she said, "Come on, Bill, let's be honest. What is there to talk about?"

Bill dropped his arms in defeat. "We've never really talked about all that happened with Amy."

Nona sighed. "You have to know that Amy's the last person I want to talk to you about."

"I just want you to know that I had no clue she was crazy and would come after you."

Nona walked to the wicker rocker and sat down. "I don't blame you for what she did to me. Can't we move past all of that and get on with our lives?"

Bill sat down in the other rocker. He leaned in close to Nona. "That's just it, Nona, I want you to be a part of my life again."

Seeing the sad look on his face, for a second, Nona almost felt sorry for him. Thankfully, the second passed. She couldn't forget what he'd put her through with his affair and throwing her aside after forty-plus years of marriage. He could just take those sad eyes of his somewhere else.

Nona stood up and, putting both hands on his shoulders, looked directly into his eyes. "That's never going to happen, Bill."

Nona walked to the front door. Before opening the door, she turned, and looked back at a stunned Bill. She gave him a wink. "So, move on, darlin'."

As Nona stepped into the house and shut the door behind her, she knew that she'd finally closed the door not only on Bill, but on the life they'd once shared.

Layne could not get Dixie's dream out of her mind. She'd never believed that dreams predicted the future, but Dixie's nightmare had given her an unsettling feeling. Maybe she was reading too much into it, but she was worried about her friend. She was concerned that Dixie was too involved in Jason's life, and that wasn't good for either one of them.

Layne had watched Jason grow up, but had truly fallen in love with him when she taught him in fifth grade. He'd stolen her heart with his great sense of humor and easygoing personality. The fact that he was one of the cutest kids in her class with his dancing blue eyes and dimpled cheeks made him hard to resist. Jason was one of those kids everyone liked– students as well as adults. Layne had been so proud of Jason as she watched him excel throughout his middle and high school years. He was the quarterback on the championship football team and earned himself an athletic scholarship to Layne's alma mater, Merritt Atlantic College.

Jason had been so full of promise back then, but something had changed his junior year in college after he injured his knee. He'd had surgery along with physical therapy and was told his knee had healed well enough for him to play football his senior year even though he complained of a great deal of pain. He was on the team, but sat on the bench most of the year. He no longer had that spark that he'd once had. Layne remembered how he'd struggled with deciding on a major that suited him. He'd eventually earned a degree in Liberal Studies, which hadn't served to put him on a designated career path. She knew that Jason had worked through several jobs, but he couldn't seem to stick with one long enough to find success. What disturbed her most about Jason was how he so easily manipulated Dixie into believing that it was never his fault when he quit a job or was fired from one. Over and over, Dixie would pick up the pieces of Jason's life and put everything back together trying to give him a fresh start. Layne knew that Dixie did it out of love for her son, but she worried that love had blinded her friend to what Jason was doing to her own life.

Thinking about Dixie's son as she was driving to Whitlock, the assisted living facility where her mother lived, brought Layne's thoughts back to her own son, Aaron. She was well aware that out of her three children, he was the one she'd spoiled. Maybe she'd spoiled him because he was the youngest and she'd been a more relaxed parent with him. It didn't hurt that he usually tried to make her happy too. Which was why she was so surprised by his hostility when she told him of her objection to the wedding venue.

Layne was delighted that at thirty-five, Aaron was finally getting married. She was even thrilled with Jenny, the woman he was marrying. Aaron and Jenny had met when Mark was in the hospital and Jenny had been assigned as their support nurse. What didn't thrill her was where they'd decided to get married. Instead of getting married in Aaron's home church right here in Kerry where they both lived now, Jenny wanted to get married all the way up in Bowers, Indiana. She'd grown up there but hadn't been back in over a decade. It just didn't make sense to Layne why she would want to go all the way up there to get married.

After all, Jenny didn't have any family left in Bowers. Her mother had died suddenly of a heart attack soon after Jenny graduated from high school and her father had remarried a woman from Washington, DC and moved there. The only family that Jenny had anywhere near Bowers was her older sister Emma who lived in Indianapolis. Layne thought it was inconsiderate of Jenny to ask all of Aaron's family and friends to make the long twelve-hour drive to Indiana to attend their wedding when all she had to do was have her one sister's family and father come down to Kerry.

Layne hadn't spoken to Jenny about this yet. Mark had warned her that it would be a bad idea to interfere after the way Aaron had reacted, but Layne wasn't convinced. She and Jenny had a good relationship and she felt she could convince her future daughter-in-law to change her plans for a wedding in Bowers, Indiana, to one right here in Kerry, Georgia. That was one thing she was going to discuss with her mother today on her visit. Layne pulled into the parking lot outside of Whitlock, gathered up the things her mother had asked her to bring, locked her car, and headed inside.

When she walked into her mother's room, she found her mother leaned back in her recliner napping with the TV blaring. Layne sighed as she turned down the television. She wished her mother would wear her hearing aids instead of turning the television up so loud.

Layne gently touched her mother's shoulder to wake her. "Hey, Mama, it's Layne."

Her mother slowly opened her eyes and began to focus on Layne. "Did you bring the things I asked for?" She sat up, fully awake.

Layne sat down in the chair next to her mother's recliner and began to take the box of greeting cards and packet of pens from her bag. "Of course, but I don't know why you need more cards. I just brought you a box of twenty-two a couple of weeks ago."

Her mother rolled her eyes. "Because I sent all of those out," she said.

Layne looked at her. "Who are you sending all these cards out to, Mama?"

"To the elderly, of course." Her mother took the box of cards from Layne.

Layne almost laughed at the irony of her ninety-two-year-old mother sending cards to the elderly, but thought better of it knowing how her mother would react. Instead, she simply smiled.

"I know what you're thinking, Layne." Her mother smiled back at her. "But do you know how many elderly people there are here who have no one to care about them? A few of us have started sending them cards to let them know someone cares. Even mean ol' Miss Francis is involved."

Layne leaned over to give her mother a hug and a kiss on the cheek. "You know you're something special, Mama. I brought something else just for you."

"You did?"

Layne pulled out a Hershey's dark chocolate candy bar with almonds, her mother's favorite. "Ta da!"

Mama looked at her suspiciously. "You must want something."

"Only your advice." Layne handed her mother the candy bar.

Her mother set the candy bar on the table next to her chair. "Okay, let's have it."

Layne told her mother about her concerns with where Jenny wanted to have the wedding and Aaron's surprising reaction to her objections about it being so far from Kerry. As Layne talked, she could feel the anger rising in her voice. Her mother listened without interruption to all Layne had to say. When Layne finished, she looked to her mother. "One of the things that I really hate the most is that with the wedding being so far away, it'll be difficult for you to get there for one of the biggest days in your youngest grandson's life."

Her mother didn't hesitate. "That's just it, Layne. I may not be there for that day, but, God willing, I'll be there for a bunch of the days they'll have after the wedding while living right here in Kerry."

With a sly smile, she added, "Hopefully, I'll be there for an even bigger day in Aaron's life when he brings home his firstborn child."

She reached out and took Layne's hand in hers. Patting it, she added, "You don't want to mess up your relationship with your son and his future wife over one day. Give them that one day, Layne. You'll have a bunch of others."

Her mother's words stunned Layne. She'd been so sure her mother would take her side in this, but now she realized just how selfish she was to want everything here in Kerry. She gave her mother's hand a squeeze. "I don't know what I'd do without you."

Her mother chuckled. "Well, let's hope you won't be finding out anytime soon."

After leaving her Skinny Dippers meeting Betty Jo headed to her daughter Lily's house. Lily had called earlier that morning to remind her mother that this was the day she was taking Kendall, her eleven-year-old daughter, to the orthodontist to have braces put on. Lily had sent her a "before" picture and Betty Jo couldn't wait to see what Kendall looked like "after." She knew from experience having had braces herself when she was twelve that her granddaughter's mouth wouldn't be feeling great. So she'd stopped off at The Grill to pick up a bowl of Kendall's favorite soup, chicken noodle.

Betty Jo knocked softly on the side door as she called out in a sing-song voice, "It's Gigi with something special for the most beautiful granddaughter in the world."

She waited a few minutes for someone to come to the door before opening it herself and going in. She set the soup down on the kitchen island and went in search of her daughter and granddaughter.

Betty Jo met Lily coming down the hall. "Shh." Lily put her finger to her lips. "I just got her settled down. Go back to the kitchen where we can talk."

"How is she?" Betty Jo asked.

Lily shook her head. "Well, she's not happy, that's for sure." Lily sat on one of the bar stools and patted the other one for her mother to sit next to her. "She let me know she is never going back to school and that I've ruined her life by making her get those 'ghastly things' on her teeth."

Betty Jo chuckled, "That sounds about right for the typical eleven-year-old-reaction to metal objects being placed in her mouth."

"Personally, I think she looks adorable." Lily smiled. "But I sure can't tell her that. If I did, I'm afraid she might just throw something at me."

"It'll pass," Betty Jo assured her daughter. "You're just lucky you got your dad's teeth and never had to endure braces."

"I know," Lily agreed, "and I wish Kendall could have been spared, but she is her Gigi's granddaughter."

They both laughed.

"How are the Fearsome Foursome this fine Tuesday morning?" Lily asked as she got down two cups from the cabinet and poured each of them a cup of coffee.

Betty Jo hesitated and then sighed. "I wish I could say everyone is great, but that wasn't the case today."

As they drank their coffee, Lily listened intently as Betty Jo told her about Dixie's nightmare.

"Oh, Mom, I just hate that Dixie had such a disturbing dream about Jason."

Betty Jo remembered how much fun Lily and Jason once had together. Lily was a year older than Jason and the two of them had been so close when they were younger. When Lily was upset, Betty Jo could always count on Jason to make her laugh. They'd gone out on a couple of dates, but Lily always swore it was only as friends. It had been Jason who warned Lily not to marry Matt, her ex-husband. But, when Lily had married Matt despite Jason's warning, it seemed that Jason no longer wanted to have anything to do with her. Betty Jo knew it hurt Lily's feeling when he hadn't even come to see her after Kendall was born.

Lily set her cup down. "What's going on with Jason that would cause his mother to dream such a terrible nightmare?"

"I'm not exactly sure, but it can't be good."

Betty Jo stayed for another thirty minutes talking to Lily, hoping that Kendall would come out of her room. When it was clear that she was not going to come out even to see her grandmother, she left.

As Betty Jo pulled into her driveway, she smiled seeing her husband Don's blue 1959 Chevy Apache pickup truck parked in the driveway. He loved that truck, even though he'd been driving it when he had the accident that almost killed one of his best friends. After that wreck, Betty Jo begged him to get rid of it, but Don was determined to restore it one more time. She had to admit he'd done a great job of returning it to its original state. With his truck in the driveway, that would mean that Don was in his workshop working on his latest project– building a cedar-strip canoe.

Don had talked about building a cedar-strip canoe for years. She remembered how he and their son Ethan had started building a cedar-strip kayak years ago when Ethan became interested in kayaking as a young boy, but their busy lives got in the way. They'd never finished it. She thought the shell of their incomplete venture that now hung in the rafters of Don's shop was his motivation for building this canoe.

Instead of going straight into the house, she decided to head out to Don's shop to check on his progress. As she neared the shop, she could hear the high-pitched whine of his table saw.

Betty Jo took a deep breath, filling her lungs with the woody, sweet aroma of cedar. She loved that smell. It made her feel like she was in the middle of a deep, dark forest.

Betty Jo watched as Don finished cutting a cedar strip. When he turned to put it in the pile with the others, he jumped back in surprise to see her standing at the door watching him. He turned off the saw and took off his safety glasses. "Hey," he said. "When did you get back?"

"Just now." Betty Jo went over to take a closer look at his cedar strips. "How many of these do you have to cut?"

"A lot more." He smiled at her as he brushed the sawdust from his pants.

Betty Jo smiled back. "Did you eat the apple I put out for you?"

Don stopped smiling. "Yes, Betty Jo. I ate the apple."

Since Don had been diagnosed with Type 1 diabetes, Betty Jo had kept a constant watch on his diet and insulin levels. She didn't want another diabetic incident like the one that had caused him to lose consciousness and run head-on into Mark's truck. She knew Don thought she was overly concerned and could tell he didn't like the extra attention his diet was getting. He'd let her know on many occasions that a man over seventy should be allowed to take care of himself. Betty Jo let him know she didn't agree. As a nurse, she was sure she could do a better job of watching after his diet than he ever would.

She reached out and gently squeezed his arm. "You know I love you, right?" she asked.

"I know, and I guess you know I love you too."

Then pulling her close, he kissed her. When their kiss ended, they held one another relishing a quiet moment together.

Chapter Three

Dixie looked down at her watch as she left the Dream Bean Coffee Shop. She was having such a good time with her friends that she hadn't realized how late it was. If she didn't hurry, she was going to be late for her appointment with Whitney to have her hair colored and cut. People had always commented on her thick, auburn hair–which Whitney had been able to match perfectly to the hair color of her youth. Being short and with a less-than-thin body, Dixie felt that her hair was her best feature. It had taken her a few years to discover Whitney, who knew instinctively what hairstyle would look best on her. Dixie always felt much better about life when she left Whitney's Southern Roots Salon.

Dixie had just started the engine of her metallic-blue 2016 Impala when her cell phone rang. She glanced at the screen and was surprised to see it was Hailey calling. Hailey rarely had time to even take a restroom break let alone make a personal phone call during the day. She waited for her car's Bluetooth to pick up the call before answering.

Dixie pulled out of her parking place. "Hey, Hailey. Is everything okay?"

"Everything's good with me, Mom. I'm calling to check on you.

When Dad stopped by this morning to drop off the bread, he mentioned that you had another one of your sleepless nights."

Dixie sighed, "I wish your Dad hadn't said anything about that. It was nothing, really. Just one of those restless nights I sometimes have."

"Well, the girls love it when you have one of your restless nights and decide to bake your famous cinnamon raisin bread instead of tossing and turning in bed." Hailey laughed. "They happily left for school after having some of their Nonnie's special bread for breakfast."

"If they're happy, then I'm happy."

"I need to get back to my patients, but I just wanted to call you to make sure you're okay and to thank you for the bread."

"Well, I'm glad you called," Dixie said. "Love you!"

"I love you too." Hailey ended her call.

Dixie couldn't help but smile as she drove to Whitney's. Hailey's call and breakfast with her best friends had been exactly what she'd needed to erase the lingering effects of her worrisome nightmare. Of course, she was concerned about what was going on with Jason, but she was beginning to realize that it wasn't serious enough that it should keep her from a good night's rest. He just needed a little time to regroup and refocus on his life goals.

Dixie took it as sign of good luck when she found a parking place right in front of the salon. She looked down at her watch as she quickly got out of her car, and laughed to herself when she saw she was actually three minutes early. It was beginning to look like it was going to be a good day after all.

After getting her hair styled just the way she liked it, Dixie ran a few errands before heading home. After having such a good morning, she was beginning to feel optimistic about Jason's situation. That feeling lasted until she pulled in her driveway. There stood Jason, dressed in only his T-shirt and boxers, with a look of anger mixed with disbelief on his face. He was watching as his prized race-red 2016 Ford Mustang GT convertible was loaded onto the bed of Big Willie's Repo roll-back tow truck. Dixie parked her car and stared at the scene before her. At first, she couldn't make sense of what she was seeing. Then it began to dawn on her what was happening.

They're taking Jason's car away!

She sprang out of the car and into action. "Stop!" she screamed as she ran toward the truck. "You have no right to take this car!"

A large man, whom she assumed must be "Big Willie," stepped out from the side of the truck. "Yes, ma'am, this paper right here gives me that right." He retrieved a paper from his front shirt pocket and handed it to Dixie.

Dixie snatched the paper from his hand. With alarm, she read the first few lines:

Citizens Fidelity Bank and Trust Company of Kerry

THIS IS YOUR AUTHORIZATION TO ACT AS OUR AGENT TO COLLECT AND /OR REPOSSESS ON SIGHT THE PROPERTY OF THE NAMED BELOW, WHO HAS IN HER/HIS POSSESSION:

Below that it listed Jason's full name with the complete description of his 2016 Ford Mustang.

With trembling hands, Dixie folded the paper and started to hand it back to Willie. "That copy's for your son, ma'am."

"I'm sorry," Dixie said as she took back the paper. "I didn't fully understand the situation."

Big Willie smiled. "No problem, ma'am. I pretty much get that reaction most of the time." He tipped his cap and turned back to his job of repossessing Jason's car.

Throughout Dixie's confrontation with Big Willie, Jason stood in silence at the back of the truck. As she walked toward him, he reached out his arms to her. "Mom, there's been some kind of mistake here."

Dixie slowly walked past her son's outstretched arms. She was so mad she couldn't even look at him. "Get some clothes on."

Dixie continued into the house, leaving the disturbing scene behind her.

Dixie walked straight back to her bedroom and closed the door. She sat down on the end of her bed. She couldn't remember when she'd ever felt such anger towards her son. She held her hands together tightly, trying to stop them from shaking as tears began to slide down her cheeks. She took deep breaths, willing herself to calm down.

Dixie wondered why Jason hadn't talked to her about not being able to make his car payments. She just couldn't believe he'd let things go so far that the bank would repossess his car. She could have stopped the whole thing from happening if he'd just come to her. Suddenly it was all becoming clear to Dixie that it wasn't just anger she was feeling toward Jason. She was disappointed in her son.

Dixie had always felt such delight in her children, which was surprising to her since she hadn't always wanted to be a mother. In fact, when she and Alex were dating and things began to be serious, she'd let him know that she didn't want children. It took Alex some time to come to terms with her feelings about not having children, but he'd finally decided their lives would be good as long as they had one another. It was after she'd given birth to Hailey that she'd learned Alex had always believed he could convince her to have children after they'd been married a few years.

Dixie let Alex believe he'd been the one to change her mind about having children, but in truth it was her sister Scarlett who'd convinced her to become a mother. Scarlett was two years older than Dixie and, even though they were very different, they'd always been close. When Scarlett became a mother, Dixie witnessed the pure joy that her nephew Finn brought to her sister's life. That's when she began to change her mind about remaining childless. But now she was questioning if she'd been the best mother for Jason. Maybe Alex was right about her being too lenient with Jason.

Dixie wished with all her heart that she could talk to Scarlett right now. She missed her sister so much that at times she thought she could actually feel the hole her sister had left in her heart when she died. The two sisters had been so close that they'd always known what the other one was thinking or feeling without saying a word and Scarlett was the one who knew how to make Dixie feel better about whatever situation she'd gotten herself in to. Breast cancer had taken her sister from her over twenty years ago, just like it had robbed her of her mother only days before starting her freshman year at the University of Georgia.

Dixie vividly remembered the day their mother had died. She recalled how her father had gone to work as if it was an ordinary day while his two daughters held their mother's hands and watched her life slowly pass away. It took Dixie years to understand why her father had left them that day. He hadn't had the courage to stay and witness the ending of his beautiful Georgina's life.

Their father, Walker Parker Randolph III, was a prominent business man who'd inherited the Randolph Lumber Company. Dixie had always admired her father's strength. It had always been her father she went to for advice and support. She'd looked upon her mother as a frail Southern belle. All that changed as she watched her mother battle breast cancer with strength, courage, and an unfaltering trust in God. It became obvious to Dixie that her mother had been the strong one all along. Her father's weakness became clearer in the days following her mother's death. He shut himself up in his room away from everyone, including his daughters. His only companion was his whiskey bottle.

That left Scarlett and Dixie to make the arrangements for their mother's funeral. The days that followed her mother's death went by in a blur for Dixie. It was Scarlett who took over and made the difficult decisions. She was also the one to pull their father out of his room and sober him up long enough to attend his wife's funeral and burial. Sadly, she wasn't able to keep him from crawling back into his misery of isolation and drunkenness.

Dixie decided to abandon her college plans to stay home to take care of their grieving father. With Scarlett leaving in only a few days to begin her junior year at Agnes Scott and with their mother gone, Dixie felt she couldn't desert him. It was clear to her that her father needed her.

Two days after the funeral, their father still hadn't left his room. As far as Dixie knew, he'd not eaten anything since the funeral. She was worried about him and decided she'd make his favorite breakfast– three eggs over easy, two homemade buttered biscuits, three slices of crispy fried bacon, cheese grits, and coffee with one sugar and two creams. She'd been so sure he'd come out of his room for this special meal. Using her mother's best china, she placed the breakfast on one of her mother's silver trays and carried it up to his room. She set the tray down on the hall table and gently knocked on her father's door.

"Daddy, it's Dixie," she'd called out. "I've made your favorite breakfast just for you."

When her father didn't come to the door, she knocked a little harder and called out in a stronger voice, "Daddy?"

When her father still didn't answer, she tried the doorknob. It turned easily in her hand. She remembered how she'd taken the tray from the hall table and opened the door. The scene she saw before her when her eyes became accustomed to the dark had made her gasp. It looked as if her mother's clothes had been torn from her closet and thrown about the room. The sheets had been stripped from the bed and lay tangled on the floor. At first, she couldn't see her father, but when she looked more closely through the chaos, she almost dropped the tray. He was slumped against the wall in the corner of the room. She set the tray of food on the bed and went to him. She remembered kneeling next to his lifeless body. At first, she wasn't sure he was breathing, but then, when she shook him, he let out a mournful moan.

She pulled him toward her and cried out, "Oh, Daddy, what have you done?"

In her mind's eye, she could still see her father's eyes as they fluttered open for a moment. She remembered how sure she was that he would answer her, but without a word he fell back into unconsciousness. As she held him in her arms, rocking him back and forth, she screamed Scarlett's name over and over and over, not even realizing when Scarlett came into the room or when she called for an ambulance.

It seemed to Dixie that she'd held her father like that for a very long time, but Scarlett assured her it was only minutes before the ambulance arrived. Dixie had never been able to recall how they'd gotten to the hospital or what the doctor's name was who'd come out to announce that their father had died due to a deadly mixture of sleeping pills and alcohol. The only thing she remembered were Scarlett's comforting arms around her telling her over and over that everything was going to be alright.

The pain of that moment when the two sisters realized they had lost both parents in a matter of days stayed with Dixie. That moment when she became an orphan was one of the most defining moments of her life. She had to decide whose example she would follow, her mother's or her father's. That was the moment she made the choice that she would be strong and trust in God for her sister as well as for herself.

That choice had been tested repeatedly in her life. Her determination to be strong and trust in God was tested when she left her sister to attend UGA the day after her father's funeral. Her strength and trust in God was tested to its breaking point when she lost Scarlett to the same deadly disease that had taken her mother. Now she realized it was being tested once again with Jason.

Dear Lord, I ask for Your help with my son. I don't know what is going on with him, but I know that You do. I pray that You will be with him, watch over him, and give him strength to rebuild his life. In Jesus' name, Amen.

Dixie got up from where she'd been sitting, went into the bathroom, washed the tears from her face, and gathered up the power she'd always felt through her strength and trust in God as she opened the door ready to face her son.

Chapter Four

Dixie walked into the kitchen to find Jason dressed and sitting at the kitchen island with his head in his hands. When she entered the room, he looked up at her.

"Mom, I'm so sorry," he began in a low voice filled with regret. "I just don't know how this happened."

Dixie walked over and stood next to him. She held her hands with fists clenched and close to her side to keep herself from reaching out to wrap her son in a comforting embrace. It was breaking her heart to see the hurt on his face. She knew this was a new experience for both of them, and she wasn't confident that she was brave enough to do what she believed was best for Jason. She cleared her throat before speaking.

"Jason, you know exactly how this happened. You decided to ignore the obligation you had to pay for your car."

Dixie could see the shock in Jason's eyes as he registered her tone and her words. He started to say something, but she put up her hand to stop him.

"I don't want to hear any of your excuses," she continued. "I only want to hear what your plans are for getting out of the mess you find yourself in."

Jason stared at his mother in disbelief. Dixie was well aware that, based on past experiences, her son expected his mother to come to his rescue, and that's exactly what she wanted to do. She held back the words that threatened to escape from her lips.

Oh, Jason, don't worry. I can call the bank and get your car back. It's all going to be okay. We'll work it out.

Instead, she gathered up what courage she could muster, resolving to be strong for the both of them.

She sat down on the stool next to him. "I know this is hard for you, but it's time you took control of your life."

Jason sat silently with his head down for several minutes. Then suddenly he stood up, almost knocking his stool over as he pushed away from the island. "Don't you think I've been trying to do just that, Mom?" he said with a bitterness that took Dixie by surprise. "But nothing ever works out for me. It's not fair."

He turned, grabbed the extra set of her car keys on the hook by the garage door, and rushed out of the house. Stunned by his outburst, it took Dixie a minute before she could react. By the time she'd gotten up from her stool and out the door, Jason was backing her car down the driveway.

Dixie stood dumbfounded in the middle of the driveway as she watched her son pull onto the street with tires squealing. With shaking hands she pulled her cell phone from her back pocket and dialed Alex's number. She didn't allow Alex to finish his greeting before saying, "Alex, come home now." She hit the End button and sat down in the driveway to wait for her husband. She didn't have to wait long before she saw his white Ford 150 come into view. Alex slammed on his brakes, stopping short when he saw Dixie sitting cross-legged in the middle of the driveway. He jumped out of the truck without shutting off the engine and ran to her.

"Dixie, what's wrong?" Alex's voice was heavy with concern mixed with fear as he reached her side and gathered his wife up in his arms.

"Jason just stole my car."

Alex held Dixie closer, not seeming to comprehend what she'd just told him. Dixie knew her words that Jason would "steal" her car were not making sense to him. He must think she was having some kind of breakdown or something.

Alex helped her to her feet. "Dixie, honey, I think you might be a little confused. Maybe you should lie down for a bit. Let me help you to the house."

Dixie pulled away from him. "Alex, there's nothing wrong with me. Listen to me!" She grabbed his arms. "I'm trying to tell you that Jason stole my car because his was repossessed today."

Alex looked at her with confusion. "Repossessed? Why?"

"Because our son's in denial, that's why. I think it's a good idea to go to the house, but you might be the one who wants to lie down after you hear this story!"

It didn't take Dixie long to tell Alex all that had happened since she'd arrived home to find Big Willie's Repo hauling away Jason's Mustang, and about how she was beginning to come to the realization that always picking Jason up after he'd fallen down may not have been the best thing for him in the long run. Jason's reaction when she'd made it clear she wasn't going to bail him out this time confirmed it.

Dixie concluded her story with, "Then he grabbed the keys to my car as he went out the door, got in my car, and squealed out of the driveway on two wheels in MY car! If that's not stealing my car, then I don't know what stealing is."

Alex listened to her story without interruption. When she finished, he sat staring at her.

Dixie knew she often overreacted to certain situations and Alex always tried to get her to see what had happened from his point of view. Knowing how Alex thought, he'd probably try to convince her that Jason was just borrowing her car and would be back with it after he calmed down. But not this time. No matter what he said to try to convince her otherwise, she knew her son had stolen her car.

Dixie was shocked when Alex pulled out his cell phone and said, "I think we should call Mark right now and report your car stolen."

Mark, as well as being their friend, was the Kerry County Sheriff.

"Wait!" Dixie cried as she reached out to stop Alex from making the call. "I'm not sure we need to report my car stolen just yet."

Smiling, Alex put his phone back in his pocket.

"Okay, Alex, I get it," Dixie sighed, rolling her eyes. "You know I don't want Jason to be arrested for stealing my car."

Alex got up from his chair to give her a hug. "I know that, and I also know this was a first for both of you."

Dixie looked at him questioningly.

"It's the first time you've ever stood up to Jason. I'm sure he didn't know what to do. So, he got away from you as fast as he could. I'm sure he'll be back with your car before long,"

"Oh, Alex, do you really believe that?" Dixie returned his embrace.

"I'm sure of it."

With his arms still wrapped around her, he asked, "Are you okay for me to go back to work?" With a laugh he added, "I just left my truck in the middle of the driveway, running and with the door open."

Dixie joined him in laughter. Then she added more seriously, "Thanks for coming to my rescue so quickly."

Alex kissed the top of her head. "Anytime. It's all going to be alright, you know."

"I know," Dixie agreed. But after Alex left and she was alone again with her thoughts, she began to wonder if it really was going to be "alright" after all.

When Jason peeled out of the driveway, he had no clue where he was going. All he knew was he wanted to get away from the shocking confrontation that had just taken place as fast as he could. In all his life, he'd never experienced anything like it. The mother he knew and depended on had always been understanding and supportive of everything he'd ever done, even if what he did wrong. Until today, he had no reason to question that was how she always would be. His mind began to race, trying to think of anyone who would come close to giving him the support and backing she had.

Jason's first thought was to go to Hailey, but he knew he'd pretty much burned that bridge the last time he'd gone to his sister for help. She'd let him crash on the couch in the kids' playroom for a little while, but she wasn't forthcoming with the financial support he needed. He knew a lot of that was because of her husband's influence over her. Jason was pretty sure Josh had never really liked him, let alone trusted him.

Maybe Josh didn't trust him because he was afraid that Jason might take away his job if he became a part of the Bradley Contracting Company. Jason had never taken an interest in the company, but he was confident he'd be welcomed with open arms if he changed his mind. After all, Josh was only the son-in-law, not the son.

Throughout his life, Jason had heard his father proclaim to anyone who would listen, "My proudest day will be when my boy Jason follows me into the business I built from the ground up." Josh had to be a more than a little worried that Jason might decide it was time to make him the proud father he'd always wanted to be.

Jason knew what he had to do and which man he had to win over if he was going to be able to get the support he needed. He had to convince his father that the best thing he could do for his family would be to welcome Jason into his business. Surely, now that he had a college degree, he wouldn't be expected to do the low-paying physical work that he'd had to do all through high school. Clearly, he wouldn't be expected to work for that piddly amount he'd been paid back then. He was sure if he played out his plan just right, he would be able to persuade his father to put him in a salaried position where he'd be making the big bucks.

Jason was well aware that Alex Bradley was a tough nut to crack. The first thing he needed to do was convince him that he had turned over a new leaf. Maybe he could persuade him that the confrontation he'd just had with his mother was his motivation for wanting to join the family business. He smiled to himself. He could really come out on top if he could also make his mother believe that she'd been the reason for his change in attitude toward the contracting business.

Jason was on his way to Bradley Contracting Company headquarters when his phone rang out with an old-fashioned bell tone from the passenger's seat. He picked it up, glanced at the screen to see who was calling, then put it back down, ignoring the call. He knew what the caller wanted. He'd call him back after he had a job secured with his father and, hopefully, an advance on his salary in his pocket.

Don't worry. You'll get your money soon enough. You just need to be patient a little longer.

Chapter Five

Alex had been working on plans for the Martin house remodel when he'd gotten the strange call from Dixie. As he sat back down at his desk to finish those plans, he found he couldn't concentrate on the design. He shook his head wondering how Jason had gotten himself into so much financial trouble. Jason had left or been fired, he wasn't sure which, from a well-paying job that should have given him enough money to make his car payment up until a month ago. Alex knew the bank wouldn't repossess his car if he'd only been a month behind on his payments. He had to be several months behind. What had he spent his money on instead of taking care of his obligations? He began to consider what other bills Jason might have neglected paying. He knew Dixie had co-signed a couple of his loans in the past, but didn't know for sure if any of those loans were current. He hoped that Dixie wouldn't be getting any past-due letters.

Knowing his mind wasn't on designing, Alex decided the best thing to keep from worrying was to go out to the site where Josh was supervising a complete renovation of one of the older iconic motels in town, Kerry King's Inn. They'd been working on the job for three weeks already and had encountered more problems than they'd anticipated. It was becoming a headache for Alex, but Josh was confident that they'd finish on budget and on time. Josh was usually right about these things. Alex knew he tended to see the negative side of things, but was thankful his son-in-law countered that with looking at the positives. That made the two of them a good, balanced pair to work together on a project.

Alex had just reached out his hand to open the door to leave his office when Jason pushed his office door open.

"Jason, what are you doing here?"

Jason smiled at his father. "I'm here to see you, Dad."

"Are you in your mother's car?"

"Yes, sir." Jason dropped his head. "I really messed up this time, Dad."

Knowing his son as well as he did, Alex was suspicious. What did Jason hope to gain by confessing his wrongdoing? Wanting to learn more about his true motive, he put his arm around Jason's shoulder. "Why don't we get out of the doorway here and sit down and talk about it, Son?"

Jason looked up at his father. Alex could see there were tears in his eyes. "Thanks, Dad, I'd really like that."

Jason followed his father back to his desk. He sat down in the chair across from him and waited with his head down.

"Your mother told me what happened with your car and all. What I want to know is how you allowed yourself to get so far behind with your payments that the bank would repossess your car? I know you were making good money at your last job."

Alex saw a tear running down his son's cheek when Jason slowly raised his head. "I know I made good money, but I let that go to my head. I started buying things I didn't need, but I really wanted. I loaned some friends money that they never paid back. I just always thought I could catch up on my payments, but the more I missed the bigger those payments got. I was too embarrassed and ashamed to ask for help." He lowered his head as he finished his explanation.

Alex said nothing as he sat looking at his son's bowed head. He knew Jason well enough to know that he was trying to play on his sympathies, make him feel sorry they'd taken his car away. He folded his hands behind his head as he leaned back in his chair. He wondered what Jason's next move might be if he just went along. Maybe his son really was ashamed. Doubtful, but always a possibility.

"So, now, Son, what are you going to do about this situation you've found yourself in?" Alex leaned forward, putting his elbows on his desk.

Jason looked up at his father as he wiped the tears from his eyes. "That's why I'm here, Dad. I've come to beg you for a job. I want to work with you in the Bradley Contracting Company."

Alex smiled to himself. Jason knew those words were the very words he'd always hoped to hear, even if they weren't spoken with true sincerity. If Jason was willing to actually say those words, then he knew he had Jason right where he wanted him.

Alex reached his hand out across the desk to Jason. "Nothing would make me happier, Son."

Jason firmly grasped his father's hand. "I'm happy too, Dad."

Alex stood and came around the desk. "Well, let's go head on over to Kerry King's Inn. There's a lot of work to be done there and we're behind schedule." Then he added enthusiastically as he motioned for his son to follow him, "I know you want to get started right away."

"You want me to start today? Now?" Jason asked incredulously.

Alex patted his son on the back. "Now's as good a time as any, wouldn't you say?"

Alex knew he had successfully trapped his son. If Jason didn't go with him right now, he'd come across as insincere. It would look like he didn't really want to go to work for him. Even if that were true, Jason wouldn't want him to suspect it at this early stage of his plan. If he was going to stick with his plan, he'd have to go to work today.

Jason got out of his chair and followed his father. "You're right about that. Let's do this."

Jason was finding it hard keeping up with his father as he showed him around the Kerry King's Inn remodel. His Brooks Brothers leather loafers were not the best choice of footwear for walking around a construction site. But ruining his shoes was almost worth it just to see the look on Josh's face when his father told him that Jason would be working with him.

"Josh, Jason is going to be working with us now. I want you to show him what we've got going on here."

It was obvious that Josh hadn't expected this move out of Jason, but he covered it up well.

"Glad you're joining us, Jason." Josh shook Jason's hand. "Lord knows there's plenty for you to do here. We're still demoing the bathrooms, pulling out the tubs on the second floor. I'm sure Gav could use a hand with that."

Jason stared at Josh as if he had just spoken another language. Didn't Josh understand that he was to be working *with* him, not *for* him? And certainly not doing physical labor. Surely, his father would clear this up. He looked at his father.

His father looked at him. "Okay, then, I'll be back at six to pick you up." He turned to leave.

Jason was beginning to understand what his father's expectations were. He couldn't allow his father to do this to him. "Dad, I thought I was going to work with you."

His father walked back over to Jason and put his arm around him. "It was my understanding that you wanted a job, right?"

"Yes, b-but—" Jason stammered.

"Well, this is the job."

Jason knew that if he didn't do the job that he was asked to do, the chances that his father would ever help him again were slim to none. He had to think of something fast.

"It's just that I'm not prepared for this job, Dad." Jason pointed down to his shoes. "Look at what I'm wearing."

Alex stepped back to take a look at his son. He gave a chuckle. "You're absolutely right, Son. You can't work in those shoes, and you don't even have gloves. Sorry, I wasn't thinking."

Jason smiled to himself knowing that his father was finally understanding that he should be in management, not doing the actual physical labor.

Then turning to Josh, his father said, "Josh, do you have an extra pair of steel-toed boots in your truck and maybe a pair of gloves that Jason could use until he can get his own?"

"I got my old pair of size twelves in the truck and a new set of leather gloves I picked up this morning," Josh said.

Alex patted him on the back. "Well, there you go, Son. If I remember correctly, you wear size eleven and a half. Josh's boots should work for you for a few days." He turned away from Jason and walked back to his truck.

Jason stared after his father, watching in disbelief as he walked away from him. *You may think you've won this battle, old man, but you haven't won the war. I'll do what you've asked me to do, for now.*

Chapter Six

ixie had planned on going to the grocery store to finish the shopping for Aaron and Jenny's party, but without her car those plans were put on hold. She realized she wouldn't be able to follow through with any of her plans for that afternoon. Instead, she spent most of her time worrying about Jason. Relief flooded her body after getting Alex's phone call that Jason was with him at work and had even asked him for a job. Although this was surprising to Dixie, it was also good news.

Dixie decided to spend what was left of the afternoon working in her flower bed. She loved yard work and enjoyed caring for her flowers, plants, and shrubs. Her love for gardening was evident by her colorful flower beds filled with petunias, snapdragons, Lily of-the-Nile, and her newly planted "Gertrude Jekyll" roses. She'd been blessed with a green thumb, an inherited talent from her mother. Dixie was proud that her yard had been voted as Yard of the Month by the Kerry Garden Club more times than any other in Kerry.

It always amazed Dixie how quickly weeds could sprout up to threaten the health and beauty of her plants. She'd hired a lawn service to come on Friday afternoons to cut the grass, trim the shrubs, and edge the sidewalks, but her yard wouldn't look good if weeds invaded her flower beds. She needed to get those weeds out today or they might take over.

Dixie was carrying the last of the weeds she'd pulled up out of her flower garden to the compost bin when she saw Alex pull down the driveway with her car following close behind. She stood watching as Jason got out of her car and walked toward her. She was more than a little angry with him and wasn't exactly sure what she wanted to say to him, so she waited where she was for him to come to her.

Jason stopped in front of his mother and stood with his arms to his side and looking straight at her, he began in a low voice, "I am so disappointed in myself, Mom. I should have asked for help when I knew what trouble I was in with that car." He swallowed hard as if he was trying to keep himself from crying. He lowered his head. "I was just so angry with myself and I took it out on you. I'm sorry for the way I acted and the words I said."

Raising his head, he paused before asking, "Can you forgive me, Mom?"

All the anger that Dixie had felt just minutes ago toward her son for his hurtful actions melted away as she heard his words. She reached out her arms to him as tears began to fall. "Oh, Jason, of course I forgive you."

Jason went into his mother's embrace. As Dixie held her son, she hoped that his asking for her forgiveness meant he was truly sorry for what he'd done and wasn't just his way of bringing her back to his side. They stood there together until Alex broke them apart saying, "Your flower beds look good. I brought home the pressure washer. What needs done?"

Dixie pulled off her gloves and wiped her tears away. It took her a minute to gather her thoughts before she could answer her husband. "Let's see," she said as she looked around, "the driveway and deck have to be pressure washed today. I want the deck to be good and dry before they bring the tables and chairs Saturday morning."

Jason smiled at his father. "Looks like Mom's just kicked into her 'time-to-get-it done' mode."

Alex returned a knowing smile. "Yep, and when that happens, it's best for everyone to do just what she says without question!"

The three of them spent what was left of the afternoon and into the evening preparing the yard for Saturday's big event.

That night, Dixie fell into bed exhausted after showering and eating a slice of the pizza that Alex had picked up for their supper. She'd been too tired to worry about having another nightmare and had slept the whole night through. When she opened her eyes the next morning and looked over at the clock, she couldn't believe it was after seven. She wondered if Alex had already left for work or if he'd slept late as well.

Alex had moved out of the master bedroom and taken over Hailey's bedroom after she'd married. He claimed he moved out to give Dixie relief from his snoring, so she could finally get a good night's sleep. The true reason for Alex's moving out was hard for both him and Dixie to admit—they each wanted a place where they could get away from one another. At the time, their marriage was going through one of those rough places that marriages often go through. Even though things were better for them now, and they managed to share a bed at least once every few weeks lately, neither one wanted to give up their separate rooms and go back to sharing a room.

Dixie slipped on her robe and headed out of her bedroom to check to see if anyone else was up. As she walked down the hall, she could hear voices coming from the kitchen. She wondered who Alex would be having a conversation with this early in the morning.

As she got closer, she was surprised to find that Alex was talking to Jason. She hadn't seen Jason out of bed before ten any day since he'd moved back home. For a minute, she wondered what had gotten him out of bed this early, but then she remembered that Alex had told her Jason had asked for a job. She stood just outside the kitchen listening to their typical father/son exchange.

"Boots okay?" Alex asked Jason.

"Seem to be."

"I'll give you an advance of a week's wages so you can get your own."

"You don't have to do that. These will work for now."

"Need your own."

"Okay. Thanks."

When Dixie entered the room, they both glanced over at her then wordlessly went back to eating their cereal.

"Good morning." Dixie gave each of them a kiss on the cheek. "Looks like it's going to be a beautiful day." With a smile on her face she put a coffee pod into the coffeemaker.

Alex got up to put his bowl in the sink. "Yep, looks like it."

"Sure thing," Jason agreed as he went to the sink, setting his bowl down on top of his father's.

"You two are something else." Dixie shook her head. "You know a little enthusiasm wouldn't hurt either of you."

Alex smiled as he leaned over to kiss her cheek. "I thought I was being enthusiastic. Gotta get to work."

"Me too." Jason followed his father out of the door.

Dixie took her coffee with her as she sat down at the breakfast table where she could see her husband and son as they got into Alex's truck and drove away. She hoped that Jason's change of heart and decision to work for his father was going to be a good thing, a positive thing. It hadn't been very good the last time, but that was when Jason was still a teenager. He was a grown man now. She bowed her head and prayed a short prayer for both father and son.

Dixie turned her attention to making a list of what all needed to be done today to get ready for Aaron and Jenny's party. She worked better when she had a list. Plus, she loved that feeling she got when she could check off an item as completed. Once she'd finished with the list, she smiled as she checked off the first item– make a list. She needed to hurry to get the second item, shower and dress, checked off.

After putting the dirty dishes in the dishwasher, Dixie was making her way back to her bedroom when the chimes of her front doorbell stopped her. She glanced at the clock on the wall to see that it wasn't even eight o'clock yet. She wondered if the company she'd hired to put up the tent, tables, and chairs on Saturday might have gotten their dates mixed up and were here today. She stepped back into the kitchen to peek out the window. A small black sporty looking car was parked in the driveway. She didn't know anyone who had a car like that and was considering whether she should answer the door or ignore it and hope whoever it was would just go away. She jumped as the doorbell sounded once again.

"Coming," Dixie called out, realizing how silly it would be to ignore whoever was out there ringing her doorbell. She pulled her robe closer to her as she unlocked her front door and cautiously opened it to find an attractive, tall, well-built young man with a full head of blond hair that curled out over his diamond-studded earlobes pacing back and forth on her front porch. She stared at him, wondering if maybe he was someone she'd once taught. He didn't look familiar, but she'd mostly taught fifth graders and they tended to change quite a bit from child to grown man.

Guardedly, she smiled up at the man as she asked, "Can I help you?"

"Good morning, Mrs. Bradley!" The man smiled back at her as he reached out his hand to introduce himself. "I'm sorry to disturb you so early. I'm Eddy, a friend of Jason's."

Dixie was relieved that he was a friend of Jason's and not some random person coming to her house at this early hour. Shaking the hand he offered, she racked her brain trying to remember if Jason had ever mentioned a friend of his named Eddy. "Nice to meet you, Eddy. I wasn't sure who it was ringing my door bell this early."

Eddy continued smiling. "I'm sorry we haven't met before now. I totally understand why you might have been a little apprehensive about answering the door at this hour to a complete stranger. I just got back in town last night and was heading out to breakfast. I came by to see if Jason might want to join me."

Looking past Dixie into the living room, Eddy asked, "Is he here?"

"Oh, I'm sorry, Eddy. You just missed him."

Dixie saw a look of disappointment pass over Eddy's face before he quickly replaced it with a smile. "I was sure I'd catch him if I stopped by early."

"Normally, you'd have caught him at home," Dixie said proudly, "but he's working now."

"Working?" Eddy said with a chuckle. "Well, that's good to hear. I knew he was looking for a job, but I hadn't heard he'd found one."

"I don't think there's any way you could have known. He just started."

"Guess I'll have to catch up with him later. I'm sorry to have bothered you." Eddy turned to leave.

Eddy was almost down the porch steps when he turned back to ask, "Do you know what time he'll get off work? I was thinking maybe we could meet for supper instead."

Dixie opened her mouth to answer Eddy's question when an idea suddenly came to mind. "Why don't you join us for supper tonight?"

Dixie could see that her invitation caught Eddy off guard, but after a minute of consideration, she watched as his face lit up. "Why, thank you. I'd enjoy that very much, Mrs. Bradley."

Dixie smiled back. "Great! We'll see you around seven then."

"See you then."

As Dixie watched Eddy get in his car, she wondered where Jason had met him and why he'd never mentioned him. Was he a friend from college? Or could he be a friend from when he worked and lived in Atlanta? Maybe Jason hadn't mentioned him because Eddy had been away for a long time and had just returned. He hadn't exactly said that he lived in Kerry, but that's what she assumed. Eddy seemed like a nice young man. Dixie decided it'd be good for Jason to reconnect with Eddy. After all, no one could have too many friends. She hoped Jason would be pleased that she'd invited him for supper tonight. If he wasn't, it could be an awkward supper for all of them.

As Dixie closed the front door, she looked at the wall clock. She quickly headed to her room to shower and dress. She didn't have any time to waste if she was going to make her dentist appointment that she'd already rescheduled not once, but two times. She'd never liked going to the dentist and put it off for as long as she could.

As she brushed her teeth, Dixie smiled at the memory of how her mother had bribed her to go to the dentist when she was a child with the promise of a sweet treat at Louie's Ice Cream Parlor afterwards. The thought entered her head that maybe that's what she needed this morning–a bribe of something sweet after her appointment. She frowned, remembering that she'd already treated herself to something sweet after her Skinny Dipper's meeting.

What else is sweet without adding calories to my diet?

The sweetest treat she could think of would be to have lunch with one of her granddaughters. As she finished getting dressed, she realized that she was looking forward to her dentist appointment now that she would follow it by having lunch with a sweet grandchild. It was going to be a good day despite her dentist appointment.

Chapter Seven

ixie felt much better after having her teeth cleaned by Mattie, the dental hygienist at Dr. Cheek's office. Looking down at her watch, she realized she had just enough time to get to Weldon Academy to have lunch with her oldest granddaughter, Kaiden. If things worked out just right, Kaiden's teacher might ask her to stay to read to the class when they returned to their room.

After registering at the front office, she headed to the lunchroom to meet Kaiden's class. As she opened the door to the lunchroom, she heard her granddaughter call out in surprise, "Nonnie!"

Dixie turned to see Kaiden hurrying toward her. She wrapped her up in a big hug. At that moment she couldn't think of anything that could make her any happier than hugging this precious grandchild of hers. She felt blessed beyond words.

"Hey, Kaiden!" Dixie said, releasing her, "How would you like to have your Nonnie as your lunch date?"

"I'd love it." Smiling, Kaiden took her grandmother's hand as they walked together into the lunchroom.

After getting their lunch, they headed to the special table in the center of the lunchroom that was set up for students who had a guest for lunch. Sitting down and looking out over the lunchroom rocketed Dixie back to her years of teaching fifth grade here. It seemed like it had only been yesterday when she was bringing her own class to lunch. She cherished those fond memories of her years of teaching.

Dixie taught in public school for thirty years and enjoyed teaching most of those years. When she'd first started teaching the emphasis had been on preparing students to be successful in their lives and become productive citizens. Then the focus had changed and the demand for high student test scores had taken the joy out of teaching for her, and she wholeheartedly believed it'd taken the joy out of learning for the students. Dixie couldn't buy into teaching to a test, so she'd left public school. Luckily, she'd found the joy of teaching once again when, after a year of staying at home and nearly going crazy, she'd been offered a job at the Weldon Academy, a private school that didn't subscribe to an "end-of-the-year test" mentality.

Technology had sent Dixie running to retire the second time. She'd known it was time to let the younger generation take over when they'd placed an interactive white board in her room and expected her to use it. It was hard for her to believe that she'd been retired from Weldon for three years now. Some days she still missed teaching. That was why she sat up straighter when she saw Kaiden's teacher, Miss Bonwell, walking toward her.

"It's good to see you, Mrs. Bradley," Miss Bonwell said as she took a seat next to Dixie. Miss Bonwell was definitely one of the younger generation. So far, Dixie had resisted the urge to ask her how old she was. She looked to be about eighteen, but Dixie was impressed with her teaching style and the rapport she had with her students.

Dixie returned her smile. "Hey, Miss Bonwell, it's good to see you too."

"I know you're a busy woman," Miss Bonwell began apprehensively, "but would you have some time to read to the class after lunch?" Then she added, "And please, call me Tabitha."

Kaiden began to bounce up and down. "Please, Nonnie, please," she begged.

Putting her hand on Kaiden's shoulder to calm her down, Dixie said with a laugh, "I was hoping you'd ask, Tabitha. I'd love to read to the class."

"Great!"

Tabitha leaned in closer to Dixie and said with a smile, "I heard that Jason was back in Kerry."

At first Dixie wasn't sure she'd heard her correctly. "Jason, my son?" she asked, puzzled as to how Tabitha would even know who Jason was or care that he'd returned to Kerry. As far as she knew, Tabitha was new to Kerry. She looked at her, confused.

Tabitha gave an embarrassed laugh. "I'm sorry. I bet you're wondering how I know Jason."

Dixie slowly nodded her head.

"I went to Merritt Atlantic College with Jason," Tabitha said, putting her hand on her chest. "I was two years behind him and I doubt if he even knew I existed. I was kind of a nerd and he was this big football star, and..." Her voice trailed off as she looked down at the table.

Dixie waited patiently for her to finish her sentence.

"And I sort of had a crush on him," she added uncomfortably.

Dixie smiled and reached over to pat her hand. "As pretty as you are, I'm sure he noticed you."

Tabitha looked up at Dixie and asked excitedly, "Do you think?"

"I'm sure of it," Dixie said. "I had no idea you even knew Jason. You should stop by the house sometime to say hello to him. I'm sure he'd enjoy seeing you." Dixie didn't say what she was really thinking–*Please, please, stop by. You're just the type of girl I want Jason to be with.*

Tabitha took a minute to consider. "Maybe I will."

After lunch, Dixie went back to the classroom with Kaiden. She read a book to the class that went along with their theme for the week about sharing. She was glad for a distraction from the chaos that seemed to be consuming her life.

Dixie ended up with all three of her granddaughters after school. Kaiden had begged her to take her to the Dairylicious for ice cream. They'd gotten Alexa from her classroom and the three of them had gone by the Brighten Montessori to pick up three-year-old Rae. All three had behaved well, but they were just so full of energy that it was hard for Dixie at her age to keep up with them. Rae ended up with more ice cream on her face and clothes than in her stomach. Hailey wasn't going to be very happy with her. Maybe she could get her home and cleaned up before Hailey got home.

Dixie hurried the girls into the house and had almost gotten Rae cleaned up when she heard the back door that led from the garage to the kitchen open. "Mom, what's going on?" Usually Maddie Winslow picked up the girls and kept them until Hailey or Josh got home. Dixie had called Maddie to tell her she was taking the girls after school, but she'd forgotten to let Hailey know.

Alexa ran out of the guest bathroom where she'd been watching Dixie's efforts to clean up Rae. "Mama, Rae's a mess," she called out. Then she added, "Again!"

"Quit being a tattletale!" Kaiden scolded.

"You're not my boss."

"Yes, I am, because I'm the oldest."

"Girls!" Hailey yelled, putting a stop to their sisterly arguing.

Dixie walked out of the bathroom with Rae in tow. "It's nothing, really. We stopped off for some ice cream and Rae got a little on her clothes. No big deal." Dixie smiled down at her granddaughter.

Rae gave a thumbs-up and a smile in agreement. "Right, Nonnie." She turned and ran down the hall to the playroom to join her sisters.

Hailey shook her head as she watched her. "That girl's going to be the death of me."

"Or a breath of fresh air for all of us," Dixie said, smiling.

"I hope so," Hailey walked back into the kitchen. "How about a cup of tea?"

"Sounds good. I've been wanting to talk to you anyway."

Hailey gave her mother a long, knowing look. "What's Jason done now?"

Dixie sat down heavily on one of the island stools. "The bank repossessed his car."

Hailey stared at her mother in disbelief. "You're kidding me."

"No. Not kidding."

Dixie could see anger flash through Hailey. It was clear she was troubled by the whole incident with Jason.

"I could just strangle Jason for all of the heartache he's caused you and Dad. I don't want to upset you any more than you are, Mom, but I just don't understand how you put up with the things he does."

Dixie watched as her daughter busied herself with getting out two cups and heating up water for tea. When she'd finished making the tea, she brought a cup over to Dixie and sat down at the island with her.

"I don't get it, Mom. What did he think would happen if he didn't pay his car payment? Did he think they'd just let him keep it without paying for it?"

Dixie took a sip of her tea before answering. "I honestly cannot tell you what Jason was thinking, Hailey. What I can tell you is that I don't think I've ever been that angry with him."

Hailey appeared to be shocked by her mother's words. "Mom, I've never known you to ever be truly mad at Jason."

Dixie thought about this for a minute. "Well, this time I was mad, and he knew it, too." She took a deep breath. "But there's one good thing that's come out of this bad situation."

Hailey put down her tea and looked at her mother expectantly.

"Jason asked Dad for a job," Dixie announced with a smile.

Shaking her head, Hailey asked, "And you really think that's a good thing?"

"That's what I'm hoping and praying for."

Hailey got up, emptied her cup in the sink, and rinsed it out. She turned back to her mother and said in a soft voice, "I'm not sure that's such a good thing for Dad or Jason." She walked over to her mother and hugged her shoulders. "But, for all of our sakes, I'll hope and pray too."

Dixie reached up and gave Hailey's arm a loving squeeze. "I appreciate that."

At that moment, Rae burst into the kitchen. "Look, Nonnie, I drew a picture of you, Grandpa, and Uncle Jason." She smiled as she proudly held out her drawing for Dixie.

"That's us?" Dixie asked. She could see a series of circles and lines, but couldn't make out faces.

Rae frowned as she took the drawing back from Dixie. "You've got it upside down." Turning it over she handed it back. Now, Dixie could see three faces, but the thing that touched her heart was seeing the big smiles her granddaughter had drawn in the middle of each face. "I love it!" Dixie picked up Rae to give her a hug and a kiss.

Dixie turned the picture around to show Hailey. "Did you see this wonderful drawing that Rae did for me?"

Hailey walked over to the refrigerator, covered with many pictures that looked like the one she'd just received. "I've seen several of those wonderful drawings, Mom."

"Well, I guess we have a little artist on our hands," Dixie said as Rae wiggled out of her arms.

Opening the refrigerator, Hailey said, "I wish I could open this refrigerator and something that everyone liked to eat would jump out and present itself for our supper."

Trying to visualize such a thing, Dixie laughed out loud. "Wouldn't we all!"

As she sipped the last of her tea, she remembered one of the things she'd meant to ask Hailey. "Has Jason ever mention a friend of his named Eddy?"

"Eddy? I don't remember his ever talking about anyone by that name, but remember how in high school he was constantly surrounded by friends or those who wanted to be his friend? This Eddy could be someone from high school. I know when he was staying with us, he'd go out in the evenings. I assumed he was meeting up with friends, but he never mentioned any names. Why?"

"He came to the house this morning saying he was a friend of Jason's and wanted to take him to breakfast."

"Breakfast?" Hailey asked. "That's a little bit odd, don't you think?"

Dixie considered this for a minute. "Not really. He knew that Jason hadn't been working and thought he'd take him out to breakfast. Since they couldn't have breakfast together, I invited him to supper tonight."

Hailey stared at her mother. "Mom! Are you telling me that you invited a total stranger to have supper with y'all tonight without checking with Jason first? How do you even know for sure that he is a friend of Jason's?"

Dixie was beginning to question her idea of inviting Eddy for supper. She'd never considered that Eddy might not be telling the truth about being one of Jason's friends. Biting her lip, she asked, "Oh, Hailey, I didn't even think of that. What if you're right?"

Hailey chuckled, "Well, you'll know soon enough." Then reaching over to take her mother's hand, she added, "I'm sure everything's going to be alright."

Dixie gave Hailey's hand a squeeze. "Let's hope so. It may have been the wrong decision on my part to invite Eddy for supper tonight." Then she added with a laugh, "It won't be the first time I've been wrong, and I doubt it'll be the last!"

Chapter Eight

After leaving Hailey's, Dixie stopped by Harris Grocery to pick up some cube steak for supper. She had a special recipe that she liked to make with cube steak, cream of mushroom soup, and onion soup mix. Since it was one of Jason's favorite dishes, she hoped it would be something that Eddy would like as well. It seemed to Dixie that Jason hadn't had much of an appetite lately and was even losing weight. Surely, he'd be hungry after a full day of working. She hurried home to get the meal started. After getting the meat ready and four potatoes wrapped in foil placed in the oven with the timer set, Dixie headed out to her potting bench to plant the flowering plants she'd bought a few days ago but hadn't had time to put in the rustic woven baskets.

Dixie put on gardening gloves and added a layer of soil to the bottom of the baskets. As she began to break up the six-packs of yellow garden pansies and radiant marigolds to place them in the baskets along with some baby kale and herbs she was using as fillers, her mind drifted back to the conversation she'd had with Hailey about Eddy. If Eddy was truly one of Jason's friends, it was odd that Hailey hadn't heard of him. She thought Hailey knew all of Jason's friends. She would ask Jason about him first thing when he got home.

"Dixie?"

Dixie had been so deep in thought that she jumped at the sound of Alex's voice.

"Good grief, Alex, you scared me half to death," she scolded him.

Alex walked over to join her. "Sorry, but I looked everywhere for you and called your name several times. I was beginning to be concerned." He leaned over to give her a kiss on the cheek.

Dixie shook her head. "I'm sorry. I guess I was off in another world, but I'm back in this one now."

"Well, that's good, because you've got a couple of hungry men on your hands."

Dixie looked around at the darkening sky with the realization that she'd been working on the baskets much longer than she'd intended. She was glad she'd set the oven on a timer or the meal might be ruined. "I'm so sorry," she said as she took off her gardening gloves. "It'll only take me a few minutes to clean up here. I can have supper ready in less than ten minutes."

"What can I do to help?"

Alex's offer of help still took Dixie by surprise. He had never been one to help much in the kitchen, but lately he'd been a willing assistant.

"You can get the meat and potatoes out of the oven and set the table for four."

"Four?"

"I invited one of Jason's friends over for supper tonight."

"Really?"

"I sure did. His name is Eddy. He stopped by this morning looking for Jason." Dixie stopped what she was doing to look up at Alex. "It's been such a long time since we've gotten to know one of Jason's friends, so I decided to invite this one to supper."

"Jason hasn't mentioned anything to me about his friend coming for supper." Alex said, giving her a suspicious look.

Dixie smiled at Alex. "That's because Jason doesn't know Eddy is coming."

Shaking his head, Alex said, "Are you sure he wants this Eddy fellow to come to supper?"

Dixie said with more confidence that she felt, "I'm sure he's going to be happy to see an old friend."

"I hope you're right," Alex said as he headed back to the house. "I'll leave it to you to tell Jason."

Dixie quickly finished arranging the plants in the baskets, put her tools away, and was in the kitchen putting the final touches on the salad just as the front doorbell rang out. She glanced at the clock. It was a quarter to seven. Her plan had been to tell Jason about their special guest for supper after she'd finished with the salad. Now that Eddy was early, she wouldn't get the chance to talk to Jason first.

As Dixie quickly set down the salad bowl to hurry to the front door, she heard Jason call out. "I'll get it."

Dixie was walking into the living room as Jason opened the door.

"Eddy?" Jason said in a shocked voice. "What are you doing here?"

Dixie walked up to stand beside Jason. "I invited him for supper," she said as she opened the door all the way so that Eddy could get by Jason to enter the house. "Come in, Eddy."

Eddy stepped around Jason and handed Dixie the bottle of red wine he'd brought. Looking over at Jason, he said, "I believe I've caught Jason off guard. I take it he didn't know I was coming."

"That's totally my fault," Dixie said. "I got so caught up in preparing my garden for a party we're having this Saturday that I forgot to tell Jason you were coming for supper tonight."

Jason closed the door and turned to Eddy, "I'm sorry. I just wasn't expecting to see you at my front door." He patted Eddy on the back. "How great is it that you accepted Mom's invitation for supper."

Dixie could see that the smile Jason offered Eddy had been forced and the pat he gave him seemed much harder than a friendly pat. She was glad when she saw Alex walk into the room.

Alex held out his hand to Eddy to introduce himself. "I'm Alex, Jason's father."

Eddy shook his hand. "Glad to meet you, Mr. Bradley."

The four of them stared at one another before Dixie broke the uncomfortable silence.

"Supper's almost ready," she said. Turning to Jason she added, "Jason, you can show Eddy into the dining room while your father and I finish up in the kitchen."

"Glad to," Jason said as he led the way to the dining room. Eddy followed close behind.

As Alex followed Dixie to the kitchen he said, "Well, that was awkward. I still can't believe you didn't talk to Jason first before inviting this Eddy fellow over for supper."

Dixie said with regret, "You're right. I should have talked to Jason first. I don't think Jason finds Eddy as much of a friend as Eddy finds Jason."

"Well, whatever, we have to make it through this supper," Alex said as Dixie handed him the cube steak to take into the dining room.

Dixie followed with the baked potatoes and green beans. As she walked in the dining room, she was disturbed to find Jason and Eddy leaning in toward one another deep in what appeared to be a heated conversation. They straightened up at once as Alex and Dixie walked in.

Eddy looked up at Dixie and said with a smile, "It's a good thing you invited me here tonight, Mrs. Bradley. It seems that Jason had the wrong idea about why I came by this morning. He thought I was upset with him, which is far from the truth."

"We've got it all worked out now, Mom," Jason said nodding his head, "thanks to you."

As she set the potatoes and green beans on the table, Dixie said, "I'm glad y'all worked it out. Friends are so important in our lives. I have three of the best friends ever and don't know how I would survive without them."

"I don't know if I could survive without Eddy," Jason said.

"Thanks," Eddy said.

Dixie gave each of them a satisfied smile. Inviting Eddy over for supper had been the right thing to do after all.

"Let's pray," Alex said, bowing his head. "Dear Lord, we thank You for friends, new and old. We ask that You bless this food to our bodies and our bodies to Your service. Amen."

Rubbing his hands together, Alex said, "Let's eat."

As Dixie poured each of them a glass of the red wine that Eddy had brought, she asked, "Eddy, what is it you do for a living?"

Eddy finished chewing the bite of cubed steak he'd just put in his mouth before answering. "I have several small businesses here and in Bradford."

"What kind of businesses?" Alex asked.

Jason spoke up before Eddy could respond. "His businesses deal mostly in providing services. Like lawn care. He even has a couple of moving vans for in-town moves."

Turning to Eddy, Dixie asked, "What's the name of your moving company?"

Eddy grinned. "Good Moves."

"That's a great name for a moving company." Dixie chuckled.

"I'm sure that you're a busy man, keeping up with several businesses," Alex said.

"Yes, sir," Eddy agreed. "There's never a dull moment."

"Did you grow up here in Kerry?" Dixie asked.

"No, Ma'am. I grew up in Yankee territory."

"He doesn't know many people from Kerry," Jason said. "We met through a mutual friend."

Dixie was struck with an idea. Since the last one she'd had concerning Eddy was working out so well, she hoped this next one would.

"You should come to the engagement party we're having here Saturday night," she said. "That would give you a chance to meet some of Kerry's finest."

The look that passed over Jason's face made Dixie believe she'd made a grave mistake with her invitation.

"Mom, I'm sure Eddy's too busy to attend that party," Jason said with a deep frown.

"I'm not busy at all Saturday night," Eddy said to Jason. Then turning to Dixie, he said, "I'd love to come to your party."

"Great!" Dixie said. She looked over at Jason, who looked away

Eddy left right after finishing supper, saying he had some business to attend to. As soon as he left, Jason hurried to his bathroom, carefully pulled off the marble trim that surrounded the front panel of his whirlpool tub, and reached in behind the panel where he'd hidden the pills that would give him the serenity that he desperately needed right now. He took out one pill before carefully replacing the container, panel, and trim. Sitting on the edge of the tub, he popped the pill into his mouth and swallowed it with ease.

Jason could hear his mother and father clearing the table and cleaning up after the meal. He hoped it wouldn't take much longer before they headed to bed. His plan was to borrow his Dad's truck as soon as they were settled in their rooms for the night. He needed to find Eddy. He had to make him understand that he'd get his money.

Jason took a deep breath and stood up. He took his time dressing for the evening, then, putting his head in his hands, he waited for the drug he'd just taken to work its magic. He didn't have to wait long before he was feeling better, calmer. He headed back down the hallway and stood at the doorway to the kitchen. His parents were turned away from him, but he could hear them talking. After listening to their conversation, it was clear that they both liked Eddy. Usually, people did not easily fool his parents, but he could tell that Eddy had completely scammed the two of them tonight. Now that he thought about it, their liking Eddy could work to his advantage if he played it just right. But he would need to be cautious and patient, or the whole thing could blow up in his face.

Jason cleared his throat, drawing his parents' attention to him.

"Thanks for inviting Eddy over for supper and that great meal you made, Mom," Jason said as he went to give his mother a hug.

Hugging him back, she said, "At first, you seemed upset that I'd invited him."

Jason put a smile on his face. "I was just shocked when I saw him standing there on the front porch tonight."

"We really liked him," his mother said. "Why haven't you mentioned him before?"

"Like he said. We had a misunderstanding."

"So, everything's okay now?" His mom looked concerned.

"Yeah, looks like it."

Jason turned to his father, knowing this would be the tricky part. He had to play his father just right if he was going to be driving his truck tonight. He knew his dad would be more likely to give him the keys to the truck if he believed he was going to spend time with his sister. "I would sure like to visit Hailey and the girls. I haven't seen them in almost a week. I was just wondering, Dad, if you'd let me borrow your truck to go see them."

"That's a good idea! While you're there, you can tell Hailey all about Eddy," his mother said. "I was telling her about him this afternoon. You can fill in the details."

His father hesitated a minute before giving Jason his permission to use his truck. "The keys are hanging on the hook by the garage door."

As Jason retrieved the keys, his father added, "Don't be out too late, Son. We've got a big day tomorrow."

It took all of Jason's resolve to turn and give his father a thumbs-up instead of another finger before leaving.

Chapter Nine

Mark was finishing up with his usual paperwork at his desk when he got a call from dispatch about another robbery. This would make the ninth robbery in as many days. So far, they didn't have a workable lead. What demanded Mark's immediate attention was that this robbery also involved an assault. The earlier robberies had only involved property, no one had been assaulted. Mark's immediate concern was that the crimes of the perpetrator or perpetrators seemed to be escalating and now they were targeting victims. Were they gaining confidence, believing that they couldn't be caught?

The ambulance was pulling into the driveway just as Mark arrived. He noted that two deputy cars were on scene, and one he recognized as his son Aaron's. He followed the paramedics to where there was a female victim slouched on the bottom step of the side door entrance. Deputy Snyder was holding her head gently in his lap and pressing a cloth that was quickly turning red to her forehead.

Mark stood back, taking in the scene before him. He noticed that Deputy Snyder continued to gently cradle the victim's head as the paramedics tried to gain access to the victim. It was then that he realized the identity of the victim. It was Mrs. Valida Snyder, Deputy Snyder's mother.

Mark walked over to Deputy Snyder, leaned in close, and gently placed his hand on his shoulder as he said, "Scott, it's time to let the paramedics do their job."

Deputy Snyder looked up at Mark. He gently placed her head into the hands of a paramedic and stood up to join Mark.

"She's in good hands," Mark said as the two anxiously watched the paramedics. After a few minutes, he asked, "Was your mom able to give you any information about what happened?"

"No, sir. She was pretty shook up and wasn't making much sense."

"What can you tell me about what happened here?"

Referring to the small notebook he'd removed from his shirt pocket, Deputy Snyder began his report. "At 6:12 pm I responded to a dispatch call of a home owner reporting a robbery at 431 West Ridge. Recognizing the address as my mama's house, I turned on my lights and siren and got here as fast as I could. When I arrived, I discovered my mother there on the back steps, unconscious." He paused, taking a deep breath to regain his composure. "I immediately called for an ambulance. My mother regained consciousness for a few minutes, but was unresponsive to my questions."

"I see that Deputy Weaver's on scene."

"Yes sir, he arrived shortly after I called for an ambulance."

The paramedics were lifting Deputy Snyder's mother onto the stretcher after starting an IV as well as securing her neck with a brace.

"You go with your mother," Mark said to Deputy Snyder. "We'll take care of things here." Mark watched as they placed Mrs. Snyder in the ambulance and Deputy Snyder got in beside her.

Mark walked toward the garage where he was sure he'd find Aaron.

He entered the garage through the buckled garage door. It appeared that a jack of some kind had been used to lift the garage door far enough to gain entrance. The garage was empty except for a few hand tools left hanging on the pegboard above an attached workbench. He found Aaron standing in the middle of the garage taking pictures.

"Any idea what happened here?" Mark asked.

Aaron stopped what he was doing and looked at his father. "All I can tell you for sure is that the garage seems to have been accessed just like the four other garages that were broken into."

"Looks that way," Mark said as he looked around the garage.

"Can't know what's been taken until Scott gets back to tell us what's missing," Aaron said, shaking his head.

"I can help with that."

The deep voice startled both Mark and Aaron. They looked up and saw an elderly gentleman standing on the other side of the damaged garage door.

"I live right next door," he offered. "Been Valida's neighbor for well over forty years, Sheriff Weaver, and I know everything that belongs in this garage."

Mark smiled as he extended his hand. "Well then, you're the right man to help."

"Name's Orville Thompson," the man said, stepping up to shake Mark's hand. "I can't believe this happened. I was only gone for thirty minutes to get some groceries and came back to find this had happened to Valida."

"It's not your fault, sir," Aaron said.

"Maybe not, but if I'd been home I'd have seen who done it. Maybe I could've stopped them."

"And gotten yourself hurt," Mark said.

Orville considered this for a moment, then shook his head. "Maybe, but I can tell you that if I'd been here I bet her brand new 50" Magnum Dixie Chopper mower would be right here where we're standing."

Aaron removed a small blue spiraled notebook from his breast pocket and took out his pen before asking Orville, "Do you notice anything else missing?"

For the next half hour, Aaron followed Orville as he took an inventory of the garage contents. Along with the Dixie Chopper, Orville noted there were several power tools missing. Aaron would check his list later with Deputy Snyder to make sure his list was complete.

Mark left Aaron in charge of the scene and headed to Kerry Memorial General Hospital to check on Deputy Snyder's mother. Walking in the doors of the hospital brought back unsettling memories of the weeks he'd spent there. He shook them off as he entered the emergency room where he found Deputy Snyder. Mark recognized the deputy's wife Kate and his sisters Anna and Denise surrounding him.

Deputy Snyder stood when he saw Mark approaching. "Hey, Sheriff. Thanks for coming."

"How's she doing, Scott?" Mark asked, putting a comforting hand on his shoulder.

"They've taken her for a CT scan," Scott said. "We'll know more after that."

"Hey, Sheriff," Kate said. Mark leaned over to give her and then Scott's sisters a comforting embrace. He'd known Scott's family since they'd moved to Kerry when Scott was in the fifth grade. Layne had taught each of them. He hated that this had happened to their mother. Miss Valida was a well-liked member of the Kerry community. Mark couldn't imagine who would want to hurt her.

"We're going to find who did this to you mother," Mark said. "I want y'all to keep me informed about her condition."

Turning to Scott, he added, "Aaron is at your mother's house now with one of her neighbors who's helping him inventory what's missing and might have been stolen."

Scott smiled, shaking his head. "That'd be Mr. Orville. If anyone knows what's in Mama's garage, it'll be Mr. Orville. Since Dad died, he's taken care of the place and watched out for Mama."

"It's good to know we've got the right man helping with that, but we'll want you to have a look around when you can to see if you notice anything else and also to verify the list of missing items Mr. Orville is helping with," Mark said.

"I'll do it as soon as I know what's going on here," Scott said.

"No hurry, Scott. You take care of things here." Mark turned to Kate. "Is there anything I can do for y'all before I go?"

She smiled wearily at him. "Nothing I can think of right now, Sheriff."

"Well, you let me know if you think of anything, and remember to keep me informed about your mother's condition." Mark turned to leave.

"There is one thing you can do," Scott said, stopping Mark.

Mark turned back around. "What's that?"

"You can say a prayer for Mama," Scott said, looking directly at him.

"Yes, I can, and I will."

Mark had called Layne as he'd driven to Mrs. Snyder's house to let her know that he'd be late for supper, but hadn't imagined that things were going to take as long as they had. He knew Layne would be worried, but he also knew that after all the years he'd been involved in law enforcement she'd be understanding. He hadn't eaten since breakfast and hoped she'd saved him some supper.

"I'm home," Mark called out as he walked into the unusually quiet house. He went to the hall closet, where he locked up his gun and then went in search of his wife.

"Layne?"

"Out here."

Mark went through the kitchen and out the patio doors to the deck where he found Layne sitting in one of the deck chairs. He leaned over and gave her a kiss. "What are you doing out here alone in the dark?"

"Thinking."

He sat down in the chair next to her, taking her hand in his. "What were you thinking about?"

Layne looked over at her husband. "About how blessed we are."

"Well, you're right about that."

Layne sighed, "You know how I've been upset about Jenny wanting to have the wedding way up in Indiana."

"I think I may have heard you mention that a time or two," Mark said with a smile giving her hand a playful squeeze.

"Well, Mom helped me see that I was being silly about the whole thing. It doesn't matter where they get married. It's where they choose to live that truly matters." She smiled over at Mark, squeezing his hand in return. "And we're blessed that they've chosen to live right here in Kerry along with Blair and Nathan's families."

"You're right about that."

They sat in silence, pondering the many blessings of having their children and grandchildren close by.

"I'm hoping for one more blessing," Mark said, breaking the silence.

Layne looked over at her husband questioningly.

"That you're going to bless me with supper. I'm starving!"

Chapter Ten

After Jason got in his father's truck, he headed for Hailey's knowing that his mother would check with his sister to see if he'd actually stopped by. He also knew that Hailey didn't like for her daughters to eat candy, but it'd become routine for him to bring them a treat when he visited, so he made a quick stop at a convenience store on his way over.

As he pulled up into Hailey's driveway, he noticed that there were very few lights on in the house and Josh's truck was the lone vehicle under the carport. He realized too late that he should have called to make sure his sister was home before telling his parents he was going to her house. Now, he was faced with a difficult decision. Should he stay and visit with Josh– who obviously didn't like him–and the girls, or leave and face his mother's questions? After a short deliberation, he decided his best choice was to visit with Josh and the girls. He didn't need to raise any suspicions in his mother's mind.

Jason walked through the carport to the side door and knocked. It took a minute before he saw the kitchen light go on and Josh's annoyed face appear through the glass in the door. As Josh opened the door, Jason saw that Kaiden, Alexa, and Rae had followed their father to the door to see what stranger had come to pay them a visit on a school night. All three girls squealed with delight when they saw that their uncle was their mysterious visitor.

Three -year-old Rae rushed into Jason's arms, almost knocking him backwards. "Uncle Jason!" she screamed as she reached up and curled her arms around his neck. The other two girls wrapped their arms around him before he even got inside the door.

"Well, if it isn't my three beautiful nieces!" Jason said, trying to get in the door as best he could.

"Come on, girls," Josh said, pulling the oldest two away from Jason. "At least let your uncle get in the house before you attack him."

Jason continued inside, picking Rae up in his arms. "I heard that there were some girls who lived here who were being candy deprived," he said in a teasing voice as he pulled three candy bars from his jacket pocket and held them out. He was met with even more squealing as they each grabbed a bar.

"Thanks, Uncle Jason," they called out as they took off with their treats into the family room.

Jason turned back toward Josh who was still holding the door open. Jason thought for a moment that he was holding it open wanting him to leave. But Josh shook his head, closed the door, and said, "You know your sister's not home," as he walked past him to join his daughters.

Jason followed. "Yeah, I saw that her car was gone. Did she get called out?"

"Yep."

Jason ignored the irritation he could feel coming from Josh and sat down with the girls on the couch. He spent the next thirty minutes talking and playing with his nieces. He was beginning to get anxious about the time. He couldn't wait around any longer if he was going to find Eddy tonight. He wasn't sure how he was going to make his exit. Luckily, Josh helped by reminding the girls that they had school tomorrow and it was bedtime. They gave their uncle kisses and hugs as he got up to leave.

Josh walked him to the door. "I'll see you tomorrow at work," he said with the tone of a question in his voice rather than a statement.

Jason turned to look straight at Josh. "I'll be there."

As Jason drove away, he wondered what he'd done that had turned Josh against him. When Josh and Hailey had first married, the two of them were great friends. It was since he'd moved back to Kerry that he'd noticed a change in Josh's attitude toward him. Maybe he wore out his welcome when he stayed on their couch those few weeks. He'd been very careful to keep his habit hidden, so there was no way that his brother-in-law knew anything about it. He was confident that if Josh did know anything, he'd have brought it to Hailey's attention, and she would've busted him. Maybe Josh had always felt threatened by the possibility that Jason would someday go back to work at Bradley Construction, a company that his dad had always wanted him to be a partner in. He decided that Josh was the one with the problem, not him, so he put it out of his mind. He needed to be concentrating on what he was going to say to Eddy when he found him, not Josh's insecurities.

Jason headed to a house a few miles outside of Kerry where he'd always been able to find Eddy when he needed him. He knew Eddy wouldn't stick around Kerry for very long. He didn't go looking for clients. They went looking for him to get that special customer service. Jason laughed to himself remembering how he'd been turned onto Eddy by his former high school sweetheart, Angie McKelvey. It was his good luck to have run into her at a party one night when he was hitting bottom. He'd been using Coby Drugstore to have his scripts filled, until Zeke, the son-in-law of his mother's friend and pharmacist at the drugstore, became suspicious and began asking too many questions. He needed help and there Angie was, offering relief. She'd even driven him to the house for his first buy. He'd never asked Angie or Eddy how Eddy got his pills, never wanted to know. All he cared about was that Eddy always had what he needed.

Lately, Jason had been low on funds. He'd pawned a few things that he didn't think his parents would notice were gone, but that money hadn't lasted long. He'd known that Eddy wouldn't carry him for too long, but he'd never imagined that he'd show up at his house and talk to his mother. He had to convince Eddy that he could be trusted to pay him back with interest. He couldn't risk him showing up at his house again.

Jason reached his destination a little after ten o'clock. There were lights on in the house. He followed the same procedures that Angie had showed him that first night and he'd used every time to make contact– flash bright lights four times, text a number, then wait. He didn't have to wait long before the light on the front porch went on and off four times in rapid succession. .Jason stepped out of his father's truck and walked toward the front porch.

"What are you doing here?"

Jason was startled by the deep voice that came from the shadows. He stopped and scanned the area in front of him. It took a minute for his eyes to adjust to the darkness to make out a lone figure standing off to the right of the lighted front porch.

"You know why I'm here. Don't play games with me."

The figure stepped up into the light coming from the front porch. Jason watched as Eddy came walking towards him. He'd been wondering what he would do if he didn't find Eddy at the house tonight. He didn't know where else he would find him.

"Well, if it isn't my good friend Jason come to see me. I was worried you were thinking that supper with your parents would settle your debt. It was so nice of your mommy to feed me and even invite me to a big party, but that ain't gonna settle your debt with me, your best friend." Eddy smirked as he stepped up onto the porch.

Jason ignored the taunt as he moved closer. "I'm gonna pay."

"You got the money?"

Jason slowly shook his head. "Not right now, but I'll get it."

Eddy leaned his head back and laughed long and loud.

Jason moved closer. "I promise."

Eddy suddenly stopped his laughter and looked down at Jason. "Oh, you promise?" he said sarcastically.

Jason remained silent, sensing Eddy's rising anger.

"Do you know how many times I've heard that?" Eddy said in a voice filling with fury.

Jason stepped back, suddenly worried that Eddy might not be as understanding as he'd convinced himself he would be.

"I-I've got a job," Jason stammered.

"A job?" Eddy repeated as if it was a small thing.

"I'm making good money and can pay you back in no time," Jason said.

Eddy was off the porch with his face in Jason's so fast that he didn't have time to react. "'No time' is now!"

Fear filled Jason's entire body. He hadn't expected this reaction from Eddy. He'd imagined he'd be invited into the house to sit down and they'd talk this out. He now realized he'd misjudged the situation and how dangerous this could become.

Thinking fast while trying to keep his voice light and friendly, Jason said, "Come on, Eddy, don't get mad. What I meant by 'no time' was that I'd have it for you tomorrow. That's what I came to tell you that I don't have the money tonight, but I can get it to you tomorrow."

Eddy took a minute to study Jason's face before taking a step back and asking skeptically, "You'll have my money tomorrow?"

"Tomorrow," Jason confirmed, nodding.

Eddy smiled and gave Jason a playful push. "Why didn't you say that right off? I thought you were going to try to stiff me for another week."

Forcing a smile, Jason said, "I wouldn't do that to you, Eddy."

They walked back to the porch. As Eddy leaned over to sit on the top step, Jason froze when he saw him take a small handgun from his pocket and place it on the step beside him. He tried not to stare, but recognized it as a J-frame, just like the one his roommate in college used to have.

"Then, I'll see you tomorrow with the twelve hundred fifty you owe," Eddy said.

Eddy's words took Jason's attention away from the J-frame. "I-it's a thousand I owe," he stammered.

"It's twelve hundred fifty," Eddy said, grinning at Jason. Shrugging, he added, "Gotta charge interest."

Jason found it hard to breathe, but knew it'd be futile to argue and could be dangerous. "Okay, then, twelve fifty it is," he said weakly, turning to leave.

"Ya know you can get the same relief for less," Eddy called after him.

Jason turned around. "Yeah, I know."

"Just sayin'."

Jason turned and started back to his truck. He could feel Eddy's eyes on him as he walked away. As he started the truck, his whole body began to shake. He knew what Eddy was referring to as getting the "same relief for less"– heroin. Angie had turned to heroin, but he wasn't ready to turn to heroin as a means of cutting costs. It had gotten harder to come up with the money he needed to stay healthy, but now that he had a job it'd be easier. However, he had no idea where he'd come up with twelve hundred fifty dollars by tomorrow night to hand over to Eddy.

Chapter Eleven

etty Jo was looking forward to a quiet evening alone with Don. She'd been called by Memorial General Hospital to work several evenings the past few weeks. Even though she'd retired from nursing almost three years ago, she found herself working several days a week covering for nurses who couldn't make their shift. She enjoyed the work most days, but found it more challenging to work evenings and night. She especially didn't enjoy the evening shifts when she didn't get to spend any time with Don. Since the near tragic accident caused by his diabetes, she treasured their time together.

Today, she'd worked day shift, so she could be home with Don in the evening. On her way home from work she decided to pick up ribeye steaks, his favorite, at Harris Grocery. While the steaks were being cut and sealed in their closely guarded secret marinade, she walked around the store to pick up the other items she needed for supper. When she headed down the produce isle, she was surprised to see Nona coming toward her.

"Well, fancy meeting you here," Betty Jo said as she gave Nona a quick hug.

"I'm picking up steaks for tonight's supper for Daddy and me,"

Nona said. Then with a smile she added, "And Monty. In fact, Monty's the one who's going to grill these steaks for us."

Betty Jo breathed a sigh of relief when Nona said that Monty was grilling and not her ex-husband Bill. She knew Bill kept trying to wiggle his way into Nona's life, and Betty Jo didn't like that one bit. "That sounds like fun."

"I believe it will be."

"Seems like you've been seeing a good bit of Monty lately," Betty Jo said in a teasing voice,

"Come to think of it," Nona said, "he's been over quite a lot lately. Daddy enjoys his company."

"Oh, so it's your father who 'enjoys his company,'" Betty Jo said with a sly smile.

"Okay, you got me." Nona laughed. "I do too!"

"Then it's good for all of you."

"I guess it is," Nona said.

Betty Jo heard her name called out over the intercom letting her know that her steaks were ready for pick-up. "Gotta go. Have fun tonight. See you tomorrow," she called to Nona as she headed to the butcher's counter.

Hearing that Nona was having Monty over for supper made Betty Jo smile all the way home. She felt that after what Nona had been through this past year, she deserved all the happiness life could give her.

She'd hoped that Don would be home to help her carry in the groceries, but found he'd taken his truck to pick up something for his boat-building project. After carrying in the groceries by herself and putting them away, she headed upstairs to change clothes. She was on her way back down the stairs when she heard Don's truck pull into the driveway.

Great timing. Now he can start the grill.

"I'm home," Don called out as he came into the house.

"Just in time to start the steaks," Betty Jo said. "Where've you been? Picking up more parts for the boat?"

"Nope, I've been down at Dane's house," Don said, "and it's not a boat. It's a canoe."

Betty Jo walked over to the refrigerator to get the steaks out. "What were you doing at Dane's?"

"They were robbed last night."

Betty stopped what she was doing to give Don her full attention. "Dane Hudson?" Dane Hudson lived one street from their house and had been their neighbor for over twenty years.

"That's the one."

"A robbery in our neighborhood?"

"Someone stole his brand-new Polaris Ranger. Looks like they drove right up into his driveway sometime last night, loaded the Ranger up from the carport where he had it parked, and drove off." Don shook his head in disbelief. "Neither Dane nor Evelyn heard a sound, slept right through the whole thing. He had no idea he'd been robbed until he went out this morning to get in his truck and saw that his ATV wasn't where he'd parked it under the carport."

"That's awful! Was anything else taken?"

"Not that they know of, but they're still checking."

Betty Jo started getting the steaks ready for the grill when Don stopped her. "Let's hold off on the steaks for a little while."

"Why?"

"I'd like to check things out to make sure all our equipment is secure."

"Oh, Don, do you think we might be in danger of being robbed?"

"You never know," he said. "I'd rather be safe than sorry."

Don gave her a reassuring hug. "I'm sure there's nothing to worry about. It's just best to be cautious."

"Well, it makes me nervous that there's been a robbery so close," Betty Jo said as Don went out the door.

Nona was pulling up in her driveway later than she'd planned, hoping that she wouldn't find Monty's car already there. It had taken longer than she hoped it would to get all she needed for grilling. She'd had to go to two stores to find the charcoal that Monty said he preferred. It wasn't like Nona to care what someone else preferred, but for some reason she found she wanted to make Monty happy. Plus she wanted a great grilled steak. She slammed on her brakes when she saw the car she most dreaded seeing– a graphite Mercedes Benz E350 Sports Sedan– parked right up next to the back door of the house she shared with her father. Bill was here, again!

Disturbing memories came flooding back as she recalled other times she'd found Bill's car parked in her driveway with Amy as his passenger and all the havoc that had followed as they worked to wreck her life. She took a deep breath as she said a quick prayer. *Dear Lord, give me strength.*

With renewed determination to face the situation she would find inside, Nona got out of her car, grabbed the two bags of groceries, and pushed open the back door. She put the groceries on the kitchen counter and went in search of her father and Bill. She could hear voices coming from her father's study.

Nona stood outside the door for a minute listening in on their conversation.

"That's an interesting idea, Bill," she heard her father's booming voice say. "I'm not sure why I hadn't thought of that."

She heard Bill give a short laugh before saying, "I'm not either, but it's a good investment. I promise you that."

Nona had heard enough. She took a deep breath to calm herself before she gently tapped on the study door and said in a soft voice, "Daddy, are you in here?" In truth, Nona had wanted to throw open the study door and scream obscenities at Bill, but the last thing she needed to do was upset her father. With his advancing Alzheimer's, she worked hard to keep things calm and avoid confrontations.

"Come in, Nona, you're just in time," her father said as he motioned her into his study.

Nona saw that her father was sitting behind his large oak desk leaning back in his chair, while Bill was sitting in one of the leather chairs across from him, smiling up at her as she entered the room. She ignored Bill and went behind the desk to give her father a kiss on the cheek. She stood with her hand on her father's shoulder, not returning Bill's smile.

"In time for what, Daddy?" Nona asked.

Her father patted her hand as he explained. "Bill has informed me of a business he believes would be advantageous for me to invest in along with the two of you."

"Invest along with the two of us?" Nona asked, confused. The livid look she gave Bill as she stood behind her father should have stopped him from saying anything, but it didn't.

"That's right," Bill said, still smiling.

Nona wasn't sure what was going on with Bill, but she knew she wanted to bring it to an end. "Well, okay then, we can talk about this later," she said, hoping that Bill would get the hint it was time for him to leave.

Surprisingly, Bill seemed to get her hint. "That sounds good," he said, getting up from his chair. "I'll check in with you sometime tomorrow, Mr. James."

Her father stood to shake Bill's hand. "I look forward to it."

"I'll walk you out," Nona said to Bill as she followed him out into the hall. She softly closed the door to her father's study behind her.

"What in the world was going on in there?" Nona asked as soon as they were away from the study.

"When I got here today to check on your father," Bill began, "I found him in his study going through some papers. He was agitated and mumbling to himself about some investment he wanted to make, but couldn't find the paperwork. I decided that the best thing I could do to calm him down was to pretend I was the one who had brought the investment to him and had all of the papers at my office."

Nona eyed him. "Where did he get the notion that he wanted to make an investment?"

"I don't know, but I made up some stuff, and that seemed to calm him down."

"I guess I should thank you," she said, "but what I don't understand is why you're always coming to check on him. I asked you to stop coming."

"He was my father-in-law for many years and I worry about him," Bill said. He reached to take her hand in his. Nona jerked her hand back.

"I'm not buying that, Bill," Nona said, opening the back door for him to leave. "You never seemed to even like my father when we were married. I know for a fact he never cared much for you. So stop coming by to check on him."

Bill walked through the door. Looking back, he said, "I do it for Grace, Nona. She worries about him."

Nona yelled, "Not buying that one either!" and slammed the door behind him. She hadn't meant to slam the door that hard, but it felt good to release some of her anger. She had promised herself she wasn't going to let Bill upset her anymore, but she'd broken that promise all to pieces. She leaned over, putting her hands on her knees, and took three deep breaths, willing herself to calm down. She'd almost reached calm when there was a knock at the door.

If he thinks I'm going to let him back into this house, he's got another think coming!

She pulled open the door with such force that it almost crashed into the wall. "What in the world could you possibly want?" she asked through clenched teeth.

Monty stood at the door with a bottle of wine in his hands. He drew back and looked at Nona with confusion. "I want to bring you wine to go with our dinner," he said bewildered, "but I think I've made a mistake,"

Nona was mortified. She watched in dismay as Monty took two steps back. "Oh, Monty," she explained, "I'm so sorry. I thought you were Bill coming back after I'd just kicked him out." She reached out her arms to him. "I feel terrible that I said that to you."

"I'm not feeling that great about it either," Monty said as he came closer.

"I promise that those words were never meant for you," Nona said. "Please come in." She stepped back from the door for him to enter.

Nona followed Monty into the kitchen where he set the wine down on the counter and turned to her. "Am I still welcome?"

"Of course, you are more than welcome," she said with a smile. "It's just that I found Bill in the house talking to my father about making some kind of investment when I got home." She looked into those deep green eyes of his and sighed. "And I was upset."

Monty reached out and with one smooth motion pulled her in and kissed her deeply. Nona gave in to his kiss, allowing it to take away all thoughts of Bill and the lingering anger she felt.

When they finally parted, Nona stayed in his embrace resting her head on his chest and listening to the rhythm of his heart. She felt as light and happy as she had in a very long time. They stayed like that for several minutes until they heard the echoing sound of footsteps coming down the hall.

Her father entered the room. "Are we eating tonight or standing around hugging one another?"

Both Nona and Monty laughed.

Chapter Twelve

After Jason left, Dixie and Alex finished up in the kitchen. Both were pleased with the way things went having Eddy over for supper. Once they'd finished with the kitchen, Alex went outside to make sure his golf cart that his granddaughters loved to ride around in and his ATV he used to get around in the woods when he hunted were parked safely in the garage and the garage door closed. He'd heard that there'd been several robberies around town over the past few days. Even though everything was insured, he'd told Dixie he didn't want any of his property to be added to those statistics if he could help it.

While Alex was checking on things outside, Dixie headed to her room. She'd had a long day and was ready to bring it to an end. As she got ready for bed, her thoughts kept returning to Jason. She saw it as a good sign that he'd asked his father for a job, but somewhere deep down his reasons for wanting to work with his father were also worrying her. When he'd first come back home, he'd been adamant about not working with Alex in the construction business. Now, he appeared to be happy to be working there. Something about the complete turnaround he'd made in such a short time was bothering her. It made her question what had brought on such a sudden change.

Dixie wondered if it could have been the shock of having the car he loved repossessed. If it was disturbing to her, it must have been traumatic for him. Maybe that event had made him realize he needed to get his finances in order, and the best way to do that was to start making money by getting a job. Dixie at once felt better about the whole situation now that she'd figured out a reasonable answer for what had caused his change of heart about working for his father. With that problem solved, hopefully she could have a peaceful night's sleep.

She pulled back the covers and got into bed. She propped up her pillows, put on her reading glasses, and picked up her book from the nightstand. She was looking forward to getting lost in a good story when she heard a soft tapping on her bedroom door.

She pulled off her glasses as she called out, "Alex?"

"Can I come in?" her husband asked.

"Of course, come in."

Alex cracked the door open only enough to put his head in the room. "I wanted to wish you a good night."

Dixie smiled at her husband. "You can come in and give me a kiss with that good night, if you want."

Alex smiled back as he opened the door. "It'd be my pleasure," he said as he sat next to her on the bed.

Alex bent over and kissed her full on the mouth. Then he got up and walked out of the room, softly closing the door behind him without even a backwards glance.

Dixie stared after him. Alex usually kissed her on her forehead, her cheek, or the top of her head. She couldn't recall the last time he'd given her a kiss like that one, on the mouth. She was reminded that she liked it very much when her husband kissed her on the mouth. *Maybe I should tell him sometime.* She put her glasses back on and picked up her book.

"Mom!"

Dixie was annoyed that someone seemed to be intent on waking her up. She thought that if she kept her eyes closed they might go away. Suddenly, the realization came to her that something was wrong. She sat up, trying to bring herself out of a deep sleep. Opening her eyes wide, she asked in as clear a voice as she could, "What's wrong?"

"Mom, wake up!" Jason said as he continued to gently shake her shoulder.

"Jason?" Why was Jason in her room shaking her?

"Mom, you were having a nightmare," he said.

"A nightmare?" Dixie couldn't seem to make sense of what was going on.

Jason took his hand off her shoulder, "I just got home and was walking past your room when I heard you call my name. But when I opened your door, you were tossing and turning and mumbling a bunch of garbled words I couldn't understand." Jason ran his hand through his hair, shaking his head. "With the way you were acting, I realized that you must be having a nightmare. You scared me."

Dixie rubbed her eyes as she came fully awake. "I'm sorry," she said. It was then that she recalled the dream, the nightmare, she'd had. She tried to shake it out of her mind.

Jason was watching his mother closely. "It was a nightmare, wasn't it?"

Dixie nodded without looking up at her son.

"Do you want to talk about it?" Jason asked.

She offered a weak smile. "I'm not sure I remember enough of it to even talk about it," she lied.

"Do you want me to get Dad?"

"No, there's no reason to disturb him."

"Do you think you can go back to sleep?" Jason patted her hand.

Dixie looked up at her son's face. She was touched by the concern she saw on it. "I think so."

"Do you want me to sit with you until you do?"

Taking his hand in hers, she said, "I'll be fine. You go on to bed."

Jason stood. "If you're sure…"

"I'm sure," Dixie said, hoping she sounded reassuring.

"Okay, then. I'll see you in the morning."

Jason turned and left her room.

Dixie was left alone in the dark recalling the details of the dream that had brought an end to her night's rest.

How could I possibly tell him that the nightmare I had was about him?

Sleep escaped Dixie after Jason left the room. She read her book and played a few dozen games of solitaire on her tablet, all in an effort to distract her from remembering her nightmare. But no matter how hard she tried to occupy her mind with other activities, bits and pieces of the dream crept into her thoughts. When she closed her eyes, she was bombarded with vivid images from her nightmare. After several frustrating hours of fighting it, she decided it might help if she wrote down what she could remember about it. Maybe writing it down would help her make some sense of it so she could put it out of her mind. She sat up on the side of the bed, turned on the light, got a notebook and pen from her bedside table, and began to write down what she could remember about her bad dream.

It's a regular school day. I'm sitting on a stool at the front of the room reading a book to my students. I'm not sure what the name of the book is, but it has a picture of a dark-haired boy riding a bike on the front with a tornado coming at him. My students aren't listening to me. Instead, they are playing games and talking as I'm trying to read this book to them. I talk louder and louder, but they continue with their games and talking and pay no attention to me at all. I'm getting angry and frustrated when all of a sudden, the door slams open and there stands Jason. I look over at him, wondering why he's coming into my room in the middle of the day. The students get quiet and look over at him. This makes me even angrier because they're paying attention to him and not to me. Jason begins to laugh out loud. It takes me a minute before I realize that he's laughing at me. He's saying something to me, but all I hear is his laughter getting louder and louder. I can't understand what he's trying to tell me. I walk toward him so I can hear him better. He's telling me I'm not supposed to be teaching anymore. I'm supposed to be driving the school bus. The students then begin to laugh and make ugly faces at me. I'm so embarrassed and feel like a fool, realizing I don't belong there. I'm in the wrong place doing the wrong thing.

I run out of the room crying and see that now everyone is in the hallway laughing at me. Some of the students put out their feet to trip me. I fall down, but keep getting up, trying to get out of the school where I can get on the school bus. The farther I go down the hallway, the longer it seems to get. I can see Jason way down at the end of the hallway. He's doubled over with laughter as he watches me trip and fall. I finally make it to the end of the hallway, but Jason isn't there. I can see a bright yellow school bus parked outside the school. I understand this is the bus I'm supposed to be driving. When I turn around to look back down the hall, it's empty.

I run out of the school, get on the school bus, and look at the driver's seat. Jason is sitting in the driver's seat. I start to cry again because I know I'm supposed to be the driver. He frowns at me and pushes me to take the seat behind him. He takes off before I can sit. I almost fall down in the aisle. I finally sit down and look out the window to see where we're going. I can tell that Jason is going too fast on the curvy road now that it's beginning to rain. Before I can say anything, I see that we're heading straight toward the river where the bridge has been washed away. I can see the metal bridge floating away from us down the river. I scream out Jason's name over and over, but he doesn't seem to hear. He keeps going faster and faster toward the river. Just as we were about to plunge into the river, Jason woke me up.

Dixie sighed deeply as she finished writing. As she read over what she'd written, she began to shake. She put the notebook to the side, lay back on the bed, and wrapped herself up in the blanket, hoping to find warmth. She was wondering why the dream had been upsetting to her. In truth, she found it terrifying. There were no monsters, no gruesome injuries, no one died in her dream. Yet the dream filled her with terror. It was Jason's laughter and the look on his face as he pushed her to sit on the bus that had most disturbed her. She'd never been good at interpreting dreams, but wished she knew someone who was. She read through her dream once more hoping to make some sense of it. Maybe it was simply one of those senseless dreams. It had helped to write it all down. She might share it with Hailey someday to get her take on it. For now, she put her notebook back into her nightstand, turned off the light, and hoped for a few more hours of sleep.

The sunlight coming in her bedroom window woke Dixie. Usually, she was up before the sun, but not today. She looked at the clock on her nightstand. It was past eight. She quickly got out of bed, putting on her robe as she headed out of her bedroom toward the much too quiet kitchen. She found it empty. Alex had left for work without waking her. She took a cup out of the cabinet and headed for the coffeepot. She was surprised to find a note taped to it.

Dixie, Jason said you had another nightmare. Knew you'd need the rest, so we'll pick up breakfast at The Grill. Alex

Dixie was relieved to know that Jason had gone to work with Alex. She knew he hadn't gotten home until late and worried that he'd sleep in. Maybe he was truly turning over a new leaf and taking the responsibility of his job more seriously this time. In the past, he would have slept until noon or maybe even later. She fixed herself breakfast and ate as she watched an episode of *Fixer Upper_* on *HGTV*. She decided right then that if she ever won the lottery and became a millionaire, she'd hire Joanne as her interior decorator. She knew she needed to turn off the TV and get ready for the day, but it felt good to simply sit and do nothing for a little bit. After the trauma of last night, she needed some "brain fluff"– as her sister used to refer to TV. Dixie checked the clock and decided that she had enough time to watch another episode before she needed to shower and dress. She poured herself another cup of coffee and leaned back in her chair.

Chapter Thirteen

It had taken Dixie longer to get ready than she expected. It was one of those days when she just couldn't find anything to wear, or, rather, anything she wanted to wear. She was supposed to meet Layne, Betty Jo, and Nona for their medicure at eleven and it was five after. She pulled up to the nail salon beside Layne, who was still sitting in her car. Getting out of her car, she tapped on Layne's passenger window. Layne lowered the window. "What are you doing just sitting here in your car?" Dixie asked.

Layne blushed. "I was singing along with one of my favorite Carole King songs—"You've Got A Friend." I just couldn't make myself get out until it was finished."

"I totally understand," Dixie said."That's one of my favorites too."

Dixie looked around the parking lot for Betty Jo's and Nona's cars. "I thought I was going to be the last one here, but I guess the other two are running late too."

Dixie and Layne walked into the salon together. They were selecting their polish when they heard Betty Jo and Nona enter, both talking excitedly.

"Are you telling me they just took Dane's golf cart out from under his carport?" Nona was asking Betty Jo.

"That's what Don said," Betty Jo confirmed. "They must have lifted it up onto a trailer, because neither Dane nor Evelyn heard anything, and their bedroom faces their driveway."

"That's unbelievable!"

"That's the third robbery I've heard about this week," Nona said as Layne and Dixie joined them.

"We're ready for you ladies." The salon receptionist interrupted their conversation as she directed each to a seat for their pedicures. They took off their shoes and placed their feet in the warm water.

Layne picked up their conversation where they'd left off. "Mark said that in the past two weeks there have been over nine robberies reported of golf carts, four wheelers, and ATVs taken."

"Do you know if he has any leads?" Betty Jo leaned over to ask Layne.

"If he does, he hasn't shared them with me," Layne said. "All I know is that they come in the middle of the night and no one ever hears or knows anything until they get up the next morning."

Dixie said thoughtfully, "It sounds like they must be professionals who know what they want and not just some random robberies."

"Just make sure you lock everything up tightly before you go to bed each night," Layne warned. "You never know where they might strike next or what they'll decide to steal."

"I just hope they'll catch whoever is doing this before they decide to come to my house to take something," Nona said. "I've had enough drama in my life and don't need anymore."

"Speaking of drama," Dixie sighed, "I've had my fair share this week."

Nona, Layne, and Betty Jo looked at her expectantly as they waited for her to explain.

"I got home after Skinny Dippers to find Big Willie's Repo hauling away Jason's Mustang." She paused dramatically. "Yes, ladies, my son's car was repossessed."

"Oh, no, Dixie," Layne said sympathetically.

Dixie gave them a full account of the events of the repossession including how Jason had "borrowed" her car. "The only good thing that came from the whole fiasco was that Jason actually went to his father's office to ask him for a job."

No one spoke.

Dixie shook her head. "Y'all are probably thinking the same thing I've been thinking." Then she said the words she'd been thinking since Alex told her Jason wanted to work for him, "'How long will he stick with this job?' Right?" she asked, looking at them.

Once again, silence.

"It's okay," Dixie said with resignation. "I'm not sure he'll stick with it for very long either, but I can always hope."

"So true," Betty Jo agreed. "We can all hope."

"And pray," Layne added.

Nona remained silent. Dixie knew what she was thinking. *What's Jason really up to now?*

After finishing with their "medicure," the four friends decided that since it was such a beautiful day they'd walk to The Grill for lunch. Once they were seated in the back-corner booth, Dixie took out the set of index cards where she'd listed everything she could think of that needed to be completed before the party.

Dixie passed the cards over to Betty Jo. "Take a look at these to see if I've left anything out."

Betty Jo looked through the cards. When she finished, she passed them to Nona. "Here, Nona, you take a look." Looking over at Dixie, she said, "I think you've covered all the bases."

"There's no doubt in my mind that she has," Nona said as she took the cards from Betty Jo. With a grin she handed the cards back to Dixie without looking through them. "I know you well enough to know you've checked and then double-checked to make sure everything is taken care of."

"I know it's going to be a wonderful party," Layne said, smiling at her friends. "Jenny is so excited. Her sister Emma is flying in tomorrow morning and staying through the weekend. I haven't heard if her father and stepmother will make it or not."

"I hope for Jenny's sake that they will at least try to make it," Dixie said. "Isn't this the only party she's having before the wedding?"

"As far as I know it is," Layne said. "Jenny tries to make us all believe that she's fine with her dad not coming, but I can tell she really wants him here."

Layne looked up to see one of her favorite former students, Emma Grace, who'd recently started waiting tables at The Grill, heading straight for their table. She liked it when Emma Grace was their waitress. As usual, she had a big smile on her face. "Hey, Miss Weaver," she said with a thick Southern drawl.

"Hey, Emma Grace. Good to see you," Layne said smiling back at her.

"What can I get for you ladies today?"

They gave Emma Grace their orders. She took up their menus, turned, and hurried off to get their drinks.

"She's such a sweet girl," Betty Jo said as she watched her leave.

"Always has been," Layne agreed.

"Sometimes sweetness is just a facade," Nona said.

The other three turned to look at Nona. "What in the world do you mean by that?" Layne asked.

"I just mean people aren't always what they seem to be."

Layne reached across the table and took Nona's hand in hers. Giving it a squeeze, she asked, "What's going on?"

Nona sighed. "It's this whole business with Grace. She still won't talk to me. It's been months now since I've seen or talked to my daughter, who I thought was sweet and kind and loving, at least most of the time. I can get through some days without letting it bother me too much, but on other days…" Her voice trailed off as she shook her head. "Today is one of those other days."

Nona took a long drink of the iced tea that Emma Grace set in front of her before continuing. "Y'all know how Bill has been coming around to 'help' Daddy when he knows I'm not going to be there. Well, Daddy happened to mention to me yesterday that Bill is going up to Atlanta this weekend to watch Grace get some award for a public service project she headed up. I guess it's some big honor that the *Atlanta Journal-Constitution* awards each year. It just hurts that she didn't even let me know about it, let alone invite me."

"It just doesn't make sense," Dixie said. "You gave that child everything and then more on top of that."

"I found it hard to believe when she didn't even call to check on you after all that happened with Bill's Amy," Betty Jo said, "but not sharing that with you is pure spiteful!"

Nona looked down. "I know! Guess she doesn't care enough about me to want me to share in the good or bad."

Patting Nona's hand, Layne said, "I believe one day she'll regret the way she's treated you."

"Yeah, right," Nona said. "Probably when I'm dead."

"Well then, I hope you come back and haunt her!" Betty Jo said.

They all laughed at Betty Jo's comment, grateful for the release of tension it brought.

"I'll say an extra prayer for y'all that God will heal your relationship," Layne said once they'd regained their composure.

"Thanks, I'd appreciate that," Nona said with a smile.

They were quiet for the next few minutes, enjoying their lunch.

"Did I mention to y'all that I had a visitor at my door early the other day?" Dixie said, breaking the silence.

"Who would be crazy enough to come to your door early in the morning?" Betty Jo asked.

Dixie put down her sandwich and took a sip of her tea. "Well, it turned out to be a friend of Jason's. He seemed like such a nice guy that I asked him to come back that evening for supper."

"You invited a perfect stranger to supper?" Layne asked. "What were you thinking?"

Dixie frowned as she thought about how the evening had started out when Jason opened the door. "At first, I was sure I'd made a big mistake, but it ended up that I'd done the right thing by having him over for supper. Alex was pretty upset with me for inviting him without talking it over with Jason. It turned out there had been a misunderstanding between the two of them, but they were able to work it out over supper."

"You're saying that you invited someone over to your house for supper who only claimed to be a friend of Jason's?" Nona asked doubtfully.

Dixie nodded her head. "I did."

"You're a braver person than I am," Nona said. "I guess with all that I went through with Amy, I'm more suspicious of people. I don't know if that's a good thing or not."

"You may be right about that, but I know how lonely Jason has been, and I guess I just wanted to know he had a friend."

"I don't know if you were brave or just plain stupid, Dixie," Betty Jo said with a teasing tone in her voice. "Sometimes you are too trusting."

Dixie chuckled, "Well, I hope y'all won't be upset about what else I did."

"Oh, no," Layne said. "What else did you do?"

"He's not from around here and doesn't know many people, so I invited him to Aaron and Jenny's engagement party," Dixie said.

"If he's a friend of Jason's," Layne assured her, "then he's more than welcome to come to the party."

"Thanks, I was hoping you'd say that, "Dixie said with a smile.

Their conversation returned to the arrangements for the engagement party as they finished their lunch.

Chapter Fourteen

In the light of day, Jason recognized the mistake he'd made last night by promising Eddy that he'd have the money he owed him today. He'd made that promise out of fear, but if he didn't come up with twelve hundred fifty dollars, what he was afraid of happening to him last night just might become a reality tonight. He didn't know where he was going to get that much money in such a short amount of time.

Jason's first idea was to ask Hailey for a loan. He was sure their mother had shared the news of his car being repossessed with her, so she'd understand that he didn't have enough money to cover his bills. He'd make up some story about needing the money to pay off a credit card. However, the more he thought about it, he realized that she would say something about it to Josh. Then Josh might mention it to his father, who would then discuss it with his mom. That would lead to his mother asking more questions and he'd have to come up with even more lies in order to answer her questions. He didn't think he could handle all of that. He needed another plan, but every plan he thought of would lead right back to his mother asking too many questions.

Jason found that one of the good things about hard work was you didn't have time to dwell on your problems. He'd worked hard all morning tearing out the plumbing in the third-floor bathrooms of the motel they were renovating. By the time Josh called the lunch break, Jason's back and arms were aching from helping haul the enameled cast-iron bathtubs out of the demolished bathrooms down three flights of stairs. He hadn't had time to think about his problems all morning, until now. He sat down on the motel steps, pulled out his turkey salad sandwich from the paper bag, and began to contemplate possible solutions to his money problems.

He was just about to bite into his sandwich when he heard Josh call out, "Jason, where are you?"

For a split second, he considered not answering, but knew that wouldn't be in his best interests. "Over here," he called back.

He watched Josh come around the corner of the building. "There you are," he said, sounding out of breath. "Your dad needs you at the office."

"Now?"

"Yes, now."

"Can I finish my lunch first?"

"You can eat it in my truck on the way over," Josh said, holding up the keys to the company truck that he usually drove.

Jason shoved his sandwich back into the bag as he stood up. "I thought it was the law that you had to give me a lunch break," he griped.

"Not if you're the boss's son," Josh said with a hint of bitterness.

Jason ignored his comment and snatched the keys from Josh's hand. As he drove, he wondered what his dad could want with him in the middle of the work day. He hadn't mentioned anything when they ate breakfast that morning at The Grill. In fact, Jason had thought that it was one of the few times since he'd moved back home that he'd enjoyed his father's company. Usually, when it was just the two of them together, his father's message seemed to be how disappointed he was with him. That hadn't been the case this morning. It'd almost been like old times when his father had been proud of him as the star football player in high school.

He pulled the truck up next to the office door, got out, and was walking up the steps as his father came out the door. "Thanks for coming over so quickly, Son," he said as he hurried past him. "I've got something I want to show you."

Jason fell in behind his father who was already around the corner heading to the back of the building. He stopped so suddenly that Jason almost ran into him.

"What do you think?" his father said as he lifted his hand toward an old green 2007 Ford F-150 Lariat truck in less than perfect shape parked at the back of the building.

"Nice," Jason lied as he walked around the truck. "Looks like it's in pretty good shape." He couldn't imagine why his father called him to come all the way over to his office just to look at this pile of junk.

"I thought maybe you could use a ride of your own, so you wouldn't have to borrow mine," his father said, smiling over at his son.

At first, Jason didn't quite understand. Doing something like giving his son a truck was very much out of his father's character, but when Jason looked over at him it began to sink in that his dad had actually bought this old, beat-up truck for him.

"Mine?"

"I need you to have your own transportation," his father said, "to help out with the business, for pick-ups and deliveries and such."

Jason wasn't sure what he should do. Was his father expecting a hug, or for him to jump up and down, or a simple thank-you for giving him this piece of junk?

Jason decided his best play was to keep it simple. "Thanks, Dad," he said as he put his hand out.

As his father enthusiastically shook his hand, Jason knew he'd played him just right.

After finishing their lunch at The Grill, Layne, Nona, and Betty Jo headed back to the nail salon to where they'd parked their cars. Dixie decided to leave her car there and walk the short block to Sandy's Southern Office Supply, where she'd ordered a special gift for Jenny—personalized stationery monogrammed with her new initials, *JLW*. Her mind was occupied with making lists of what she needed to have completed before the party. As she walked, she casually glanced at the cars parked on the street. Her attention was taken away from her mental lists when she noticed a small black sports car, the same car that'd been parked in her driveway only yesterday. She was sure it was Eddy's car She paused beside the car, trying to see if the driver was sitting behind the steering wheel, but the windows were heavily tinted, making it impossible to see inside. She continued down the block to Sandy's hoping she'd run into Eddy somewhere along the way.

When Mandy, the store owner's daughter, saw her enter, she called out, "Good afternoon, Miss Dixie. I've got your stationery ready and wrapped for you."

Dixie walked to the counter where Mandy had placed the wrapped package. "Thanks so much, Mandy! I'm so excited about giving this to Jenny tomorrow night."

"I think it's such a sweet gift," Mandy said with a smile. "I'm glad we could get it done for you before the big party."

"I'm sure looking forward to the party."

Dixie quickly turned around at the sound of the familiar voice. She was happy to find Eddy standing behind her. "Fancy meeting you here."

"I can't wait for your party, Mrs. Bradley," Eddy said. "I forgot to ask who's this engagement party for."

Mandy clapped her hands together with excitement. "This one's a huge engagement party for Jenny and Aaron, the cutest couple in town, with half of Kerry going. Even I got invited. You'd be a fool not to want to go to this party! Mrs. Bradley gives the best parties in town."

"Oh, it all sounds like so much fun," Eddy said.

"I'm so sorry, Eddy," Dixie said. "I forgot to ask you if you knew the couple we're honoring. It's Jenny Levins, who's a nurse at the hospital, and Aaron Weaver, who's a deputy sheriff here in Kerry."

"Deputy sheriff you say?"

"Yes. In fact, he's the son of our good friend Sheriff Mark Weaver," Dixie said with pride.

"Jason never mentioned that he was friends with the sheriff and his deputy son," Eddy said as he slowly shook his head, "No, I don't believe I know either one of the honorees."

"Well," Dixie said with a smile, "you can get to know both of them at the party on Saturday night.”

“Thanks to you, I will,” Eddy said as he turned to leave.

As Dixie watched him leave she began to wonder if he knew anyone in Kerry. She turned to Mandy and asked. “Do you know Eddy?”

“That guy?” Mandy shook her head. “He’s been in here a few times to buy paper, printer ink, and stuff like that.”

“I know his first name’s Eddy,” Dixie said. “Do you by any chance know his last name or where he lives?”

“No, ma’am,” Mandy said. “He always pays in cash, so he’s never shown me his driver’s license or offered a credit card.”

Dixie thought about that for a minute before taking her package from the counter. She thought it unusual for people Eddy’s age to use cash instead of a credit card. “Thanks, Mandy. See you tomorrow night,” she called as she left the store. She looked down the block and noticed that Eddy’s car was no longer parked where it had been when she entered the store. She needed to find out more about Eddy from Jason. She at least needed to find out his last name before the party. It’d be awkward to introduce him to others without knowing what his last name was. She’d also like to know where he lived. He’d mentioned having a business in Bradford, but hadn’t said if he lived there or in Kerry.

After finishing up with her errands, Dixie headed for home. She was surprised to find an older green Ford pickup truck parked in the driveway. She couldn’t imagine who it could be. She pulled up next to the truck. She was taking her packages out of the back seat of her car when she heard the side door close. She looked over to see Jason coming toward her with a big smile on his face.

“Well, what do you think?” he asked.

“About?”

“About my new ride,” Jason said with what seemed to be pride as he leaned against the truck.

Dixie gave him a confused look. “That’s your truck?” she asked, setting her packages down on the driveway as she walked up to examine the truck.

Jason nodded.

Cautiously, she asked, "How?"

"Dad!"

"Dad?"

"I'd just stopped work to eat lunch when Josh told me Dad needed to see me at his office. I took Josh's truck over to the office wondering the whole way over what Dad might want, and when I got there, he gave me this truck." Jason talked as if he was finding the whole experience hard to believe.

"Oh, my gosh, Jason," Dixie said, feeling such happiness for him, "it's just not like your father to do something like this."

"I know! That's why I'm still finding it hard to believe this is mine."

Dixie slowly walked around the truck, taking it all in. Jason opened the doors so she could check out the interior. She was impressed with how nice it was for a used truck. Obviously, the previous owner had kept it well maintained.

"Wanna go for a ride?" Jason asked.

"Of course, but give me a minute to put these packages in the house before something gets ruined."

Jason helped his mother carry the packages in the house. They headed back outside and Dixie climbed up into the passenger's seat. Jason backed out of the driveway and took the road that led out of town. They rode in silence for several minutes, enjoying the smooth ride.

"I love it," Dixie said, looking over at her son. She realized she hadn't seen Jason this happy in a very long time.

"So do I. How about we see how fast this truck will go?" Jason pressed the accelerator.

Dixie put her hands on the dashboard to brace herself. "Let's not!"

Jason slowed down. "Just kidding, Mom!"

Dixie looked over at her son's smiling face. "It's good to see you happy, Jason. I've been worried about you lately."

"I know you have," Jason said, "but you really don't need to worry about me. Things are going to be better now that I'm working again. I'm going to get my life back on track. You'll see."

"I believe you will," Dixie said, feeling more hopeful about Jason's situation than she had in a very long time.

"I still can't believe that your dad bought this for you." Dixie shook her head. "It's so unlike him."

"I can't either," Jason said, "and I want to honor his generous gift by keeping it in great shape."

"Of course you do," Dixie said.

Jason turned to look through the back window at the truck bed. "I was just thinking that with this truck I could help Dad out by hauling things around for him, but I sure would hate to see the bed get all banged up and dented any more than it is from hauling equipment and stuff around."

"That'd be a shame," Dixie said, looking back at truck bed. Then looking over at Jason, she asked, "Isn't there anything you can do to keep it from getting even more banged up?"

Jason took a moment before answering. "Well, I guess a bed liner could be installed to protect it from getting damaged."

"Is that something you really need to have or is it something that you really want?"

"It's just that all I'm going to be carrying around in the bed of this truck could really mess it up. A bed liner would protect that from happening and also help keep the truck's value."

It made sense to Dixie that the less damage the truck had the more it would retain its value. "How much would it cost to have a bed liner installed?"

Jason kept his eyes focused on the road straight ahead. "They cost anywhere from fifteen hundred to two thousand. It all depends on the quality."

Dixie was taken aback. "Wow, I had no idea a bed liner would cost that much. I was thinking it'd be more like five hundred at the most."

Dixie noticed Jason wince at her remark.

Dixie couldn't imagine why he'd told her a bed liner would cost well over a thousand dollars more than Alex's had. It'd only been a little over six months since Alex had Maxwell's Auto Service install a bed liner in his truck for around $350. She looked at Jason, wondering why he'd given her such an elevated price.

Dixie said, "I think getting a bed liner is something you need to discuss with your father. I'm not the one to make that decision."

Dixie noticed Jason's knuckles turning white from gripping the steering wheel tightly. Then taking a deep breath he said through clenched teeth, "Okay, I'll do that."

It was obvious to Dixie that her son was upset with her.

"Since we're near the cleaner's downtown, would you mind stopping for a minute, so I can pick up my dry cleaning for the party?" Dixie broke the uncomfortable silence.

Jason didn't answer his mother but pulled into a parking place right in front of the cleaners.

"Thanks," Dixie said pleasantly. She reached in her purse, fishing out her wallet to take into the cleaners. As she got out of the truck, she added, "I'll only be a minute."

With anger mounting, Jason watched his mother as she entered the cleaners. He thought about driving off and leaving her there. It would serve her right. He wanted to bang his head on the steering wheel and scream out obscenities. He couldn't believe his plan to get the money he needed by tonight had gone so wrong. He couldn't believe he hadn't been able to convince his mother to give him at least the twelve hundred dollars he desperately needed by tonight. He'd always been able to talk his mother into almost anything he wanted. Was he losing his touch? With his fist balled up, he hit the seat next to him with such force that it knocked over the purse his mother had left behind on the seat between them. He picked it up from the floor, wanting to throw it out the window, when his eyes were drawn to something that had fallen out onto the floor of the truck. It was his mother's checkbook. He put her purse back on the seat and reached down to retrieve the checkbook. Jason couldn't believe his good luck. Her checkbook falling out right in front of him at this very moment was like a sign from the universe that he was supposed to take one of her checks.

Without another thought, he tore a check from the checkbook and quickly placed the checkbook back in her purse. He'd just shoved the check in his pants pocket when his mother opened the truck door with her dry cleaning in hand. He couldn't believe that he hadn't even noticed that she'd left the store.

"See, that didn't take long at all," Dixie said as she closed the truck door and put her wallet back in her purse.

"No, not long at all, Mom," Jason said, smiling. "In fact, it was just time enough."

Chapter Fifteen

After taking the ride with Jason, Dixie hung up her dry cleaning in her closet, changed into her gardening clothes, and went to work out in her yard the rest of the afternoon and into late evening. She wanted everything to look perfect for the party. Alex came home from work earlier than usual and helped her. Jason called to say he wouldn't be home for supper. He was going to Hailey's to show her and the girls his truck and would grab something to eat. After finishing in the yard, Dixie was too tired to cook. Instead, she warmed up some leftovers she found in the refrigerator. Since it was just the two of them, they ate at the kitchen island and watched the evening news.

When they'd finished eating, Dixie put their dishes in the dishwasher and fixed a cup of coffee for each of them. They took their mugs out to the back deck.

"Do you think you have everything ready for tomorrow night?" Alex asked.

"I hope so." Dixie sighed. "I've done all I can do until tomorrow morning when Nona, Betty Jo, and Don get here to help with the final touches."

"Do you need my help?" Alex asked.

"Do you really want to help?"

"If you need my help, then I'm offering it."

"Well, then I'm going to take you up on it. I'm sure Don could use your help with getting the flowers out of his truck." Then she added, "Thanks."

"You're welcome."

Dixie set down her cup and turned to Alex. "I've noticed that you've been awfully nice lately, with offering to help out with the party and giving Jason a truck."

Alex sat up straight in his chair and looked at Dixie. "Giving Jason that truck was as much for me as for him. I didn't like him asking to use my truck all the time. Plus, it'll help me out now that he can help with deliveries and hauling things around."

"Well, for whatever reason, it was a nice thing to do." Dixie leaned over and kissed him on the cheek.

Alex smiled. "What can I say? I'm a nice guy."

They sat out on the deck and talked for another hour. They decided to turn in early since they both had a big day tomorrow.

After turning off the lights in the kitchen, they walked together down the hall to their bedrooms. They stopped in front of Dixie's bedroom door. Alex leaned down to kiss her on top of the head, but Dixie put her hand on his chest. She looked up into his dark brown eyes and said, "You know I really liked the way you kissed me last night. I think we need to be doing that more often."

"I agree."

He leaned down, gently wrapped her in his arms, and gave her a kiss that almost took her breath away. They looked at one another, smiled, and kissed several more times.

Putting her head on his chest, Dixie softly said, "That was nice." Then added, "Do you want to come in?"

"That sounds nice," Alex said, smiling down at his wife.

Dixie opened her door and together they walked into her bedroom.

After dropping his mother off at home, Jason headed for the bank. He wanted to get there before they closed for the day. He sat in the bank parking lot contemplating the amount he should write on the check. He wished he'd taken the time to look at the balance his mother dutifully recorded each time she wrote a check. He was confident that she had more than the twelve hundred he needed. He decided he wouldn't be too greedy and would just make it out for fifteen hundred. That way he could pay his debt to Eddy and have money to replenish his supply. He didn't have a problem forging his mother's name to the check. He'd forged her name on his absence excuses all throughout high school and no one had ever questioned him. He hoped his luck would hold out and no one would question this signature.

Jason hoped he could just zip through the drive-through, but there was a long line of cars. He decided it would be faster if he went inside. He took his place in one of the many teller lines. He realized his mistake when he found himself in line behind Lily Breedlow Morton, whom he'd been avoiding since he'd moved back to Kerry. He considered making a quick exit but realized he'd missed his opportunity to escape when Lily turned around.

"Jason!" Lily screamed out as she gave him a hug.

Jason hugged her back. Even though Lily was a year older than him, he'd had a crush on her throughout middle and high school. Lily could always make him laugh, which made for some great times together, until Matt Morton came on the scene. Suddenly, Lily didn't have time for him. Jason knew that Matt was not the one for Lily. Matt used her and seemed to enjoy humiliating her in front of other people. He'd warned her to not marry Matt, but she'd ignored his warning. They hadn't been close since. She'd called him a few times, but he'd never returned her calls.

"I can't believe I ran into you at the bank of all places," Lily said. "I've been trying to get with you since you moved back, but you never return my calls."

"I meant to call you back, but you know how it is when you get busy," Jason said, a little embarrassed. "It's good to see you."

"It's great to see you!"

They stood looking at one another for an awkward moment until

Jason spoke up. "Well, I'm kinda in a hurry. I've got to get this check cashed and…" He trailed off.

"Oh, sure," Lily said. "I've gotta get out of here too. I have to get Kendall from soccer practice and all."

Lily looked down and saw that she was still holding Jason's hand. "Oh, sorry," she said, releasing his hand. "Guess I'll see you tomorrow night at the party."

Jason smiled politely. "I'll be there," he said as he turned away from her and headed to the open teller window.

Lily smiled back and gave a little wave as she walked out the door.

Jason wasn't sure why, but seeing Lily–one of his very best friends from long ago–filled him with guilt. His mind went back to the great memories he had of Lily. Since his mother and her mother, Betty Jo, were good friends, they were often together growing up. They became close friends in middle school. Jason had felt like he could tell her anything and she'd understand. He was pretty sure she'd felt the same way about him. As he thought back to those days, he realized that might be the reason he hadn't called her back–she might sense what was truly going on in his life. He couldn't risk that.

Jason worked hard to hide his dependence, but it was getting more difficult with each passing day. He'd never meant to become dependent on his medications. After all, they'd been prescribed to him by doctors after surgery for a torn ACL his junior year in college. The pain had been unbearable after surgery. The doctor had prescribed oxycodone to ease the pain, and it had worked, but not for the entire twelve hours he'd had to wait until he could take another pill. The pain was even worse when he started physical therapy, so the doctor had increased the dosage until it was almost double what he'd started out with in the hospital. He found that if he took the pills after eight hours, he didn't experience that lapse in relief from the pain.

For months, if he didn't take his oxycodone, the pain returned with a vengeance. It wasn't like he'd wanted to become dependent on oxycodone. He just didn't want to hurt. After those months of using oxycodone, the team doctor suggested he try taking a high dose of ibuprofen instead. He had tried that for a day, but found it didn't even begin to touch his excruciating pain. He'd felt nauseous with a violent headache, which made him think he might be coming down with a severe case of the flu. However, once he started back taking the oxycodone, his flu symptoms, along with the pain, disappeared. Since then, he'd learned that what he had been experiencing was called "Dope Sickness." He knew if he ever stopped taking his oxycodone, he'd be sick or unhealthy like that again. He wanted to stay healthy and the only way to do that was to stay on oxycodone.

For years, he'd been able to find doctors who'd prescribe oxycodone for him and pharmacists who'd willingly fill his prescriptions. Until he'd gone to Coby Pharmacy when he moved back to Kerry. That's when he'd been lucky enough to run into Angie, who'd turned him onto Eddy, who was able to supply him with the oxycodone he needed. He'd prided himself on being able to handle the price he'd had to pay for his pills, but when he found himself unemployed through no fault of his own, money had become tight. Thankfully, once again his mother had come to his rescue, even though she didn't know it. With her money, he could now get square with Eddy, and with the job he had working for his dad, he'd be able to maintain his supply.

"What can I do for you, sir?" the teller asked.

Jason had a story ready about his mother needing cash to buy things for a party she was giving if he was questioned about the large check he was cashing, He smiled his friendliest smile and read her nameplate, hoping he wouldn't need to tell his story.

"Hello, Ms. Turner. How are you today?"

With a smile, Ms. Turner took the check from Jason. "I'm doing fine. Thank you for asking." As she began pulling cash from her open drawer, she asked, "How's Mrs. Bradley doing? She's always been one of my favorite customers. You must be Jason, her son."

"Yes, I am. She's fine," Jason said, wondering if he should say anything else. He decided it was best to keep it simple by saying as little as possible.

The teller reached through the window and began counting out the fifteen-hundred dollars into Jason's hand. When she finished, she looked up at him and said with a smile, "Please tell your mother I said hello."

"I sure will," Jason said as he turned to leave. He was amazed at how easy it'd been to get the fifteen hundred he needed. The consequences of his actions never entered his mind.

Jason pulled into Eddy's driveway, flashed his headlights four times, and sent a text to the number he'd been given that first time he'd made a buy. He put the phone down and waited. After five minutes of waiting, he was beginning to get worried that something was wrong. He'd noticed that there were no lights on in the house when he pulled up, but that wasn't uncommon. He'd been here several times when lights weren't visible from where he was parked, but after a few minutes of waiting someone had always appeared from the dark house to deliver the product. What would happen if he wasn't able to get the money to Eddy tonight? He didn't want to even think about what the consequences could be. It was eerily quiet outside his truck. He hadn't even heard a sound of a dog barking or of cars traveling down the highway. Jason was considering his next move when the sound of his phone vibrating on the seat next to him suddenly broke through the silence. Someone was sending him a text message.

Jason picked up his phone, turning it over to check the incoming text. It was from a number he didn't recognize. <u>Put payment in mailbox.</u> Even though it was a simple message, he read it through twice to make sure he understood. He leaned over to get the twelve hundred-fifty dollars cash out of the glove compartment, opened his truck door, and walked down the driveway to the plain black mailbox at the side of the road. He opened the mailbox to put the envelope with the money inside. Then he carefully closed the door to the mailbox and walked back to his truck.

Before getting in the truck, he looked around at the house and surrounding property. Jason had hoped he could buy some supplies with the three hundred dollars he had left from his mother's check he'd cashed. But it didn't look like anyone was around to fill his "prescription." If he remembered correctly, he had enough product to last him at least one more day. He'd just have to come back as soon as he could. As he headed home, he began to feel optimistic. Things were beginning to look up.

Jason had just reached the Kerry city limits when his cell phone rang. He didn't recognize the number displayed, so he ignored the call. Within a few seconds, his phone dinged with the announcement of a text message. He glanced down to see who had sent him a message. Once again, he didn't recognize the number, but the message displayed got his attention. It simply stated, "Answer your phone." He'd just finished reading the text when his phone rang. This time he accepted the call.

Irritated, Jason asked, "Who is this?"

"Don't tell me you don't recognize your best friend's voice."

In all the time he'd been doing business with Eddy, this was the first time he'd gotten a phone call from him. His first thought was that Eddy must not know that he'd put the twelve hundred dollars in the mailbox.

"E-Eddy," Jason stuttered. "I put the money I owed you in the mailbox just like I was told."

"I know," Eddy said. "We're cool with that, but there's another matter I'm calling about."

When Jason heard Eddy use the word "matter," it brought up images of the gun he'd seen him holding in his hand the other night. His heart began to hammer in his chest. "I'm not sure what you mean, Eddy. I thought that made us square. I have the money right now, right here with me, for another buy, From now on, you don't have to worry about me not being able to pay. I promise, I won't ever…" Jason knew he was babbling, but couldn't seem to stop himself.

"Whoa, hang on there," Eddy interrupted. "You need to chill and listen."

Jason stopped talking.

"I'm not talking about money here," Eddy said. "I'm offering you an opportunity to help me with a side business I've started."

Jason remained silent, waiting for Eddy to continue. He'd promised himself a long time ago that he'd never deal drugs, but his fear was that that was exactly what Eddy was going to ask of him. His heart continued to pound at the prospect of what "opportunity" Eddy might have for him.

"I've become what you might call the 'middleman' in the lucrative business of selling off-road motorized vehicles and lawn equipment, and I've run into a bit of a snag that I'm confident you'll want to help me with."

"Eddy," Jason began, "I don't have a clue how to sell those things."

"Don't you think I know that?" Eddy said in a harsh voice. "I'm not asking you to sell them."

For a fleeting moment Jason felt relief.

"I want you to help me steal them."

Jason thought his heart might stop. He pulled his truck over to the side of the road, opened his door, and leaned out, sure he was going to throw up. In all his life, he'd never imagined himself as a thief. Yet, in only one day, he'd stolen from his mother, and his drug dealer was asking him to steal ATVs. What would happen to him if he turned down the man who not only carried a gun, but was the one person could keep him healthy?

"Hey, Jason, you okay?" Jason could hear Eddy asking from his phone that he'd left on the seat of the truck.

Am I okay? At that moment, he knew he was as far away from okay as a man could get and still be alive.

"Jason?"

For a moment, Jason considered throwing his phone out of the truck and driving as far away from Kerry, Georgia, as he could get. Then the reality of what would happen to him if he did such a thing came into his head. He knew he needed his drugs as much as he needed the air that he breathed. The fact was that he couldn't live without them. Instead of driving away, he picked up his phone. "Yeah, Eddy, I'm okay. What do you need me to do?"

"That a boy," Eddy said. "I knew I could count on you. What I need from you is information. I was struck with an idea after I ran into your sweet mama the other day. She was talking about this party that she's not only invited me to, but half the town as well. I figure that the half of the town that was invited and most likely coming will be those who most likely have the special inventory I need to expand my business. While they're enjoying themselves at the party and away from their homes for a few hours, my crew can do their work without fear of being discovered. Since you grew up with these people and know them so well, your knowledge is going to be my secret weapon and will help you out when it comes to getting what you need from my other business. I know you'll find it's a win-win for both of us."

Jason put his head in his hands. Eddy had him exactly where he wanted him. Jason didn't see a way out. At one time in his life, he would have bowed his head and begged God to help him out of his situation, but on this night, he was too ashamed to ask God for anything.

"I'll be in touch," Eddy said. "And Jason?"

"Yeah?"

"You'd better answer the next time you see this number come up or there'll be some serious consequences. You got it?"

"Yeah, Eddy, I got it," Jason affirmed with a sickening feeling in his stomach.

Chapter Sixteen

ixie woke up feeling better than she had in days, maybe even in weeks. She'd slept soundly for the first time in several nights. She hadn't even woken up when Alex left her bed. If she had any dreams, she didn't remember them, which was a good thing as far as she was concerned. She put on her robe and headed to the kitchen. Even though she had a busy day ahead of her, she wanted to fix Alex a big breakfast this morning. She was surprised when she didn't find him in sitting at the kitchen island reading the paper like he did almost every morning. She considered that maybe he'd slept late after the night they'd had together. She was taking the bacon out of the frying pan when she heard him coming down the hall.

"Good morning, sleepyhead," Dixie said, smiling at her husband.

"And a good morning to you too," Alex said as he took his seat at the island.

Dixie put a pod in the coffeemaker. "Thought you might need a big breakfast this morning. Eggs, bacon, grits, and biscuits sound okay?"

Giving her a knowing smile, Alex said, "Sounds great. A big breakfast is exactly what I need after last night."

She handed him his cup of coffee as she gave him a kiss on the cheek. "You can go get the paper while I finish with your breakfast."

Dixie was putting his eggs over easy on a plate next to the bacon and biscuits when Alex came back with the paper, he had a confused look on his face. "I wonder where Jason is. His truck isn't out there."

"He probably spent the night at Hailey's," Dixie said, handing him his breakfast plate. "He said he was going over there to show her and the kids his truck."

"You're probably right," Alex agreed as he took the plate from Dixie. "I still think he should have called to let us know he wasn't coming home."

"Alex, Jason's a grown man," Dixie said as she sat down in the chair next to his. "He doesn't need to check in to let us know where he is all the time."

"I guess you're right."

Alex read the paper as he ate his breakfast. As he stood up to leave, he asked, "What time do you need me to be back here to help?"

Dixie had almost forgotten his offer to help. "You know, I don't think I'll need your help until later this afternoon. What about two?"

"That works," Alex said as he leaned over to kiss her on the top of the head. "See ya' then."

With that kiss, Dixie understood that things were back to normal. As she cleaned up the kitchen, she decided to give Hailey a call just to make sure that Jason had spent the night. She could tell Alex that Jason was a grown man, but man or not, he was still her son and she'd probably always worry about him. She picked up her cell phone and dialed Hailey, hoping to catch her before she left for her office.

Dixie was about to end the call when a breathless Hailey picked up. "Hi, Mom, I can't talk long, I'm on my way to work."

"Just a quick question," Dixie said. "Did Jason spend the night with you last night?"

"No, I haven't seen Jason for a couple of days. He stopped by the house the other night when I wasn't home to spend some time with the girls. He might have come by last night, but we didn't get home until late. It was STEM night at the school. Anything wrong?"

"No, I don't think anything's wrong," Dixie said. "His truck wasn't here when we got up this morning, so I thought he might have spent the night with y'all."

"His truck?" Hailey asked. "Where did Jason get a truck?"

"Dad got him a used truck to help out at work," Dixie said, emphasizing the word "used," knowing that Hailey thought they did too much to help Jason. "It's not a big deal. We can talk about it later. I know you're on your way to work."

"Can't wait to hear this one," Hailey said as she ended the call.

Dixie could tell that Hailey was irritated, but she'd have to worry about that later. Right now, she was concerned about Jason. She'd put off calling him because she didn't want him to think she was checking on him, but knew she wouldn't be able to think about anything else until she was sure everything was okay with him.

At the sound of Jason's voice, relief flooded through Dixie's body. "Hi, Mom, what's up?"

"I'm calling to remind you about Aaron's engagement party here tonight," Dixie said, hoping he'd believe that was the reason she was calling.

"I remember," Jason said. Then he added, "I hope you weren't worried about where I was this morning, like Dad was."

"Maybe just a little," Dixie admitted.

"I knew I'd need to get off work early today, so I came to work early." Jason teased, "I bet you're as surprised as Dad was when I told him."

"Probably," Dixie said with a laugh.

"Gotta go, Mom."

"Okay, have a good day," Dixie said, ending the call feeling like she was the one who was going to have a good day.

Dixie was in the final stages of styling her hair when her cell phone rang. She could tell by the tune playing that it was Nona calling. She set the dryer back in its holder to answer.

"Hey, Nona."

"Good morning to you, Dixie," Nona said with a cheery voice. "I'm on my way to get Betty Jo and wondered if there was anything you needed for us to do on our way to your house."

It was on Dixie's list to call Nona after she got ready. She smiled, knowing this would be another item she could check off. "Yes, I'm glad you called. Can you go by Darla's Bakery to pick up the specialty buns she's made for the barbecue? I was going to see if she could deliver them, but I'd feel better if y'all would just go ahead and get them."

"No problem. We should be there by the time they get there with the tent and all."

"Great!" Dixie ended the call and finished getting ready for the day.

She'd just stepped out of her bedroom when she caught a glimpse of the Kerry Tents & Events delivery truck backing down the driveway, bringing the tent, tables, and chairs. She rushed out to meet them so she could direct them where everything needed to be set up. As she stepped out the door, she was grateful to see Don pulling up.

Dixie smiled and waved at Don as he got out of his truck. "Boy, am I glad to see you," she said, giving him a quick hug. "You can help me direct."

"Lucky me," Don said with a teasing tone, returning her hug.

When the driver and his crew of two got out of the truck, Dixie showed them where to set up the tent along with the tables and chairs. Then Don took over from Dixie as overseer of their progress. Dixie went inside to finish putting the icing on her Chocolate Ice Storm Cake that she'd baked yesterday afternoon. She'd made this cake especially for Aaron. It was his favorite. In fact, he was the one who'd named it after a rare ice storm had taken out the power at Layne and Mark's house when Aaron was around ten years old. Dixie and Alex had insisted that they all come to stay with them until their power was restored. Dixie had tried out a new dark chocolate cake recipe that very day. It ended up that Aaron ate almost the entire cake. He'd named it the "Ice Storm Cake" and that's what it'd been called ever since.

Dixie walked back outside to find the tent set up and Don coming out of the truck with two sets of folding chairs under each arm. "I thought you were supposed to be supervising," she called to him.

"I was, but I can't just sit around when I see that there's work to be done," Don called back.

Dixie hadn't noticed that Nona and Betty Jo had driven up and were getting out of the car until Betty Jo yelled out, "Oh, yes you can!"

"It's not going to hurt me to carry a few chairs," Don protested.

"Put those down right now," Betty Jo insisted as she came up beside her husband.

The workers who'd been hired to set up the tent, tables, and chairs stared at the couple, not quite knowing what they should do. One of them eased in next to Don and took the chairs away from him. "I've got these, sir," he said as he carried the chairs to the tent.

Don looked at his wife with annoyance. "I'm not a helpless old man, you know."

"I know," Betty Jo said, "but you aren't a young man anymore either, you know."

"Oh, I know, because you keep reminding me of that fact," Don said.

"I only do it because I love you, you know."

"I know." Don leaned over to give her a quick kiss on her cheek.

"Okay, now that y'all are finished with that," Nona said, looking to Dixie, "where do you want these buns?"

"The kitchen island will be fine," Dixie said. Then turning to Don, she asked, "You got the flowers for the tables?"

"I do," Don said, heading to his truck.

"And I have a trunk full of Mason jars," Betty Jo added.

"Well, let's get the flowers in the Mason jars and on the tables," Dixie said, walking over to Don's truck excited to see what flowers he had brought from his own greenhouse and from the farmer's market.

Don pulled the tarp back from the bed of his truck to reveal buckets filled with a variety of wild flowers– Queen Anne's Lace, daisies, English Ivy, pink butterfly weed, sunflowers, lilies, dahlias, cosmos, and others she didn't even know the name of.

"Oh, Don, they're beautiful!" Dixie exclaimed.

"Thanks," Don said. "Now that the day is heating up, let's get them under the tent, and in those Mason jars before they start to wilt."

Don carried the buckets of flowers to the tent. While Nona and Betty Jo took the Mason jars out of the trunk, Dixie went inside for scissors, string, pins, and ribbons of teal and brown–the colors Jenny had picked out for her beach wedding theme.

"I hope I got everything we'll need to decorate these jars," Dixie said, placing her filled basket down.

"I can tell you one thing for sure," Nona said as she placed the last of the Mason jars on the table, "this is not something that I'm good at or like to do."

Don shook his head as he looked at the ribbons and things Dixie had in her basket. "I can grow the flowers, but I'm with Nona. You don't want me to arrange the flowers or decorate those jars. That's just not my thing either."

"I'm well aware of that," Betty Jo said, smiling up at her husband. "You've done your thing with the flowers. Dixie and I can take it from here."

"Well, then, I leave y'all to it," Don said with relief as he gave Betty Jo a peck on the cheek and headed to his truck.

Nona watched Don walk away. "I know y'all aren't going to let me off that easy." Turning back to Dixie she clapped her hands together. "So, what do you want me to do?"

"You can put the tablecloths on the tables they just set up," Dixie said.

"As long as I don't have to arrange flowers or decorate jars, I'm good with whatever," Nona said with a smile. Then glancing around the tent, she asked, "And where might I find these tablecloths?"

Putting her hand to her mouth, Dixie stared at Nona with wide eyes as the realization came to her that with all that had happened yesterday, that errand had slipped her mind.

Nona could see by the look on Dixie's face that she was upset. She reached out, putting a comforting hand on her shoulder, and said, "Not a problem. I'll go by the church, get the tablecloths, and grab us some lunch on my way back."

"You're the best," Dixie said, feeling relieved.

"I know," Nona said as she headed to her car.

By the time Nona had returned with the tablecloths and lunch, Dixie and Betty Jo had finished all the Mason jar flower centerpieces. "Those look really good," Nona said, admiring the arrangements. "How about we eat before putting the tablecloths and centerpieces on the tables?"

"Sounds like a plan to me." Dixie headed into the house. "While I get the tea, y'all can set lunch up on the back deck."

"I'm starving," Betty Jo helped Nona get the sandwiches and chips out of the bag. "Are these those homemade chips I've heard about from that new place in town?"

Nona handed one of the chips to Betty Jo. "They are. I decided to get lunch from The Rustic Bistro. I don't know how Susan does it down there, but these are the best chips you'll ever eat."

Betty Jo took the chip and put it in her mouth. "You're right about that. She reached for another one.

"Right about what?" Dixie asked as she walked out onto the deck with a tray holding a pitcher of sweet tea and three glasses filled with ice.

"These chips being the best I've ever eaten. Here, try one."

Before Dixie could set down her tray, Betty Jo had popped a chip into her mouth. "Oh, my, these are the best. I hope the sandwiches are as good."

Nona sat down. "You're going to love their chicken salad on a homemade croissant."

"Let's finish up with lunch. Then we can get those tablecloths and centerpieces on the table. We've still got a bunch to do before we're ready for this party."

"We've got plenty of time," Betty Jo reminded Dixie. "Let's first enjoy this lovely lunch that Nona's brought. Then we can finish up."

Layne came around the corner of the house. "Don't tell me y'all are going to start eating without me."

All three turned at the sound of Layne's voice. "Oh, my goodness," Dixie cried out as she jumped up to give her a hug. "What are you doing here?"

Layne was suddenly surrounded by her three friends. "I know that since I'm the mother of the groom y'all think I shouldn't be helping with this party, but I just couldn't stand to sit by myself at home and not be a part of this."

"Well, come on in and join us for lunch," Betty Jo said. "We have plenty to share."

Dixie went back in the house to get a plate and glass for Layne while Nona cut the sandwiches into smaller pieces. The four of them sat down to eat.

"So, what have I missed out on this morning?" Layne asked as Dixie set a plate in front of her.

Smiling at Layne, Betty Jo slapped a sandwich down on her plate. "Work! Dixie put us all to work. We haven't even had time to talk."

Layne looked around at the tent that had been set up and the flower-filled decorated Mason jars setting out on a table. "Well, it looks like your hard work is paying off. Those flower arrangements are beautiful!"

"Thanks," Dixie said, "but wait until you see it after we've finished."

"Y'all, let me bless this food so we can start eating," Betty Jo said. "I'm starving!"

The four bowed their heads as Betty Jo began her prayer. "Dear Lord, bless this food to the nourishment of our bodies and our bodies to thy service. Amen."

"Let's eat." Dixie passed the plate of sandwiches.

Nona took a bite of her sandwich, contemplating whether she should share her latest story about Bill. She hadn't mentioned it the last time they were all together, but decided that now might be the time to share. "I had another run-in with Bill the other night."

"I thought you had a date with Monty," Betty Jo said with concern.

"I did!"

"Oh, no," Layne said. "Don't tell me that Bill had a run-in with Monty."

"No, nothing like that," Nona said.

"So, what happened?" Layne asked.

"I came home to find Bill in Daddy's study discussing investments with him." Nona still found it hard to believe that Bill had made himself at home in her house.

"You're kidding!" Betty Jo said disbelievingly.

"Not kidding," Nona said, shaking her head. "Daddy was living in the past that day and thought Bill and I were still married. What just burned me up was that Bill seemed to be enjoying fueling Daddy's delusion. I've told him several times he isn't to come around anymore, but he continues to believe he has a right to be there." Nona sighed. "What makes him think he's welcome?" she asked.

"Arrogance," Layne said with authority. "It seems to me it's his arrogance that makes him believe you want him there."

"He must think he's so awesome you can't live without him," Dixie agreed.

"Well, he's sadly mistaken," Nona declared. "I plan to live happily ever after without him in my life."

"Did you still have your date with Monty?" Betty Jo asked as she leaned forward.

Nona smiled. "Oh, I most certainly did. And I have to say we had a nice evening together."

"I can't tell you how happy that makes me," Layne said, smiling over at her friend.

"I think that makes all of us happy," Dixie said.

"I just hope that Bill got the message that you don't want him anywhere near you or your father," Betty Jo added.

"I hope so too!" Nona said. "Now, let's change the subject. I'm tired of talking about Bill."

"We still have tablecloths and centerpieces to arrange," Dixie said. "So, let's finish up with lunch."

"Slave driver!" Betty Jo gave Dixie a wink.

"Looks like I'm too late." All four turned at the sound of Alex's voice.

"No, you're just in time to help," Dixie said, jumping up to clear the table.

"I meant for lunch," Alex said with a laugh.

"I think there might be a few crumbs left over," Dixie teased.

"I need more than a few crumbs."

"I think it'd do you some good to just eat crumbs for a few meals," Dixie said as she patted his stomach.

They all laughed.

"Okay, I'm here to help like you asked. What do you want me to do?"

Dixie pulled a list out of her back pocket and handed it to Alex. "I was hoping you'd ask."

Alex looked over the list.

"Any questions?" Dixie asked.

Alex sighed. "What in the world are 'fairy lights'?" He looked at Dixie with total confusion.

Dixie laughed. "They're little twinkling lights that I want strung all the way around the pool and deck. I put several rolls of them next to the tools and poles you'll need to put them up."

Alex gave her a blank look.

"Come on, let me show you what I'm talking about." Dixie began walking toward the tool shed.

Turning back to Layne, Dixie said with a smile, "You need to go home. After all, this party is for you as well as the happy couple, and we've got work to do."

"I can't tell y'all how much it means to me and my family that y'all are doing this for Aaron and Jenny," Layne said as she gave each of them a hug.

"Let's get these tablecloths on those tables and centerpieces set up. It's going to be time for everyone to be here before we know it." Nona said to Betty Jo.

Alex followed Dixie out to the tool shed where she'd shown him the fairy lights and how she wanted them strung up. It didn't take him long to know that he couldn't get this job finished in the few hours he had before the party started. He needed to call in reinforcements. He took out his cell phone to call his son-in-law.

"Josh, here."

"I'm going to need some help over here at the house," Alex said. "Dixie's got me stringing lights."

"You want me to send the crew?"

"Yeah, it's going to take the whole crew to get all of this done in time."

"We'll be there in twenty." Josh ended the call.

Alex smiled at Dixie. "Some days it's good to have your own company."

Dixie shook her head. "I never realized fairy lights would be so much trouble."

"No problem," Alex said. "It'll get done."

Dixie walked back to join Nona and Betty Jo in getting the tables decorated. The three of them along with Alex's crew spent the rest of the afternoon preparing the Bradley home for the engagement party of two people that were very special to all of them.

Chapter Seventeen

After leaving her friends at Dixie's house, Layne stopped by Kinard's Cleaners to pick up the outfit she was wearing to the party. She'd had it professionally pressed for the event. She pulled open the door and ran straight into Blair, who was pushing the same door coming out.

"Mama!" Blair cried out, dropping her cleaning bag onto the sidewalk.

Layne leaned down to help Blair retrieve her cleaning. "I'm so sorry. I was in a hurry and wasn't watching where I was going."

"Thank goodness they're wrapped in plastic," Blair said as she checked the blouse and pants for any damage. "It looks like they're okay."

"I am sorry," Layne said again.

"It's not your fault," Blair said. "It was an accident. So, why are you in such a hurry?"

"I wanted to make sure I had enough time before the party to get Mama ready," Layne said.

Suddenly, a thought occurred to her. "Why don't you come with me? In fact, it might just take the two of us to get her ready for the party. I know she'd love to see you."

Blair began talking to herself, thinking out loud, "Zeke is home watching the girls and Mrs. Coby will be there to get them in a little bit." Then, looking at her mother she said, "Sure, I'd love to help Nana get ready."

"Great! I'll finish here and meet you at Whitlock." Layne hurried into the cleaners.

When Blair arrived at the Whitlock, she went straight to her nana's room. She knew that Nana would be disappointed that she hadn't brought her daughters Rachel and Madison with her. Nana always seemed to enjoy their visits, but Blair hadn't found the time this week to bring them by.

Blair could hear the television from her grandmother's room. She knocked two times on the door. "Nana, it's Blair," she called out as she opened the door. She found Nana sound asleep in her recliner. Blair couldn't imagine how she could sleep with her television blasting. She rushed over to turn it off. The sound of silence was a relief.

Nana sat straight up. "What did you do?"

"Nana, you had it turned up too loud," Blair explained.

"Too loud for you, but not for me!" Nana said. "It's my room, not yours."

"I'm sorry," Blair said as she reached down to turn the TV back on.

"Don't turn that thing back on if you're going to be staying." Nana waved a dismissive hand toward her. "I won't be able to listen to both you and the TV at the same time."

Blair smiled at her grandmother as she leaned over to give her a kiss on the cheek. "It's good to see you, Nana," she said.

"It's always good to see you," Nana said. Then looking around she asked, "Where are my precious great-grandchildren?"

"They're at home with their daddy. They're going to be mad when they find out I came to see you without them."

"It's my fault," Blair's mother said as she entered Nana's room. "I literally ran into Blair at the cleaners and invited her to join me in getting you ready for the big party tonight."

Nana frowned. "I'm not convinced that I should be going to this 'big party.'"

"Mama, we talked about this," Blair's mother said. "Aaron and Jenny want you there to help them celebrate."

"I don't know why they'd want an old lady around," Nana said. "I can't get around that well anymore. I'll end up being a burden."

"You're not a burden to anyone," Blair said. "We all want you there."

"It won't be the same without you," her mother added.

"I'll tell you what, Nana," Blair said as she leaned in closer to her grandmother. "When you're ready to leave, Zeke can take you to our house to see the girls and spend the night. The girls will be thrilled to have their G-Nana sleep over. How does that sound?"

After a minute of consideration, Nana said, "Okay, I'm convinced. Now, let's get me dressed."

"Now, Nana, don't forget that we'll be here to pick you up at six on the dot," Blair said.

"I'm not stupid, you know. You've told me that umpteen times already. I've got it. Six." Nana grinned at Blair as she held up six fingers.

Blair shook her head. "Nana, you're something else!"

After dropping Betty Jo off at her house, Nona headed straight home. She was looking forward to a long, relaxing soak in in a hot bubble bath. She'd had a seventy-inch air-massage pedestal bathtub installed in her bathroom at her father's house as soon as she'd moved in. It was the one indulgence she'd splurged on since bubble baths were one of her secret pleasures.

As Nona pulled into her driveway, she was surprised there was no sign of her father's caretaker anywhere. Instead, she saw Monty's car parked near the back door. She couldn't imagine why he'd be there instead of Miss Althea. He wasn't due to pick her up until five thirty. She hurried out of her car and in the back door.

As soon as she entered the house, she noticed small circles of red dotting the floor of the mudroom and on in to the kitchen. Her heart almost stopped as she stepped in the kitchen. Bloody towels filled the kitchen sink. There was a stream of blood running down the front of the cabinet and pooling on the kitchen floor. There was blood splattered on the white quartz countertop all the way from the stove to the sink.

In a panic, she called out, "Daddy? Monty? Where are you?"

When she stepped in the dining room, she saw Monty quickly coming towards her with a finger to his lips. "Shh, your dad's sleeping in his chair in the front room," he whispered. Taking her by her shoulders, he ushered her back to the kitchen.

"What in the world is going on here? Why is there blood all over the kitchen? Where's Miss Althea? What are you doing here?" Nona demanded.

Monty smiled down at her. "I can tell you're a little upset by what's going on here."

"A little?" Nona said, both irritated and frustrated by Monty's nonchalant attitude. "I'm a lot upset."

"Why don't you have a seat right here at the breakfast table so I can alleviate some of your anxiety by answering your questions?" Monty said in a calm, controlled voice.

Nona sat, her heart pounding, trying not to be aggravated with Monty.

Monty took the chair across the table from her, and as he gently took her hand in his, began to explain. "As you know, I play golf on Saturdays."

Nona slowly nodded, wondering how his playing golf on Saturdays had anything to do with what had happened in this kitchen and why he was here an hour and a half early.

"I was on the seventeenth hole, ready to putt the ball in for an Eagle—an Eagle mind you, when my cell phone sang out with the little tune I have set for your cell and your landline. Needless to say, it distracted me from my putt and I missed the hole by inches." Monty used his fingers to show Nona how close he'd been to making his putt.

"Okay, Monty, I got that you missed the putt," Nona said as her aggravation continued to grow, "but I didn't call you."

"I know you didn't, darlin'," Monty said as he tenderly patted her hand. "Your father did."

Nona jerked her hand away from his. "My father? Is Daddy hurt?" Nona was panicking all over again. "Monty, just tell me what happened here!"

"Your father is fine, but poor Miss Althea had an altercation with a knife while slicing cucumbers for tonight's supper. As you can see," he said, looking around the kitchen, "the knife won."

"And my father called you?" Nona asked in disbelief.

"I surmise that my number must have been the last number dialed out on your landline. Your father said he couldn't remember any numbers, so he hit Redial, and that's how he got me."

"Daddy must have been near panic when he called you."

"Not really," Monty said. "In fact, your father seemed in total control. He explained to me what had happened and gave the phone to Miss Althea, who told me she was confident she could drive herself to the emergency room to have her hand stitched up. Her concern was that your father would be left alone. That's when I offered to come right over," Monty concluded with a smile.

"Oh, Monty," Nona said, coming around the table to embrace him. "Why didn't you call me?"

"I knew you were busy," Monty said, welcoming her embrace, "and I wasn't."

"You are the best." Nona kissed him. "Do you know that?"

"Just keep believing that," Monty said, returning her kiss.

"I hate that you have to drive all the way back to Bradford to get ready."

"It's not all that far," Monty said, looking at his watch, "but I need to leave soon if I'm going to be back by five thirty. I can at least help you clean up this mess. That's where I was heading when you walked in."

"I've got this," Nona said, dismissing his offer of help. "You go on."

"Are you sure?"

"Positive."

Monty gave her one last kiss before leaving. Nona looked around the kitchen. As she took the cleaning supplies from under the sink, she realized that she'd be taking a shower this evening instead of her bubble bath.

Betty Jo was glad to be home after a long day of setting up for Jenny and Aaron's engagement party. She was proud that their hard work had created the perfect setting for tonight's festivities. As she stepped in the house through the side door, she was perplexed to find Don sitting at the end of their kitchen table holding his cell phone in one hand. It was a rare sight to even see her husband in the house during daylight hours. She'd usually find him tending to his plants and flowers in his greenhouse or out in his shop tinkering on his latest project. Betty Jo sensed that something was wrong.

"Don?" Betty Jo said with concern as she hurried over to him.

Don looked away from his phone and up at his wife. "I just got a call from Ethan," he said with a puzzled look on his face.

Their son Ethan was a lieutenant colonel in the United States Air Force, stationed at the Pentagon. Ethan lived in the Washington, DC area with his wife, Chloe, and their three children, Kelli, Matthew, and Chase. Neither Don nor Betty Jo knew exactly what he did at the Pentagon. When they asked him, he always joked that if he told them, then he'd have to kill them. Which let them know they were better off not knowing.

"Is everything alright?" Betty Jo asked as her concern shifted from Don to Ethan.

"It looks like our son and his family are coming back to Georgia," Don said.

"What?" Betty Jo found this news hard to believe, and yet she was excited at the prospect of Ethan and his family living closer to them. When Ethan had come home after Don had been arrested and falsely accused of drunk driving, he'd told them that he was certain he'd be stationed at the Pentagon until he retired. They'd been able to get together with Ethan and his family only a couple of times a year, which was never enough for Betty Jo.

"Don't leave me hanging. Tell me what's going on." She took the chair next to Don, urging him to fill her in on the details.

Don took a minute gathering his thoughts before he spoke. "It seems that the Navy and the Air Force are going to collaborate on a project at the Naval Submarine Base at Kings Bay, Georgia. From what I can understand, they're transferring Ethan down here to head it all up."

Betty Jo couldn't think of anything that would make her happier than her son and family moving within an hour of her. She reached over to Don and wrapped her arms around his neck.

"Oh, Don, now we can truly be a part of our grandchildren's lives!" Betty Jo was thrilled. After Ethan's last visit, she'd given up hope that she'd be able to watch his children grow up. "This is truly an answer to my prayers."

"Now, hold on a minute before you get all excited and start making plans," Don said as he gently held her by her shoulders and looked sternly in her eyes. "We can be a part of our grandchildren's lives only as much as Chloe allows us to be." He emphasized the word "only."

Betty Jo sat back in her chair, her enthusiasm deflated by Don's words.

"You remember what happened on their last visit here," Don said. "Chloe wasn't very happy with you when you took the kids swimming without her permission while she was taking a nap. It wasn't a pleasant scene for any of us."

Betty Jo vividly remembered Chloe's reaction when she got home with the kids. She'd thought she was doing her a favor by getting the kids out of the house, so they wouldn't disturb her nap. It'd been one of those late summer Georgia days when the heat was so oppressing. The kids were tired of being in the house. Little Kelli and Matthew had begged to go swimming at Aunt Dixie's house. She truly believed that she was doing Chloe a favor and making the children happy at the same time–a win-win situation. However, it hadn't turned out that way. Chloe had been extremely upset with her. So much so, that they'd left the next day.

"I think that episode is all behind us. You must admit everything was much better when we visited them at Christmas. It'll all work out," Betty

Jo said, hoping it was true.

"Don't burst my happiness bubble," she said as she stood up. "Let me enjoy this moment of knowing our son and grandchildren will soon be living closer to us." She leaned over to kiss Don on the cheek. "Come on. We need to get ready for this party or we're going to be late."

Jenny was thankful that her job as a support nurse gave her little time to dwell on anything other than her patients and their families. She'd wanted to take the day off from work, but knowing that she was going to be asking for more than a week off for the wedding, she'd decided the smart thing to do was go to work today. Aaron had stepped up and taken on the job of picking up Emma at the Savannah/Hilton Head International Airport that morning. Aaron and Emma had never met. She'd been praying the two of them would hit it off from the start. Emma was not only her sister, but her best friend in all the world. She loved them both so much and had no clue what she'd do if they didn't get along.

Jenny had a busy morning and at ten o'clock had just sat down in the nurses' break room at Memorial General hospital when her phone rang. She looked down to see that it was Aaron calling.

"Did Emma's flight get there on time?"

"Oh, was that today I was supposed to pick up your sister?"

Jenny's heart sank until she caught the teasing tone in his voice. "Aaron," she said sternly, "that's not funny."

"Emma thought it was," Aaron said, laughing.

Jenny could hear more laughter in the background. "Is that my sister laughing?" she said, trying to sound upset.

"I put you on speaker so Emma could get a kick out of your reaction," Aaron said, still laughing.

"Hi, baby sister," Emma said. "I see you still can't take a joke."

"Ha, ha!" Jenny said without humor. "I can take a joke when it's funny."

"I have to say, Jenny," Emma said. "You may not be able to take a joke, but you know how to get the most handsome man in Georgia to marry you." She added, "I could just melt in those blue eyes of his."

Jenny could feel the blush rising on her face. "Emma, you're embarrassing me."

"It's okay. Aaron didn't hear what I said. He's getting my luggage."

"In that case, you just go melt in someone else's eyes," Jenny said. "He's mine."

They both laughed. Jenny's heart was happy. She could tell her sister and her future husband had hit it off just fine.

Chapter Eighteen

Dixie rarely wore makeup, but for this special occasion, she'd highlighted her cheeks with a touch of blush and even used a bit of mascara to make her dark brown eyes stand out. After running a brush through her hair, she put on the teal and coral bamboo screen print tunic and slimming white ankle pants she'd set out on her bed before taking her shower. Now, looking at the white pants, she hoped she wouldn't drip barbecue sauce on them. Somehow, no matter how careful she was, some part of her food would become a part of her ensemble. She considered changing to black pants, but knew the outfit wouldn't be as striking. She put on the white pants.

Dixie was fumbling with the clasp on her solitaire diamond pendant that Alex had given her for their fortieth wedding anniversary when she heard him call out that the caterers had arrived. She glanced at the clock. They were fifteen minutes early. *Better early than late,* she thought as she rushed out of her bedroom. She met Alex coming down the hall.

"Would you please help me with this necklace? I seem to be all thumbs." Dixie held out her necklace to him.

"Calm down," he said as he put the necklace on her. "Everything looks great."

As she turned around, he added, "And you look beautiful."

"You're looking pretty fine yourself." Dixie stood on her tiptoes to kiss him.

"Would you please make sure Jason is ready while I help the caterers set up?" she asked Alex.

Dixie continued down the hall as Alex went to Jason's door and knocked. "Jason, how's it going in there?"

Jason didn't answer. Alex leaned in closer to the door, hoping to pick up sounds of his son getting ready from inside the room. He tried the doorknob, but found that it was locked as usual. He knocked again.

"You okay in there?"

Jason was sitting on the bathroom floor desperately trying to make the panel from the bathtub fit back in place.

"Yeah, Dad," he called out, "all good here. I'll be there in a minute."

"Okay, just making sure."

Jason listened to his father's retreating footsteps. He sat with his head in his hands and his back against the tub. He'd been sure that he had five round 160mg oxycodone pills in that bottle this morning, but when he'd taken the bottle out this evening, he only counted three. He'd taken the entire front panel from the tub searching for the two missing pills. He hadn't had any luck finding them. He couldn't have taken more than one this morning or he'd be lying dead somewhere by now.

He'd have to figure it out later. Right now, he needed to be outside with his parents before they came looking for him again. He swallowed the pill he held in his hand. He wasn't sure how long this party would last, so he'd taken out an extra pill to keep in his pocket just in case. Which meant he only had one pill left. Which made him think about Eddy. Which in turn made his whole body tense and his heart beat faster. He looked at his phone, wondering when he'd hear from him again. He jumped, almost falling backwards into the tub, when he heard the ding of his phone alerting him to a new text as if he'd conjured it up by just thinking about Eddy. He thought about ignoring it until after the party, but then remembered Eddy's parting words of warning. He reached over to take the phone from the sink and glanced down at the message displayed on the screen.

need addresses

At first Jason was confused whether or not Eddy was asking for his address so he could attend the party. But then he took a closer look at the message and, knowing what Eddy's side business was, he understood that he wanted the addresses of those attending who'd have what he needed to increase his inventory of ATVs, golf carts, and lawn mowers. Was he really going to just text the addresses of friends and family to Eddy so he could steal from them? He wondered if he'd truly sunk that low. Then he remembered about what was truly at stake for him. His own inventory was low and had to be replenished as soon as possible. Plus, there was the matter of the gun he knew Eddy had.

Jason looked through his contacts for the information Eddy would need. He grinned to himself as he texted Zeke Coby's address, knowing Zeke was the one who'd cut off his legitimate supply which had, in the long run, made him Eddy's partner in this crime. It'd serve him right to go home tonight to find out he'd been robbed. He sent out three more addresses before deciding that was enough. He hoped after doing Eddy this favor tonight, he'd never be asked to do it ever again.

Jason was beginning to feel much better about things. It always amazed him how one little pill could quickly turn all his problems into minor concerns. He got up from the floor, ran a comb though his hair, straightened his clothes, and left his room, ready for a night of celebration.

Aaron's plan to shower at the gym after his workout that afternoon hadn't worked out as he'd planned. With the rash of break-ins and robberies, his father, had expanded all patrol territories, which meant longer hours. Add to that picking up Emma, and his timing was thrown way off. Once he'd dropped Emma at Jenny's apartment, he'd barely had time to patrol all the areas in town he'd been assigned. That had meant he hadn't had time to get to the gym. Which was why he'd just taken an ice-cold shower instead of the long, hot shower he would have taken at the gym.

When Aaron made the decision to give up his job as a trooper with the Georgia State Patrol to move back to Kerry to work with his father after his father's accident, he'd bought a fixer-upper with the intention of remodeling it himself with a little help from his friends and family. He'd watched his mother and father renovate their house as he'd grown up. He was confident he could do the same with this house. It hadn't turned out to be as easy as he'd hoped. His attempts to repair the water heater by himself was why he'd just taken another cold shower. He knew he had to get it fixed before Jenny moved in after they were married.

Aaron and Jenny had chosen not to move in together even though all their friends thought they were crazy to waste their money keeping up two separate residences. They were both well aware that what they were doing wasn't what most couples in their early thirties did these days. Most couples moved in together. However, Aaron doubted that most moved in together for the sole purpose of saving money. If his friends knew that he and Jenny had also chosen not to sleep together until they were married, they'd consider them both certifiable. They'd managed to keep that as their secret.

Aaron smiled as he thought back to the first time he'd seen Jenny, when she walked in the hospital waiting room to give them an update on his father's surgery. When Nurse Levins entered the room in her standard green hospital scrubs, surgical mask hanging from one ear and dark brown hair pulled back in a ponytail, his breath had caught in his throat. He'd watched as she'd given his mother an update on his father. She'd spoken with such compassion and empathy that he'd known right then that he wanted to get to know her. Luckily, she'd felt the same about wanting to get to know him. It hadn't taken long at all for him to realize that he was in love with Nurse Levins.

Aaron had been hurt more than once by someone he was sure he loved. Blair had told him many times that he fell in love too easily and that's what left him vulnerable to having his heart broken. The feelings he had for Jenny were different from any he'd ever experienced before. This was not like any of his other relationships. He didn't want to mess this one up by rushing in too quickly.

Aaron made an old-school decision to court Jenny, and that's what he did. Instead of casually dating her to see where it might lead, he pursued Jenny with the one hope that she would see him as the man she'd want to spend the rest of her life loving. It was later he learned that Jenny had also been the victim of a broken heart and felt the same way about not rushing the love that she believed was developing between the two of them. That's what had led both of them to the decision of waiting to make love until their wedding night. It had been a true test of their commitment to one another to stay with that decision. Now that Aaron thought about it, maybe it was a good thing he had to take cold showers.

Jenny couldn't remember when she'd felt this excited. First, she didn't have to go to work for the next four days. Second, her sister, whom she hadn't seen for over ten months, was at her apartment waiting for her. Third, there was a party this very night specifically to honor her and the man she loved. Jenny pulled into her parking place in the basement of her apartment complex. *Could life be any better than this? My life has truly been blessed by God.*

Getting out of her car, Jenny was suddenly hit with a wave of sadness, realizing that it could be better, much better, if only her father had cared enough to come down to Georgia to be with her tonight. She tried to push away her sadness and return to feeling as happy as she was only few minutes ago, but she couldn't seem to shake it.

Jenny took a deep breath and placed a smile on her face as she put the key in her apartment door. She almost fell in the door as Emma yanked it open. "Jenny!" Emma grabbed her up in her arms.

As Jenny returned her sister's embrace, she felt her sadness melt away. "Oh, Emma, I'm so glad you're here!" she said. "I've missed you so."

"Where else would I be?" Emma asked, releasing her sister. "I'm just sorry I let so much time go by without getting down here to meet that handsome fiancé of yours."

"I sent you pictures."

"The pictures you sent to me just didn't do him justice."

Jenny smiled at her sister. "He is a fine-looking man."

"I'm truly happy for you," Emma said. "I know Mom would be too."

Not wanting things to get emotional, Jenny hoped to change the subject. "How was your flight?"

"It was good," Emma said, taking a seat at the far end of the couch. "I love flying. It sure beats driving."

Jenny sat down in the recliner directly across from Emma. "Amen to that," she said as flipped up the recliner. "Ah, it feels good to be off my feet."

"I still can't believe you chose to work today with all that's going on," Emma said, shaking her head.

"Working today means I don't have to go back to work until Tuesday," Jenny said, looking over at her sister, "which gives me time to be with you." "Plus, I needed to work today so I can ask for extra time off for the honeymoon," she added with a smile.

"By the way, where are you two going for your honeymoon?" Emma grinned at her sister.

"What a strange word, 'honeymoon' is," Jenny said. "I wonder why it's called that and not something more romantic like 'Expedition of Love'?"

Emma laughed. "Really? 'Expedition of Love'? When did you get so corny?"

Jenny joined in her sister's laughter. "I'm not sure."

They laughed until tears began running down their faces. "I haven't laughed like that since the last time we were together," Jenny said, taking a deep breath in hopes of regaining her composure.

"It feels so good." Emma wiped the tears away. Then, looking over at her Jenny, she said, "I've missed you."

"I've missed you too," Jenny said. "And if we don't get a move on, we're going to miss my party."

Checking her watch, Emma agreed. "All I need to do is get dressed. You're the one everyone is coming to see, and if they saw you now they'd all be feeling sorry for Aaron!"

"Well, thanks a bunch!"

Getting up from the couch, Emma walked over to give Jenny a hand out of the recliner. "Come on, let's make you beautiful for your big night."

Jenny wondered how long it would take Emma to realize she hadn't weaseled out of her where they were going on their honeymoon.

Chapter Nineteen

After Dixie directed the caterers to where they'd be setting up under the tent, she took a few minutes to walk around the yard, making sure that everything was in its place and all was ready for their guests. She moved a couple of the flower-filled planters to the back of the patio so they wouldn't interfere with the flow as guests moved from the tent to the patio. She glanced at her watch. Her excitement was building. It wouldn't be long before the first guests would arrive.

Dixie had always loved parties, even as a child. She and Scarlett had enjoyed the parties her parents had given. Her mother had been a natural hostess, making everyone feel welcome. Dixie wanted to be as good at hosting parties as her mother had been, but feared she fell short. She wished her sister were with her now to help her with this party.

"Dixie!"

Dixie was taken out of her reverie at the sound of her name. She turned to see Nona and Monty coming toward her. Seeing the two of them together made Dixie's heart happy. They made such a handsome couple, with Nona in her subtle floral-print sundress with a pale pink shawl draped over her shoulders and Monty in khaki pants with a light green button-down shirt that brought out the green of his eyes.

"Where were you?" Nona asked as she leaned over to give Dixie a quick kiss on the cheek. "You must've been off somewhere in outer space. I called your name a couple of times."

"Sorry about that," Dixie said, embarrassed. "I'm back now." Holding out her hand to Monty, she said, "It's good to see you again. So glad you could come."

Monty took her hand in his. "It's good to see you too." Looking around, he added, "You have a beautiful place."

Dixie released his hand and smiled. "Why, thank you."

"What do you want me to do?" Nona asked.

"Well, you're the first ones here, so I'll give you the job of greeting our guests as they arrive. I hope the signs are clear about where they should park."

"I didn't have a problem understanding them," Monty reassured her. "It's pretty clear that everyone is to park in the side yard."

Dixie looked at Monty gratefully. "That's what Alex said. He told me not to worry, but—"

"Did I hear my name?" Alex said as he walked up to stand next to Dixie. After shaking hands with Monty and kissing Nona's cheek, he took Dixie's hand and gave it a squeeze. "You need to stop worrying and start enjoying your hard work. This party is going to be one of the best Kerry has ever seen."

"Amen to that," Betty Jo added as she and Don walked up to the group.

Don said, "It looks great. You ladies did an excellent job."

"We couldn't have done it without you and Alex helping," Dixie said.

Alex nodded. "It just goes to show you what teamwork can do."

"Our teamwork isn't over. It's going to take all of us working together tonight to make this a great party," Dixie said. "And it looks like it's time to get started."

They all looked over to see Aaron, Jenny, and another young woman walking towards them.

"Oh my, how handsome and attractive y'all look," Dixie said as she warmly embraced both Jenny and Aaron.

"Miss Dixie," Jenny said after returning her hug, "this is my sister, Emma."

"Emma, we are so happy to have you here with us," Dixie said as she hugged Emma.

Introductions were made as welcoming hugs were given all around. The evening was off to a good start.

By six thirty, all the guests had arrived. After Brother Richard blessed the food, it didn't take long for the guests to go through the serving line and be seated at tables under the tent enjoying the meal. The weather had turned out to be perfect, but what most delighted Dixie was that the gnats and mosquitoes that usually hung around, and often ruined outdoor parties in South Georgia, were nonexistent. She knew that was due to the foresight of her husband, who'd had the yard professionally sprayed all spring and summer. He'd grown up in Kerry and attended many a party where he'd often fought the bugs for the food.

Dixie, Nona, and Betty Jo walked from table to table chatting with guests and making sure their tea glasses were full. There would be beer and wine later after the band set up and the dancing began, but sweet tea was the perfect beverage to go along with a Southern barbecue dinner. The fact that the tent was fully occupied was a tribute to Jenny and Aaron and their family. The Weavers were a well-liked family in the Kerry community.

A special table at the head of the tent had been set up for Jenny and Aaron and the bridal party along with their families. Jenny had asked Emma to be her maid of honor and Blair to be her bridesmaid. Nathan was Aaron's best man and Zeke was his groomsman. Mark, Layne, and Miss Louise were sitting at the head table as well. Dixie noticed a great deal of laughter coming from that table.

Dixie looked away from the head table and began to look for Jason and Eddy. She'd tried to get them to sit at the same table with Lily, still hoping that Jason and Lily might get together, but it seemed that Jason had chosen to sit with Eddy as far away from Lily as he could. She thought he'd been acting nervous tonight. When he was in high school, she could count on Jason to be the life of the party. In those days, by the end of the evening, he'd have talked to everyone attending. She signed, realizing that wasn't the Jason of today. It seemed that he purposefully isolated himself from everyone he knew. It made her sad to see him sitting at a table with people he barely knew, but she was glad that he had Eddy with him. It appeared that Eddy was having a good time talking to everyone, but it looked to her as if Jason was trying his best to make himself invisible. She was glad that she'd invited Eddy. Jason needed someone with whom he could connect, and it looked like Eddy was that person.

"I think we've pulled it off," Nona said as she came up behind Dixie.

Dixie turned to her, taking her attention from Jason. "It looks like we have so far," she said, smiling. "Now we need to make sure the band is set up and the bar is ready for guests."

Betty Jo joined them. Brushing her hands together, she announced, "Already done."

"It is?" Dixie asked with surprise.

"Don and I took care of it. It's all ready."

"That's great," Nona said. "Now, how do we let everyone know the band is ready?"

"When the band starts playing," Dixie said, "I think everyone will get the idea."

As if on cue, the band started warming up. The three looked at one another in surprise.

"I guess that's what you call perfect timing," Nona said.

Guests began to get up from their tables and make their way to the back patio. A portable dance floor had been set up beside the patio with tables and chairs scattered about. So far, everything was going as planned. Dixie just hoped that would be the way it would continue.

Chapter Twenty

Layne had tried to keep an eye on her mother throughout the night, but she was a hard one to keep up with. It was obvious to all that Miss Louise was enjoying herself, but Layne was worried that she might be wearing down. Her mother had moved from the tent to sit in one of the chairs close to the band where she could watch couples as they danced. Layne noticed that Jason's friend had taken the chair next to her and they were talking and laughing.

"How's it going, Mama?" Layne asked, bending down close to her ear so her mother could hear her better over the music.

With glowing eyes, her mother looked up at her. "Oh, Layne, I'm having one of the best times I've had in years."

"I'm so glad," Layne said, giving her mother's shoulder a squeeze. It was good to see her mother looking so happy. She knew her mother spent too many of her days lonely and unhappy.

"Have you met Jason's friend, Eddy?" Miss Louise asked. "He's just the nicest young man."

"No, I don't believe I have," Layne said.

Leaning in toward Eddy to introduce herself, she said, "I'm Layne Weaver. I'm Miss Louise's daughter and the mother of the groom-to-be."

Eddy smiled at Layne as he said, "Congratulations on both!" Then he added, "Your mother is a real trip."

"That's a good way to put it," Layne said, smiling back. "Nice to meet you, Eddy."

Turning back to her mother, Layne whispered in her ear, "Just let me know when you're ready to leave. I don't want you to get worn out."

Layne watched as her mother's head bobbed with the beat of the music. It seemed that she wasn't ready to go just yet to Blair's house where she wanted to stay the night so she could spend some time with her great-granddaughters. Layne kept her hand on her mother's shoulder as she listened to the band.

It wasn't long before Layne felt her mother's hand on hers. She looked down to see her mother crooking her finger at her indicating she wanted her to tell her something. Layne leaned down. "Yes?"

"I'm ready," her mother said as she patted Layne's face with her hand.

Layne could see the weariness on her mother's face. Giving her a warm smile, she said, "Okay, Mama. Let me find Blair and Zeke to take you home." She searched the crowd, hoping to see Blair and Zeke on the dance floor, but they weren't dancing. She spotted Aaron and Jenny but didn't want to bother them. She leaned back down to tell her mother, "I'll be right back."

It didn't take Layne long to find Blair and Zeke sitting at a table under the tent with Nathan, Heather, and Lily. They were deep in conversation about the upcoming college football season. "I'm sorry to interrupt your important conversation, y'all, but Nana's pretty much worn out and ready to leave," Layne said.

Zeke stood up. "I can take her to our house," he offered.

"I think I better take her," Blair said as she put a hand on her husband's shoulder to sit him back down. "You've had way too many beers and probably shouldn't be driving."

Zeke sat back down without protesting. "Good idea," he said as he handed her the keys to their car.

"I'll go with you," Heather offered.

"Great," Layne said. "I'll get Mama and meet y'all out front."

Layne was concerned when she found that her mother wasn't in the chair where she'd left her only a few minutes ago. She looked around for her and spotted her on the dance floor in the arms of her youngest grandson. Layne watched as Aaron and his nana gently swayed back and forth to the music. It was a precious moment that Layne would remember forever.

When the music ended, Layne walked out on the dance floor. She heard her mother say, "Thank you, Aaron. You just made an old woman very happy." She reached up to kiss his cheek.

"Love you, Nana," Aaron said.

"I know," she said in return.

Layne helped her mother to the front where Blair and Heather were waiting with the car. After helping her mother into the car, Layne stood for a moment watching Blair's car head down the driveway. As she turned back toward the party, she could see so many of her friends and family who had come out on this night to help celebrate the love between two people who were very dear to her. Her heart was full.

Dear Lord, thank You for all of the blessings You've showered on my life.

Miss Louise entertained Blair and Heather with stories of residents at Whitlock during the fifteen minutes it took to get to Blair's house from Dixie's. Grandma and Grandpa Coby had taken Rachel and Madison out to eat and then to a movie in Bradford for the evening. The plan was for them to come back to Blair and Zeke's house to stay with the girls until their parents returned home from the party. Blair hadn't expected them to be back from the movie this early, so wasn't worried when she didn't see their car in her driveway. However, she was shocked to see a large white moving truck backed up to her carport. She didn't see anyone in or around the truck.

"Well, what in the world?" Miss Louise stopped in the middle of one of her stories.

"Blair?" Heather asked.

Blair had no idea who was parked in her driveway. Her first thought was that the people who Zeke had hired to landscape their yard had come by to drop off materials for the job. Her second thought was that it didn't make sense for them to be here this late on a Saturday night. Just as she was about to open her car door to check it out, two men came from around the side of the carport. They had ball caps pulled down low on their heads. They stopped and seemed to be as surprised to see Blair's car as the three women in the car were to see them. One of the men shouted something to the other man as he reached around his back and pulled out something that looked to Blair like a gun.

Blair screamed out to the others in the car, "Hold on!"

Blair slammed her car in reverse. Her tires squealed as she backed out of the driveway onto the street. She put the car in Drive and pressed down on the gas, begging her car to move as quickly as possible.

"Call my dad!" Blair ordered Heather.

It took Heather a minute to react. She fumbled with getting her phone out of her purse, almost dropping it on the floor of the car. By the time she had control of the phone, Blair remembered watching as her mother had purposefully taken away her father's phone from him when they'd arrived at the party. She'd explained that she knew he'd be tempted to "check in on things" if she left it with him, so she'd put it in her bag with the promise of paying no attention to any calls he might receive. Blair prayed that she wouldn't ignore Heather's call.

"They don't seem to be following us," Nana said as she turned to look out the back window.

Before Blair could answer Nana, she heard Heather shouting into the phone, "Help! Help us!"

Blair looked over at Heather. It was obvious that fear and panic had consumed her. Blair reached over, taking the phone from her. She could hear her mother's voice filled with alarm. "Heather? What's going on? Answer me!"

With her hand shaking, Blair put the phone to her ear. "Mom, I need Dad, now. My house is being robbed!"

Willing herself to remain calm, Layne scanned the area, searching for Mark. She couldn't remember where she'd seen him last. She hurried back toward the tent as Dixie was coming out of it to check on the band. The two almost collided.

Dixie grabbed Layne's arm. "Whoa! Where are you going in such a hurry?"

Tears filled Layne's eyes. "I have to find Mark."

"Layne, what is it?"

"Have you seen Mark?"

"I just left the table where he was sitting with the guys."

"Take me there!"

Layne followed closely behind Dixie. She tried to keep her mind from filling with frightening images of what could be happening to Blair, Heather, and her mother. As soon as she saw Mark, Layne cried out, "Mark, Blair needs you!"

"Blair? What's wrong?"

"She called saying something about her house being robbed," Layne blurted out. "Oh, Mark, I think something bad might be happening to them."

"Where is she now?" Mark asked.

"Oh, Mark, I don't know. She didn't say."

"It's going to be okay," Mark said, giving Layne a reassuring hug. "If she was able to call you, then she's not hurt or in immediate danger."

"Can I do anything to help?" Dixie asked with concern.

"I'm calling it in and going there," Mark said. "You go back to the party. Don't let something like this ruin a great evening."

Then looking around he added, "But whatever you do, don't let Aaron know anything about this. He'd be leading the way out there, and this should be a special night for him and Jenny."

Layne at once felt calmer knowing that Mark would handle the situation. "You be careful," she said as she leaned into him.

"You can count on it."

Mark took his phone from Layne. He needed to report the robbery or attempted robbery. As he headed out to where he'd parked his car earlier that evening, he saw Blair's car pull in the driveway. He rushed over to her car. Blair was out of the car and into her father's arms in a matter of seconds.

"Oh, Daddy," Blair sobbed into his shoulder as he held her, "I was so scared."

After Heather helped Miss Louise out of the back of the car, they all gathered around Mark.

"Well, that was an experience I've never had and can truthfully say I never want to have again," Heather said.

Mark looked toward the front porch where there were a couple of rockers.

"Let's go up to the porch where y'all can sit down. I want you to tell me exactly what happened."

Once the women were seated, Mark listened as one by one they relayed the story of what had happened. His first concern was that Zeke's parents would pull up with Rachel and Madison and find the scene as Blair had. However, Blair assured him that she'd called them, and they were keeping the girls at their house for the night.

After listening to the three of them, Mark looked at Blair and said, "I think we need to get Zeke as discreetly as we can and the three of us go to the house. If they've taken anything, you two can give us an inventory. Two deputies should already be there."

Mark turned to Heather. "I'll get Nathan to let him know what's happened. He can take you and Nana to your house to spend the night."

Heather looked up at Mark with grateful eyes. "Oh, Mark, that would be wonderful."

"Do y'all think you'll be okay to wait here while I get Zeke and Nathan?" Mark asked.

From the side of the porch, Layne called out, "We'll take care of them."

Dixie, Betty Jo, and Nona came to stand next to Layne. As soon as Blair saw her mother, she burst into tears again. Layne wrapped her up in a comforting embrace while the others tended to Heather and Layne's mother. Mark left the porch confident that the Fearsome Foursome were exactly the ones who Blair, Heather, and Layne's mother needed to look after them.

Mark found Zeke and Nathan sitting together at the edge of the patio. The problem was that Aaron was sitting next to them. Mark would have to think of a reasonable excuse to pull Zeke and Nathan away from Aaron. As he approached the group, he worked to replace the worried look that he was sure was written on his face with one of cheer. He knew if Aaron picked up on the emotions that he was feeling, his son wouldn't let up on him until he learned the truth of what was bothering his father.

Mark came up behind Aaron and slapped his hands on his son's shoulders. "Don't tell me you're sitting here talking with these two instead of out there dancing with your beautiful bride-to-be!"

Aaron turned around to look at his father. "I'm trying to catch my breath, Dad. I'm about danced out. I never knew just how much Jenny likes to dance."

Mark scanned the dance floor looking for Jenny. It took him a minute before he spotted her standing with several nurses whom he recognized from the weeks he'd spent in the hospital. He noticed that she was holding an empty wine glass.

"Looks to me like your lady is in need of a refill," he said, pointing toward Jenny.

As Aaron slowly rose from his seat, he sighed dramatically, "I guess there's no rest for the weary. Let me hasten to my love's rescue."

Mark sat down in the chair that Aaron had just vacated. Making sure that Aaron was out of earshot, he turned to Zeke and Nathan and said in an even voice, "There's nothing to be alarmed about, but I need both of you to calmly get out of your seats and follow me down to the front porch."

"Why?" Nathan leaned closer to his father. "What's going on?"

"I'll tell you as soon as we get away from here," Mark said, "but I don't want to make a scene or for Aaron to know about this." He stood up and began walking around the house toward the front porch hoping that Nathan and Zeke would follow like he'd asked. When he got to the front porch, he found a much calmer group than when he'd left them only a few minutes before.

As Mark stepped up on the porch, he was relieved to see Nathan and Zeke coming around the corner of the house. He waited for them to join him.

"Now can you tell us what's going on, Mark?" Zeke asked.

Blair sprang up from the rocker where she'd been seated and dove into her husband's arms. "Oh, Zeke, I was so scared. When I pulled in our driveway and saw that moving van. I just couldn't imagine why there would be a moving van parked right there in our driveway. All of a sudden, I saw two men come from around from behind the truck. They stopped when they saw my car. That's when I saw one of them reach behind his back for something. I was so afraid he was going reaching for a gun. I wasn't sure what to do, so I just slammed the car in reverse and gunned it out of there."

Blair broke down sobbing. Zeke whispered words of comfort as he held her.

Mark shook his head. "She did exactly what she should have done. Her actions kept everyone safe."

Mark turned to Nathan. "Nathan, you should take Heather and Nana home now while Zeke, Blair, and I go back to the house to see what, if anything, has been taken."

"Okay, Dad," Nathan agreed.

Mark turned back to Zeke and Blair. "Blair, do you think you can handle going back to your house tonight?"

Blair stepped away from Zeke's embrace to answer her father. "I think so."

"I'm glad to hear it. I think it'll be better for you to go back to the scene of the crime tonight instead of putting it off until tomorrow morning."

After making sure everyone was safely in their cars, Nona headed back to the party to continue her hostess duties. As she walked up to the patio, she spotted Monty standing off to the side talking with Jason. She watched as his face lit up when he looked at her. Nona smiled back. As she began walking over to join him, she could feel his eyes following her every step.

Monty reached out for Nona, taking her hand in his. "May I have this dance?" he said leading her out to the dance floor.

Nana was glad the band was playing a slow song. She felt such peace with Monty's arms wrapped around her and her head resting against his chest. They fit together as if they were made for one another.

"I hope everything's okay, now," Monty whispered in her ear.

"It's all good for now," she said with a true belief that everything in her life really was good, for now. She hoped and prayed it would be for everyone else.

"Do you happen to know that I guy I was just talking to?"

"You mean Jason?"

"Yeah, that's the one." Monty sighed deeply. "He's high as a kite and about to come crashing down."

Nona stopped dancing and stepped back to look up into Monty's face. "Jason? What in the world would make you think that?"

With one eyebrow raised, Monty looked down at Nona. "Because I know the signs firsthand."

Nona dropped her hands to her side and stared up at Monty with disbelief. "What are you saying?"

"We need to talk."

Chapter Twenty-one

As Mark pulled onto the street where Blair and Zeke lived, he could see the flashing blue lights from his deputy's car. He knew the scene had been secured and it was safe for him to pull his car up into the driveway. He watched as Blair and Zeke pulled in behind him in their car.

Mark stepped up to Blair's car door and opened it, reaching his hand in to take hers. In a soft voice, he said, "It's safe for you to get out, Blair."

Blair looked up at her father, her eyes filled with fear. "Daddy, I'm not sure I can."

Mark squeezed her hand as he pulled her toward him, lifting her out of the car. "Yes, you can. I'm right here with you. You know I would never let anything happen to you."

Blair slowly stood, tightly gripping her father's hand. "You're sure that guy isn't here?" she asked in a shaky voice.

"Completely sure," he said with a reassuring smile.

Deputy Miles was standing just inside the carport. He turned to Mark as he entered still holding Blair's hand and with Zeke walking beside her. "Sir, ma'am," he said as he greeted the group.

Looking at Mark, he began to give him a report. "It appears that Mrs. Coby interrupted a robbery in progress." He turned and walked under the carport, motioning for them to follow. A riding lawn mower was flipped over on its side at the front of the carport.

Zeke gave a cry. "What have they done to my lawn mower?"

He rushed to the back of the carport. "I had my Polaris 700 and my Marshall golf cart parked all the way back here. The keys to every one of those vehicles are in the house. I thought they couldn't even be moved without starting them up."

Looking to the deputy who'd followed him to the back, he asked, "How were they able to steal them without a key?"

"Well, sir, it's not that hard to move these vehicles without starting them up." Deputy Miles walked back to the front of the carport with Zeke following closely behind. "Your ATV and golf cart were most likely placed in neutral, which allowed them to be pushed to the front here and up on the trailer or bed of a truck. Then your lawn mower gears were disengaged so they could push it out of here, but it looks like it fell off the trailer. That must have been when your wife pulled up in the driveway and scared them. They probably left in a hurry and didn't have time to secure it." He pointed to the lawn mower that was flipped over on its side.

Zeke shook his head. "I had no idea that could be done."

"Most people don't, sir," Deputy Miles said. "Since they don't have the original key, they'll simply install a new ignition."

Squeezing Blair's hand and then releasing it, Mark said to her, "Your timing was perfect, Blair. You caught them in the act. I'll bet because of you pulling up when you did, we'll be able to get some clear prints this time."

"Yes, sir," the deputy agreed. "I don't believe they had time to wipe it all down this time like they've done in the other robberies."

Mark turned to Zeke. "Why don't you see if your parents will put y'all up for the night? Our techs will be out here until late collecting evidence."

Deputy Miles said, "They're going to be doubly busy tonight. Three other robberies have been called in." Looking to Zeke and Blair he added, "Those folks weren't as lucky as y'all."

"I don't feel very lucky," Blair said. "That guy scared me to death. When he raised his hand, I thought he had a gun."

"Did you get a good look at his face?" Deputy Miles asked.

Blair shook her head. "With that cap down so far on his head, I couldn't even make out the color of his hair."

Mark could see that talking about the incident was upsetting Blair. "Why don't you go on inside and pack a few things for tonight, honey? We can talk about the rest tomorrow."

Zeke followed Blair in the house, which left Mark and the deputy alone.

"Do we have any leads?" Mark asked.

"None at all." Shaking his head, Deputy Miles added, "You know, after what happened to Deputy Snyder's mother, I believe that guy really could have had a gun in his hand."

"I know, Miles," Mark said. "That's what makes me believe God was watching over Blair, Heather, and Miss Louise. He's the one who kept them safe here tonight."

Monty led Nona over to a bench beside the pool away from the crowd that had gathered around the band. They sat down next to one another. There were several minutes of silence before Monty spoke. When he did, it was in a gruff, emotional voice that he told his story.

"I'm a recovering drug addict. Few people know that, but it's a fact." Monty paused looking at Nona to see her reaction. Seeing none, he continued.

"It started out so easily. When I was at law school, I played soccer on a co-ed intramural team. I played for two reasons. One, to keep in shape, and the other was because the girl I was in love with played on my team. It was during the play-offs that I went to kick the ball, missed, and landed on my butt, hard. After ignoring the pain for a few days, Sandy, my girlfriend who later became my wife, made me go to the doctor who x-rayed my posterior and found I had fractured my tailbone, my coccyx to be precise, which resulted in a great deal of pain. This was also my last semester of law school, and there was no way I could miss any class to nurse my injury. So the doctor prescribed a sweet little pain patch that you may have heard of, Fentanyl.

"I could go into all the details about how this drug affected me and how I moved on to other drugs, but let me just say that I became dependent upon this drug and drugs similar to it. I was addicted. I couldn't live without it, and it seemed I never had to since the doctors were more than accommodating by making sure I had a generous supply. Surprisingly, I was able to function for years without any problems as far as I could tell. I passed the bar, was hired by a prestigious Atlanta law firm, married, and had a beautiful daughter all while getting high on various opioid drugs. After years of addiction, it finally caught up with me. My body needed more and more and higher and higher dosages until I was taking what would have been to the average man a lethal dose each and every day. The drug—not my wife, not my work, not even my daughter—became the only important thing in my life. Then, I crashed. I lost it all—my wife, my daughter, my job. It was all gone. The only thing I had left was my addiction."

Monty paused. Leaning over, he ran his hand through his hair. Nona put her hand on his arm, offering support. Sitting up again, he continued, "Those were some dark days, I can tell you. Days when I thought about ending my life. But then, Ruth, the sister I'd cut out of my life years before, pulled me out of that black pit of despair by showing me through her love and belief in me that I was worth saving. She led me back to God, and I found that He still loved me despite all I'd done to ruin my life. Ruth convinced me to go to rehab. Ruth, rehab, and AA helped me break free of my addiction and start a new life. Ruth is the one who set me up in Bradford with my own law practice. I owe my life to my sister."

As Nona listened to Monty pour out his heart and soul about his addiction and recovery, silent tears ran down her cheeks. Her heart was breaking for the pain and loss he'd suffered. When he finished, she took his hands in hers. "Thank you for telling me your story, Monty. I know it couldn't have been easy for you, but it helps me know and understand you so much better. Now there's one thing I need for you to do for me."

"Name it."

"Introduce me to your sister. She has to be one great lady to have done all of that for you, and I want to personally thank her."

Monty squeezed her hands tightly as his eyes filled with tears. "Nona, I wish more than anything you could have met Ruth, but—" He paused. Then with a voice filled with emotion, he said, "She passed away five years ago."

Taking a deep breath, he continued. "She died a long, hard death from ovarian cancer. I count it as one of my greatest blessings that I was able to take care of her during those final months of her life."

Nona wrapped Monty in her arms and held him as she prayed, "Dear Lord, please shower Your blessings of peace on this man who has been through so much heartache. Amen."

They remained like that for several minutes. When they broke apart, Nona looked at him. "Now, what are we going to do about Jason? Don't you think we should tell someone what's going on with him?"

Monty thought for a moment, recalling the times he'd been high like Jason was now. "I don't know that we need to do that tonight. We should talk to him about it first. For now, we need to get him to bed so he can sleep it off."

They left together in search of Jason.

As Jason stood talking to Miss Nona's friend—he couldn't remember his name—he could feel his body beginning to break down. He'd taken his second pill of the night a little over an hour ago. He should be feeling fine by now, but he was feeling anything but fine. Maybe he'd gotten one of those pills without any potency, a dud. Surely duds happened sometimes. His tongue felt like it had swollen to twice its size, which made it hard to talk. He could feel the sweat running down his back and his whole body felt shaky. He began to search the crowd for Eddy. Surely Eddy had brought a little something with him that would cure whatever was going on with him so he could make it through the rest of the night. First, he needed to get away from Miss Nona's friend before he noticed something was wrong with him.

Jason had just begun running plausible excuses through his mind when he saw Miss Nona coming their way.

"Looks like someone wants a dance," he said, giving Nona a smile as she walked up to them.

"I think you're right," Monty said as he watched Nona approach. "And I know the guy who's going to give her that dance."

As Monty and Nona danced away, Jason scanned the dance floor, looking for Eddy. When he didn't see him there or around the band, he began to worry that he'd left the party. He wasn't sure what was happening to him, but he needed help and he needed it now. When he didn't find Eddy in the tent or by the swimming pool, his worry was quickly turning to panic. His heart was beating so hard, he felt like it would beat right out of his chest.

"Nice party."

At the sound of Eddy's voice, Jason turned around so fast he lost his balance and almost fell into the pool.

"Whoa," Eddy said, reaching out to pull him back to safety. "You okay?"

Grabbing onto Eddy, Jason words began to pour out of him in a rush, "No, I'm not okay! Can't you see I'm not okay? I'm sick. I need help. Those last pills you sold me must have had some duds mixed in with them."

Eddy laughed as he peeled Jason's hands from his arms. "Calm down, man. I got ya covered."

Jason stared up at Eddy with wild, frantic eyes. "I need something now!" he shouted at him.

"No need to panic." Eddie grinned down at him as he took a silver packet from his shirt pocket. "I've got what you need right here."

With shaking hands, Jason snatched the packet from Eddy's fingers. Tears of relief filled his eyes as he ripped it open. He eagerly took the Fentanyl patch from the packet and was about to put it in his mouth when Eddy's hand flew out to stop him.

"Not the whole thing," Eddy warned as he took the patch from him. "Tell me you aren't that stupid."

Jason watched, dismayed, as Eddy tore the patch into quarters.

"I need the whole thing," Jason said in a weak voice.

"You chew a quarter now," Eddy ordered, handing the quartered Fentanyl patch back to him. "Save the rest for later."

Jason did as he was told. He sat down in a chair at the side of the pool, shoved a quarter of the patch into his mouth, and began to chew. He carefully put the remaining three quarters back into its silver packet and into his pants pocket. He leaned his head back and closed his eyes, waiting for the relief he knew the Fentanyl would bring.

Without opening his eyes, he said in a calm voice, "Thanks, Eddy. You're a lifesaver."

"I'm glad I could be of assistance," Eddy said.

"By the way, I need to restock my supply. I've only got one pill left," Jason said with his eyes still closed. "I figure you owe me big time with the haul you're going to make tonight."

"We'll settle up tomorrow," Eddy said, turning to leave. "With what's left of that patch and your pill, you'll be fine until then. I'll see you tomorrow."

"Yeah," Jason said.

When Jason opened his eyes, he saw that Eddy was no longer standing there. He looked around for him. When he was sure he was gone, he reached into his pants pocket and took out the silver packet. Eddy may be the supplier, but he wasn't the expert user. Jason knew that if one quarter could make him feel better, then a half would make him feel great. He smiled as he put another quarter of the patch into his mouth and began to chew.

Jason wasn't sure how long he'd been sitting in the chair by the pool, but he knew he didn't want to go over to join the party that seemed to be still going strong. He wasn't feeling as well as he'd hoped. Things seemed to be out of focus. He leaned his head back and closed his eyes again.

"Jason, are you okay?"

Jason wanted whoever was talking to him to leave him alone. He kept his eyes closed, hoping they'd do just that.

"Jason!"

Jason opened one eye just to peek at who it was that kept calling his name and wouldn't go away.

Realizing who it was, Jason opened both eyes wide. "Miss Nona!"

"We've been looking for you, Jason." Nona leaned over Jason, putting a hand on his forehead. "Monty and I are worried about you."

"There's nothing to worry about, Miss Nona. I'm fine."

"You don't look like you're doing so fine, Jason," Nona said.

Monty, who had been standing off to the side, walked over to stand next to Nona. "I believe I know how you're feeling right now. I've been there myself a few times. I think the best thing we can do for you is to get you to the hospital."

At the mention of the word "hospital," Jason sat straight up. There was no way he was going to go to any hospital, and if this guy thought he was going to take him to one, he had another think coming.

"I don't need to go to any hospital," Jason snorted. "I just need a hot shower and a bed. I may have had a little too much to drink is all."

"Son, I can tell you have something more than a drink or two in your system." Monty reached over to help Jason stand up. "We can take you right now."

"I'm not going with you now or ever."

Jason pulled away from Monty as he stood up. The world around him began to spin. As he was about to fall, he felt two strong arms reach out to catch him.

"Whoa! Let's sit you back down."

Jason sat back down in the chair with a thud. He thought he might be sick, so he leaned over, putting his head between his knees.

Nona gently rubbed his back. "Take it easy."

With his head still between his knees, Jason said, "Please don't make me go to the hospital. I can't."

He sat up and looked directly into Nona's eyes. "Please, just get me to the house, and I promise I'll go straight to bed."

"Oh, Jason, I don't know."

Jason reached out to take her hand and gave it a squeeze. "Please." He looked from Nona to Monty with pleading eyes.

"Okay, Jason, okay."

Nona and Monty helped Jason walk around the pool to the back door of the house. Once inside, they helped him make his way down the hallway to his bedroom.

"Thank you," Jason said as he closed his bedroom door and turned the lock. The last thing he would remember from that night was walking into the bathroom.

Things were beginning to wind down for the night. The caterers had started cleaning up and the band had just announced that this would be their last song. Dixie and Betty Jo stood to the side of the patio watching the few guests who remained. They didn't know how they had done it, but they'd been able to keep the event that had happened at Blair's house from Aaron. Luckily, he'd been wrapped up in his bride-to-be and friends and hadn't noticed that part of his family was missing.

As Dixie looked around, she didn't see Jason or Eddy anywhere. The last time she'd seen Jason, he'd been talking to Monty, but that was about thirty minutes ago. She didn't see Lily anywhere either and wondered if the two of them might have gotten together. At one time they'd been such good friends. Dixie had always thought it was a shame they'd drifted apart.

"What's wrong?" Betty Jo asked, looking over a Dixie.

"What makes you think something's wrong?"

"You have that deep furrow between your eyes that always shows up when something is bothering you," Betty Jo said as she pointed to Dixie's forehead.

Dixie sighed. "I was just thinking about Lily and Jason and what good friends they used to be and wishing they could be again."

Betty Jo shook her head. "They fell out over her marrying Matt. I can't wish she'd listened to Jason, because we wouldn't have Kendall if she had. But she's gone through some tough times because she made the choice to marry him."

"I don't see either one of them around," Dixie said, "and I was just wondering if maybe they were together somewhere."

"Don't think so. Lily left over an hour ago."

"Wishful thinking on my part," Dixie said with a smile.

"Looks like this party's breaking up," Alex said as he walked up behind Dixie and put his hands around her waist.

"And none too soon," Don said, joining the group.

"Where have you two been?" Dixie asked.

"We drove a couple of partygoers who'd had too much party home," Alex said.

Looking over at Don, he asked, "How many do you think we took home in all?"

Don rubbed his chin. "I'd say about a half dozen or so."

"Well, I'm glad they were smart enough to know they were in no condition to drive," Betty Jo said.

Alex gave a short laugh. "We might have had a hand in persuading a couple of them."

"What do we need to do tonight about cleaning up?" Alex asked.

Dixie looked around. "I think the caterers will take care of most of it. We'll have to get the centerpieces from the tables before they get picked up tomorrow. Everything else can wait until daylight. That's when we'll know what we need to do to clean up."

The four of them looked over to see Aaron, Jenny, Emma, and Layne coming toward them with tired but happy smiles on their faces.

Layne went to each of them, giving them a kiss on the cheek and a hug around the neck. "We can't thank y'all enough for this lovely party."

"It was the best engagement party I've ever been to," Aaron said as he hugged Dixie and Betty Jo and shook Alex's and Don's hands.

"Even though most of my family was using poor manners by cutting out of here early without even saying goodbye," he added.

"I'm sure they were just worn out and didn't want to stop the flow of fun," Jenny said. "I want to thank y'all for giving us this special party." Looking around, she asked, "Where is Ms. Nona? I want to thank her too."

"She probably hiding in a corner somewhere with her new friend," Aaron said in a teasing voice.

"I don't know where Nona is," Dixie said, "but we'll be sure to let her know how much you enjoyed the party."

"Thank you for giving this lovely party for my sister and for taking her into your hearts," Emma said. "She's told me so much about each one of you. It's comforting to know that even though she's chosen to live far away from her one and only sister, she has friends and family she can count on."

"We're the ones who have been blessed to know your sister. It was wonderful to meet you, Emma," Dixie said. "You are welcome anytime."

Once the young people were out of earshot, Dixie turned to Betty Jo. "Where is Nona?"

"No idea, but I hope wherever she is, she's with Monty," Betty Jo said with a smile. "I like him."

"I do too," Dixie agreed, "but I'd like to know where she is. After all that went on at Blair's, I want to make sure everyone is safe."

Immediately, Jason came to her mind. She turned to Alex to ask, "Have you seen Jason lately? The last time I saw him he was over there talking to Monty. Then it seemed that he, Nona, and Monty simply disappeared."

"Come to think of it, I haven't seen Jason in some time," Alex said. "He didn't say anything to me about leaving, but let me check to see if his truck is here."

"I'm sure he's fine. He may have taken someone home who needed a ride," Don said, hoping to reassure Dixie. "Why don't we start gathering those centerpieces from the tables?"

"I have a much better idea," Dixie said. "Why don't we wait until tomorrow morning? I'm so tired I can hardly wiggle."

"Sounds like a plan to me," Betty Jo said as she kissed Dixie on the cheek and gave her a hug. "It really was a great party. I think everyone had a good time."

"We'll be back around nine," Don said. He took Betty Jo's hand and the two of them walked out to their car.

Dixie called to them as they left, "Good night! Sleep tight!"

"His truck is right where he parked it this afternoon," Alex said. "He has to be in the house, probably sound asleep. I worked him pretty hard this past week, harder than he's worked in years. I'm sure he needs the rest."

"I'm sure you're right," Dixie said as the two of them walked toward the house. "I still don't understand where Nona went, though. It's not like her to just leave without saying something."

"I'm sure she had a good reason and will tell you all about it in the morning and in great detail," Alex said with a laugh.

Dixie gave him a playful punch on the arm. "Are you accusing us of talking too much, Alex Bradley?"

"Me?" Alex asked. "Never!"

He put his arm around Dixie as they walked into the house together.

Chapter Twenty-two

Dixie "slept like the dead" as her mother used to say after a good night's rest. It seemed that the second her head hit the pillow, she was asleep. She was thankful for another night when dreams did not invade her sleep. She hurried to take a shower and get dressed. She hoped she'd have time for a bit of breakfast before Betty Jo and Don arrived.

Dixie had noticed that Jason's door was closed as she passed it on her way down the hall to her room the night before. She'd lightly tapped on the door, but got no answer. She'd tried doorknob and found it was locked. That made her feel better, because it meant that he was in the room. Now, as she passed the closed door on her way to the kitchen, she resisted the urge to knock, knowing he was most likely still asleep. Since it was Sunday and he didn't have to be at work today, he probably wanted to sleep late.

Dixie could hear Alex banging around in the kitchen. She hoped he was fixing his famous blueberry pancakes for breakfast. Alex rarely cooked, but every now and then he'd fix pancakes. When she walked into the kitchen, she knew by the aroma of warm blueberries that she was right. She smiled.

"Good morning," Dixie said, walking over to the Keurig to fix a cup of coffee. "I smell something wonderful cooking."

"I've made us blueberry pancakes for breakfast," Alex said, pleased with himself. "You're just in time for the first batch."

Dixie sat down at the kitchen island as Alex set a plate with a stack of pancakes down in front of her.

"Yum!" Dixie said. She spread her pancakes with butter and poured on the maple syrup.

"I guess Jason is still sleeping," she said before she took her first bite.

"I guess so," Alex said as he sat down next to her with his own stack of pancakes. "I was sure he'd be worn out after working all week."

They finished their breakfast in silence. When Dixie got up to take her plate to rinse off in the kitchen sink, she saw Don's old truck pull in the driveway. "They're here," she told Alex.

"Good timing," Alex said as he put his plate in the dishwasher.

They went out to meet Betty Jo and Don. They all turned around to see Nona pulling in behind Don's truck.

"I'm sorry I bailed on y'all last night," she began as she walked toward the group. "Something important came up that I had to tend to."

"You can tell them all about it after we've gotten this mess cleaned up," Alex said sternly. "I don't want to spend all day out here. I know for a fact that y'all could talk for hours unless someone stops you. So, put a plug in it until we're done here."

Nona, Dixie, and Betty Jo looked at one another and burst out laughing.

"Well, tell us how you really feel, Alex," Nona teased.

"I'm with Alex," Don said. "Let's get 'er done!"

The five of them worked for the next ninety minutes taking apart centerpieces and putting Dixie's and Alex's yard back to the way it had been pre-party. The tent truck was there by ten and left with tent, table, and chairs by ten thirty, which left them plenty of time to change clothes and meet Mark and Layne for brunch at the Rustic Bistro, the new restaurant in town that Nona had told them about.

"Will Monty be joining us this morning?" Dixie asked Nona.

Nona smiled at the mention of Monty's name. "He's with Daddy right now. I'm to pick him up on my way to the restaurant."

"Wait!" Betty Jo said. "We haven't heard your story about why you left last night."

Nona looked at her watch. "I think it's going to have to wait for a little while. I told Monty I'd be there to pick him up before eleven."

"Don't forget you owe us that story," Betty Jo said.

As Betty Jo, Don, and Nona left, Dixie and Alex headed back in the house. Dixie had been sure they'd find Jason at the kitchen island drinking a cup of coffee as he watched some sports show on television, but he was nowhere in sight. It was obvious that Alex had the same expectation.

"I wonder why Jason is still in his room. I thought he'd be up and out before now." Alex headed down the hall to Jason's room. "I'll let him know we're leaving and he's on his own for lunch."

As Dixie started to follow, an overwhelming feeling of dread stopped her. She stood frozen as the nightmare she'd had only a few nights ago of Jason drowning and her trying to save him flooded her whole body.

Alex knocked on Jason's bedroom door. "Jason, you up?"

"Something's wrong!" Dixie cried out in panic as she raced down the hall. "We have to save him, Alex!"

Dixie saw the confused look on Alex's face as she came rushing toward him. He'd stopped with his hand in mid-air, staring at her as he asked, "Save him?"

"Break down the door, now!" Dixie demanded. "Something's wrong with Jason. I know it!"

Without asking another question, Alex took two steps back and with all his strength rammed his shoulder into the door.

Dixie silently prayed, *Dear Lord, please help.*

The door splintered away from its frame as Alex hit it with all his might. He fell into the room through the now open door. Dixie ran past him, searching the room for her son. She saw that his bed was empty. Without stopping, she ran into the bathroom where she found Jason, her sweet son, her joy, her baby, lifeless on the floor.

Give me the strength to do what I need to do to save my son.

In a moment of total awareness, she could feel God was right there with her. She knew with certainty that if she were to save her son, she could not react with fear and panic. She had to give God absolute power over her emotions and allow Him to be in control,

As Dixie got down on the floor next to Jason, she felt God's presence all around her. She looked up to see Alex's wide eyes staring down at the lifeless body of his son. She said in a controlled voice, "Alex, call 9-1-1." Alex immediately took his cell phone from the pouch on his belt and made the call.

One of the first things Dixie noticed was that Jason's lips were a bluish purple. It was also obvious that he'd vomited, maybe several times. She put her hand on his chest, checking to see if he was breathing. She couldn't feel or see his chest move. She put her hand under his nose, hoping to feel air moving in or out just like she'd done when he was a baby, but she couldn't tell for sure. She took hold of his limp wrist and felt for a pulse. At first, she felt nothing. When she pressed down as hard as she could, she felt the faint pulse of his beating heart. She recalled from a required class on CPR that she'd taken when she was teaching that a person could have a pulse, but not be getting enough air to survive. Jason didn't need CPR but he did need rescue breathing. She knew what she had to do. She leaned over him, wiped his mouth with her sleeve, then put her mouth over his to push her life-giving breath into his body. She counted to five and then gave him another breath. She would do all she could to keep Jason alive.

Dixie continued to breathe into Jason's mouth every five seconds. In between breaths, she softly said over and over, "Don't be afraid. You're safe in God's arms." She didn't allow her mind to think about what had brought her son to this point. Instead, she concentrated on giving him breath and the heartbeat she could still feel through the pulse in his wrist that she continued to hold fast.

Dixie didn't know how long she'd been on the floor giving her breath to her son or when Alex, who'd been standing behind her, left them to open the door for the paramedics. She had heard people talk about having a "God experience" when they knew that God was in control, but she'd never really believed such a thing was truly possible until that moment when she saw Jason on the bathroom floor and knew it was God who held both of them in His mighty hands.

While Dixie was breathing for her son, time stood still. As soon as the paramedics entered the bathroom and Alex pulled her up and away from Jason, everything began to move in fast motion.

As one of the paramedics leaned over Jason, she asked, "Does your son have any medical conditions we should know about?"

"None," Dixie replied without hesitation.

"Is your son a drug user?"

Dixie stared at the paramedic, unable to speak.

With more urgency, the paramedic asked, "Ma'am, could your son have overdosed?"

Dixie looked from the paramedic to Jason's near-lifeless body, and with an unexpected clarity understood what had been going on in her son's life. With certainty, she knew the answer. "Yes."

Immediately, the other paramedic took a syringe from his bag and pushed the needle into Jason's shoulder. She would learn later that it was that shot of naloxone that reversed the effects of the oxycodone and Fentanyl and had saved Jason's life. Dixie and Alex stood back and watched as the paramedics tended to their son. As soon as he was placed on a stretcher, the paramedics rushed him out of the room.

Alex took Dixie in his arms. "That was the most amazing thing I have ever witnessed," he said as he held her tight. "You saved our son's life."

"No," Dixie said in a soft voice. "It was God who saved our son's life."

Aaron had just gotten out of the shower when he heard the emergency call for an ambulance that went out through the 9-1-1 call center. He at once recognized the address as the place where he'd just had one of the most special nights of his life introducing his future wife to his friends. He quickly dressed and headed to the Bradleys' house. As he got in his patrol car, he turned on the lights and siren, hoping to clear his way to get to the there as fast as he could.

Once he was on his way, he called his father to inform him and to make sure he knew that an ambulance had been dispatched to his friend's house.

"Aaron, I know you're calling about why I left the party early last night without—"

Aaron broke in. "Dad, I'm not calling about that. I just heard an emergency call go out for an ambulance to be dispatched to the Bradleys' house."

"Are you sure you heard that address correctly? We're on our way to meet Alex and Dixie for lunch right this minute."

"I'm sure of the address, Dad, but I'm not sure why they called for an ambulance," Aaron said. "I'm on my way there right now. I'll let you know what I find."

"Has something happened to Alex or Dixie?" Layne asked with concern.

"I'm not sure," Mark said, looking over at Layne. "Aaron called to let me know that an ambulance has been dispatched to their house."

"Oh, Mark, no!" Layne's breathe caught in her throat as disturbing images began to fill her head. Bracing herself for possible answers, she asked, "What happened?"

"Aaron doesn't know, but he's on his way over there to find out. He'll let us know what he finds."

"Mark, we need to go there now!" Layne said.

Mark kept his eyes on the road. "Layne, I know you want to help, but at this point we don't know what's going on. We might be in the way if we go over there now. We need to continue to the Rustic Bistro. We can let the others know what's going on and wait there until we hear from Aaron. Then we'll be better informed and have a clearer understanding of how we can help."

Layne knew Mark believed he was right to simply wait, but her heart was telling her that Dixie needed her now. "Mark, my heart is telling me that Dixie needs me right this minute. Turn around right now and take me to Dixie."

"Are you sure that's the right thing to do?"

"I'm sure."

Mark pulled into the next driveway to turn around.

Layne took out her cell phone to call Nona. Before Nona could say a word, Layne said, "Nona, something has happened at Dixie's. We're on our way over there now. I'll let you know what's happened as soon as I can." She ended the call and prayed, "Dear Lord, please be with Dixie and her family. Give them the strength and courage they need to get through this crisis. Amen."

As Mark and Layne turned onto the street where Dixie and Alex lived, they saw the red and blue flashing lights of the ambulance parked in their driveway. Layne's heart began to beat faster. As they got closer, she could see Aaron's patrol car parked next to the ambulance. Mark pulled up in the yard. Layne was out of the car before Mark had completely stopped. As she got to the door, she was almost knocked down by Aaron. He held the door as the paramedics came rushing through with a body on the stretcher. As they passed by her, she was shocked to see that the body on the stretcher was Jason. Layne watched in disbelief as the paramedics loaded Jason onto the waiting ambulance.

As Aaron bolted past her to get to his patrol car, he called out, "Meet us at the hospital."

Aaron peeled out in front of the ambulance with sirens blaring and lights flashing to clear their way. As Layne turned back to enter the house, she found Dixie and Alex standing at the door.

Without saying a word, Layne held out her arms. Dixie fell into them and began to sob. Layne held Dixie, offering the comfort and understanding that only a friend can give. The two remained like that for only a few minutes before Alex broke them apart with the words that Layne knew to be true. "Jason needs us."

"Let's go," she said, leading the way to where Mark was waiting with the car running. As they raced to Kerry Memorial General Hospital, Alex and Dixie held tightly to one another.

"Thank heavens y'all came when you did," Alex said. "I don't know that I would have been able to drive."

"You're God sent," Dixie confirmed.

"I believe we are," Layne said as she turned around to take Dixie's hand in hers. "I believe it was God who told me you needed us."

"Glad you listened," Dixie said, offering a weak smile. Then she added so softly that Layne barely caught her words, "I felt God's hand on me when I found Jason near death on the floor of his bathroom."

"What happened to Jason? Did he have an accident?" Layne asked.

With tears rolling down her cheeks, Dixie took a deep breath. "It looks like Jason may have overdosed on drugs. When the paramedic asked me if Jason might be a drug user, things began to fall into place. Things I hadn't wanted to see suddenly became clear. I have no idea how long he's been using drugs, but I do know how long it's been since he changed from the son I once knew to the son I know now."

Knowing that Dixie's heart was breaking, tears filled Layne's eyes. She squeezed her friend's hand and continued to hold it until they reached the hospital's emergency room entrance. They could see the ambulance that had brought Jason parked with the doors open and lights still flashing. Mark pulled up as close as he could get to the emergency room door. Dixie, Alex, and Layne jumped out and hurried in.

As they entered the ER, Layne's mind was plunged back to the day of Mark's accident. For a moment those memories almost overpowered her, but then she remembered why she was here. This was not about her. She was here for Dixie and her family just like Dixie had been there for her when she needed her. She looked up to see Aaron hurrying toward them. She couldn't tell by the expression on his face if he was bringing them good or bad news. Layne watched as Dixie reached out for Alex's strong hand. Layne braced herself, preparing for bad news.

Coming to a stop in front of Dixie and Alex, Aaron said, "Jason regained consciousness in the ambulance. He's with the doctors right now."

Dixie stared at Aaron. "He's awake?"

"Yes, ma'am," Aaron said with a reassuring smile. "He's wide awake and asking questions."

Layne could see that Dixie was relieved by Aaron's news. She knew Dixie had been expecting the worst and Jason's being awake was truly an unexpected blessing from God. She saw Dixie's eyes fill with tears and she had the sudden urge to scream out for all the world to hear, *Thank you, Lord!* But she found that she was too choked up with emotion to even speak. Dixie fell back into Alex's arms as she softly cried tears of joy.

It was Alex's strong voice that spoke for both of them. "Thanks be to God."

He freed one of his hands to shake Aaron's while still holding Dixie in his arms. "Thank you for letting us know, Aaron. We appreciate all you've done."

Aaron grinned. "I was happy to help." He walked over to his mother. "Are you okay, Mom?"

"I'm fine," Layne said. "I'm just worried. I'm so thankful that Jason is alive and awake, but I know he doesn't have an easy time ahead of him. They all have a great deal to face in the days ahead."

Aaron took his mother in his arms. "Jason has something that most drug addicts who overdose don't have—loving, supportive family and friends."

Layne pulled away from Aaron and said, "That's the first time I've heard anyone use the words 'drug addict' to describe Jason. It's disturbing and terrifying to know that he's actually been addicted to drugs and none of us noticed."

"He did a good job of hiding it from all of us." Aaron said, shaking his head. "I'm in law enforcement and see guys strung out on drugs all the time. I should have picked up on the signs. They were right there for me to see."

Betty Jo and Nona came rushing to where Dixie, Alex, Layne, and Aaron, were standing. "What's going on?" Betty Jo asked.

"It's Jason," Dixie said. She went on to explain to Betty Jo and Nona what had happened.

Betty Jo looked over at Dixie. "I just can't wrap my mind around the fact that we were all right there in the yard cleaning up while Jason was lying on the floor close to death. None of us even suspected that Jason was using drugs."

Nona said haltingly, "I knew."

"What?" Dixie asked. "You knew what?"

Nona crossed her arms in front of herself. "I knew that he might be using drugs." She hurried on to explain. "Monty said something to me last night about Jason being 'high as a kite and about to come crashing down.' We thought the best thing for him would be to get to bed. So we made sure he went to bed. We thought he would sleep it off."

"You thought he was using drugs and neither one of you thought to tell us?" Dixie asked incredulously.

Nona slumped down in a nearby chair and put her head in her hands. "I'm so sorry. I should have said something. I could have prevented this whole thing. This is all my fault."

"No, it isn't!"

Nona jerked her head up, startled by Monty's strong voice. Don and Monty had entered the room without anyone taking notice.

"This is all Jason's fault!" Monty said with conviction. "He's the one who chose to take the drugs. He's the one to blame, not Nona or me. We might have stopped today's overdose, but it would have just postponed the inevitable."

They all stared at Monty.

"He's right, you know," Aaron said. "You can't blame Miss Nona or Mr. Monty for not knowing that Jason was going to overdose any more than you can blame one another. This is not the time to pass around blame."

"Excuse me," a nurse in blue scrubs said as she walked up to the group. "The doctor would like to speak with Mr. and Mrs. Bradley alone, please."

Alex took Dixie's hand as they came forward. "We're the Bradleys."

The nurse smiled as she said, "Please, follow me."

Dixie and Alex followed the nurse to where a man was standing at a computer station. As they approached, he turned.

"I'm Doctor Patterson," he said. "It appears your son has

experienced a drug overdose, most likely an overdose of opiates. Once we have the toxicology screen back, we'll have a better idea of what drugs are in his system. The paramedics administered two dosages of naloxone, one at the scene and one in the ambulance, to counter the effects of the opioid overdose. This restored his breathing to normal. He is conscious and responsive."

Doctor Patterson paused, allowing Dixie and Alex to process the information he had just given them. He continued, "I understand he was given mouth-to-mouth respiration before the paramedics arrived."

"That's correct, my wife started mouth-to-mouth as soon as we found him."

Doctor Patterson said to Dixie, "Your actions most likely saved his life, but what I am most concerned about is how long he went without oxygen before he was found. If it was for a significant amount of time, he may have some brain damage or other impairments. We'll just have to wait to see. We'll keep him overnight for observation."

"Can we see him now, Doctor Patterson?" Alex asked.

"Yes, but understand his body has been through a great deal of trauma. He's also experiencing the first stages of withdrawal," Doctor Patterson said as he turned to take them to Jason.

"He's going to be okay though, isn't he, Doctor?" Dixie asked apprehensively.

Doctor Patterson stopped. He said, "You have to understand that your son is addicted to opiates. He's a drug addict. He tells me he's been taking some form of opiate drugs for his pain for well over ten years. I suspect that the dosages he's taking now would be lethal to the average person, but his body has built up a tolerance for such a dosage. There is no easy fix for drug addiction. We can talk more about his options later. Let's get him through this crisis first."

Dixie understood that Jason had overdosed, but she hadn't allowed her mind to make a connection to his being addicted. The thought had never entered her mind that her son would ever be described to her as a "drug addict." She was afraid she might be sick right there, right now, as her world began to spin out of control.

Her brain was screaming, *This cannot be happening!* However, her eyes and ears were telling her that it was happening, no matter how much she didn't want to believe it.

Doctor Patterson opened the curtain and announced, "You can see your son now."

Dixie stared blankly at Alex as he took her hand in his. "Dixie?"

"I'm not sure I can do this, Alex," she said, grabbing onto his arm and holding him back.

"Yes, you can," Alex said. He gave her hand a squeeze. " I'm right here with you and, after this morning, you know who else is walking in there with you."

As Dixie released her grip on Alex's arm, she felt an instant peace come over her. Looking up at him with grateful eyes she said, "Yes, I do."

Dixie held tightly to Alex's hand as they walked through the curtain and up to Jason's bed. He was turned away from them. Dixie hadn't known what to expect, but she knew what had been her hope since the moment she'd found him on that bathroom floor. When Jason turned around, she knew that all she'd hoped for was looking right at her. Her son was alive.

When Jason saw his mother and father standing there, he was embarrassed and filled with shame. He knew how much his actions had dishonored his parents. He'd hoped that they'd never know the secret he'd so carefully hidden from them for over ten years. He was sure he wouldn't be able to handle seeing his own failure reflected to him in their eyes. But when he turned over to see them both standing there, he didn't see the disgust or the disappointment he'd expected. He saw only love in their eyes, which brought tears to his.

His mom reached out to take Jason in her arms. She said three words with complete forgiveness and true hope in each syllable. "I love you!"

Jason knew he didn't deserve her love after what he'd just put her through and what he knew he would be putting her through in the coming months. But when she spoke those words to him, he believed in his heart of hearts that because of this unfailing love of his mother, he'd been given another chance at life.

As Jason held onto his mother, he said the words more sincerely than he had said them in a very long time. "I love you too."

Chapter Twenty-three

As Mark was getting out of his car after letting Dixie, Alex, and Layne off at the emergency room entrance, his cell phone began to ring. After seeing the caller's name on the display, he accepted the call hoping his voice sounded upbeat, "Good morning, Blair. How are you this morning? I hope you got some sleep last night."

"I slept surprisingly well," Blair said, then added with a laugh, "That might have been because Zeke gave me some miracle drug that knocked me right out."

Mark winced at Blair's mention of a drug. After all his daughter had been through, he didn't want to say anything to her just yet about Jason's overdose. "Glad you slept well," he managed to say while keeping his voice upbeat.

"Is everything okay, Daddy? You sound a little funny," Blair said.

Mark realized that his voice might have been just a little too upbeat. He should have known that he couldn't fool his only daughter. She'd always been able to see through any screen he tried to put up. He sighed. "It appears that Jason Bradley overdosed on drugs. Your mom and I drove Dixie and Alex to Memorial General Hospital."

"Oh, Daddy," was all Blair could say.

"I just dropped them off at the emergency room and am headed there now. I'll know more once I get in there," Mark said.

"I know you want to see how he is, so I'll let you go." Blair said. "I called to let you know that Zeke and I thought we would go back home, but Deputy Miles called this morning to ask if we could stay away for another day. Something about securing evidence."

"Okay," Mark said, wondering what the deputy may have found at their house. "I'll check to see how Jason's doing and then check with Deputy Miles to see what's going on."

"You don't have to do that," Blair protested. "I'm sure you're needed more at the hospital."

Mark ended the call as he walked into the emergency room. The first person he saw as he entered was Aaron. With all that had been going on this morning, he hadn't had time to tell Aaron anything about what had happened at Blair's house last night and why he had left the party. He needed to fill Aaron in on the events of last night.

Walking up beside his son, Mark asked, "How's Jason doing?"

"He's awake and responsive," Aaron said. "He'll make it out of the drug overdose, but as for his addiction…" Aaron shook his head in frustration. "I sure would like to know who's been supplying him with drugs. When I get my hands on them…" He let his voice fade away, but Mark understood how he felt.

"Hopefully, Jason will give us a lead on who's been his supplier," Mark said, "but right now I need to give you an update on the events of last night."

Aaron gave his father a puzzled look. "Last night? At the party?"

"Not at the party, but while the party was going on," Mark said. "I know you wondered why I left the party. It wasn't because I wanted to. It was because your sister's house was robbed last night."

"Blair's house?" Aaron asked in disbelief. "What happened?"

Mark spent the next ten minutes giving Aaron the details of the robbery from the time Blair interrupted the robbery and ending with a list of what had been stolen.

"I can't believe you didn't tell me about it last night," Aaron said.

"It wasn't just your engagement party, Son. It was also Jenny's. We didn't want to ruin the evening for either one of you," Mark said, hoping Aaron would understand his decision.

"What's happening now?" Aaron asked.

"I was just about to call Deputy Miles about that. Give me a minute," Mark said as he made his call.

"Deputy Miles here."

"Miles, this is Sheriff Weaver."

Mark could almost hear the deputy snap to attention as he said, "Good morning, sir."

"I just spoke to my daughter who informed me that you've requested that she and her husband stay away from their house. Something about collecting evidence," Mark said.

The deputy hesitated for a minute before answering, "Yes, sir. We may have a break in this case with the evidence collected from the earlier robberies as well as the ones from last night."

"I'd like to know more about this evidence," Mark said. "I have some business I need to take care of, but I'll be in touch later. I'm sending Deputy Weaver to check in with you."

"Yes, sir" Deputy Miles said, ending the call.

Mark hoped the deputy was right and that they had enough evidence to find who was responsible for the robberies. In all his years as sheriff, there had never been anything like this happen in Kerry. It needed to be shut down, now.

Turning to Aaron, Mark said, "We may have a lead on the robberies. You need to get to the station to meet with Deputy Miles. He can fill you in on the details. I'll be there as soon as I check on how things are going here."

As Aaron turned to leave he asked, "Will you tell Mom and Miss Dixie why I left?"

"Sure thing."

"He's going to get through this," Alex said to Dixie reassuringly as they walked away from Jason's curtained room. "You heard the doctor. You saved his life."

"Oh, Alex, I pray you're right," Dixie said.

Nona was the first to see Dixie and Alex as they entered the waiting room.

"How is he doing?" Nona asked anxiously.

"You can tell he's had a rough time," Dixie said.

"I'm sure he has," Monty said, "but I guarantee that the days ahead are going to be even rougher."

"Let's take a minute to say a prayer for Jason." Layne bowed her head. "Most loving Father in Heaven, we ask for Your healing love and strength to surround Jason as he fights his addiction. Bless him with Your peace. Amen."

After a few minutes, Alex said to Dixie, "I still have a couple of papers I need to sign. You can wait here and go with Jason when they take him up to a room for the night."

"Wait!" Dixie called out as Alex started to leave.

Alex stopped. "What's wrong?"

"I can't believe we haven't called Hailey to tell her what's happened with Jason. Alex, we have to tell her right now before she hears it from someone else."

Alex reached for his cell phone that was usually clipped to his belt, but found it wasn't there. "I must have left my cell phone at home. I never do that!"

Dixie reached for her purse, knowing that was the last place she'd seen her phone. Tears filled her eyes as it became clear to her that she hadn't thought to grab her purse on the way out of the house. "Oh, no! My phone is at home too!"

Dixie and Alex looked at one another as if not having their cell phones with them was one of the worst problems they had come across that day.

Betty Jo, Layne, and Nona held out their cell phones.

Dixie and Alex stared at the phones for a minute as if they couldn't believe that anyone else had a phone. It began as a chuckle deep in Dixie's throat, then it blossomed into a laugh. Before long, she was bent over double laughing uncontrollably which made Alex laugh and soon everyone was laughing. Tears of laughter streamed down Dixie's face.

Every time she thought she had it all under control, she'd start up again.

After several minutes and several deep breaths, Dixie was finally able to speak. "I'm sorry, y'all! After all we've been through today, there we were acting like it was the end of the world to have forgotten our cell phones."

Alex took Betty Jo's phone. "I think it'll be better if I call Josh. He can tell Hailey."

Dixie nodded in agreement as Alex walked away from the group to make the call. "While Alex is taking care of that, I'm going to freshen up. I must look a sight."

Nona said, "I'll go with you."

"I was hoping you'd say that since I don't even have a comb or anything with me."

"We'll all go," Betty Jo offered. "I'm sure among the three of us we can get you looking presentable."

As Layne followed Dixie, Nona, and Betty Jo to the restroom to freshen up, she noticed Mark standing at the entrance to the ER talking on his cell phone. She'd wondered where he'd been since he dropped them off at the door of the ER. She could tell by the look on his face that he was having a serious conversation with the person on the other end of the call. When he finished, he and Aaron huddled together. Then Aaron turned to leave the ER as Mark came hurrying over to where the four of them were standing.

Mark walked up to Dixie, taking her hands in his. "I'm sorry, Dixie, but Aaron and I have to leave. Something's come up that requires our immediate attention."

"I understand, Mark," Dixie said, and added with a smile, "as long as you leave Layne here I'm okay with your leaving."

"You have to know I couldn't blast Layne away from your side." Mark smiled back at Dixie.

After releasing Dixie's hands, he turned to Layne. "I'll call you later to check on things." He gave her a quick kiss and left.

Alex returned after calling Layne to find only Don and Monty in the waiting room. He'd wanted to tell Dixie about his phone conversation with Josh. Not seeing Dixie, he asked, "Where did the girls go?"

"They went to freshen up," Don said with a chuckle.

Shaking his head, Monty added, "Apparently, they have to all go together."

Looking at Monty, Alex said, "You'd better get used to it. They are the Fearsome Foursome, a force to be reckoned with."

"Amen to that. No one gets between those four and lives to tell about it," Don agreed.

Alex handed Betty Jo's phone to Don. "I'll give this back to you to look after. I don't want to get in trouble with Betty Jo."

"Did you get in touch with Josh?" Don asked.

"Yes. As soon as Josh's mother gets there to watch the kids, he'll bring Hailey over to see Jason."

Leaning over and putting his head in his hands, Alex said, "It's a hard thing to accept that my own son is addicted to drugs. I just never thought such a thing could happen to us."

"I know what you mean," Monty said as he clapped him on the back. "I never thought such a thing could happen to me."

Alex gave Monty a puzzled look.

"I was once addicted to drugs," Monty said. He told Alex and Don his story about his drug addiction. After finishing, he chuckled, "I can't believe it. I haven't shared my story about my addiction with anyone in years. Now, I've told it for the second time in less than twenty-four hours."

Dixie felt better after freshening up. She'd hoped she wouldn't have to wait long for Jason to be taken to his room. She hadn't liked waiting when she was with Layne as they waited to hear news about Mark's surgery. She was finding it hard to believe that she was back in the hospital so soon waiting for her own son to be admitted. She kept looking at the door hoping that the nurse would come tell her that Jason was being moved. Waiting for the actions of others had always frustrated her.

Dixie remembered many times in her life when she'd felt powerless or useless. She'd felt powerless watching her mother and sister battle breast cancer. She'd felt useless watching her father drink himself to death. But she was finding that the thought of her son being a drug addict made her feel helpless. She hated that feeling most of all. She kept thinking of ways she should have been helping Jason, but had been so oblivious to what was going on with him that she hadn't even known he needed help.

"I can't believe I didn't check on him earlier this morning or last night before I went to bed," she said to the other women, biting her lip. "I thought I was letting him get a few extra hours of sleep, and all the while he was on that bathroom floor struggling for his life. Those few hours would have made a difference."

"You have to stop beating yourself up about this, Dixie," Betty Jo said. "There's just no way any of us could have known what was going on with Jason."

"I should have seen that something was wrong, that he was using drugs. I saw changes in him, but I didn't do anything about it." Dixie put her head in her hands. "I was always making excuses for him."

With tears coming to her eyes once again, she looked up at her friends and choked back a sob. "I just wanted him to have a happy life. I didn't want him to experience the heartaches I had gone through. I thought I was helping him, and it turns out that all I did was enable him."

Immediately, Layne, Nona, and Betty Jo were beside Dixie wrapping their arms around her, offering her their support.

"Please, don't do this to yourself, Dixie," Layne said gently. "Only through hindsight could you know what he was doing."

Dixie said bitterly, "I'm his mother, Layne. I should have seen the signs. I should have paid closer attention,"

"You were blinded by your love for him," Betty Jo said.

"We all were," Nona added.

Dixie nodded in agreement. "You're right, but it's so hard not to feel that I'm to blame for not seeing what was happening right in front of my eyes!"

Shaking her head, Betty Jo said, "I don't know if you're aware of this or not, but there is an opioid/heroin epidemic going on in America, even right here in Kerry, Georgia. Over a hundred Americans die every day from an opioid or heroin overdose. At this hospital, they get anywhere from five to ten cases a week. Some aren't as lucky as Jason. They don't make it."

Dixie stared at Betty Jo. "I've heard about drug usage going up in America, but I have never heard anything about drugs in Kerry."

Betty Jo continued, "I read in the paper just the other day that according to the most recent survey from the Substance Abuse and Mental Health Services Administration, nearly twelve million Americans have an addiction to opioid painkillers, and over twenty-two thousand die each year. That's sixty people a day."

Nona nodded. "I read that same article. It was titled, 'Painkillers Don't Kill Pain; They Kill People.'"

Dixie couldn't believe what she was hearing. "How can this be happening, Betty Jo?" she asked. "I thought doctors were the ones who prescribed opioids to patients."

"True! They do, and that's how most addictions get started, with a prescription," Betty Jo said. "The patients think that because the doctors have prescribed it, then it must be okay to take. Oxycodone is given to many people after surgery or a car accident and many of those patients are addicted before they even leave the hospital. Most families don't know their loved one is addicted until it's too late."

"I think I knew!" another voice said. "I could see that there was something wrong with Jason. I suspected drugs, but I never confronted him about it."

Dixie had been so intent on listening to what Betty Jo was saying that she hadn't even realized that Hailey and Josh had arrived. "I had no idea, Josh," Dixie said.

As Josh looked down at the floor, he said, "I'm sorry, Dixie. I shouldn't have kept what I was thinking to myself. I was afraid if I said anything to you or Alex or even Hailey, you wouldn't believe me. Then you'd be mad at me. I didn't want to risk that, so I kept quiet."

Dixie took Josh's hand. "It's okay, Josh. I don't blame you."

"Oh, Mom, I can't believe this has happened, "Hailey said, folding her arms tightly around herself. "It just makes me so mad that he would be this stupid. What could he possibly be thinking by doing this to himself, to us!" Hailey's voice was filled with resentment.

"Hailey, it's not going to do anyone any good to be mad. It won't help you and it won't help Jason," Dixie said firmly.

"I want to just want to slap some sense into him!" Hailey cried out. "I don't understand why you aren't as angry with him as I am!"

Alex had been silently standing to the side watching the heated exchange between his wife and daughter. He couldn't simply stand by and watch any longer. He stepped up next to Hailey. "You have to understand that we almost lost your brother today. When I saw him on that floor, I was sure he was dead."

Tears came to his eyes as he remembered how helpless he'd felt at that moment. Alex paused, taking several deep breaths. When he'd regained control of his emotions, he continued, "Your mother didn't hesitate for a minute. You should have seen her, Hailey. She literally breathed life back into his body. By the grace of God, your mother was able to save his life. "

Taking Dixie's hand in his, he said, "Don't you see, Hailey, your mother didn't give up on him. She never will, and neither can we."

Reaching out to take Hailey's hand, he added, "Jason needs each one of us to be there for him if he's going beat his addiction. If we give in to the anger or resentment or blame we're all feeling, it will divide us, and we'll lose him. We're a family. We have to be in this together."

With tears streaming down her face, Hailey looked from her father to her mother. Then she took her mother's hand in hers, completing the circle.

"Mr. And Mrs. Bradley?"

They all dropped hands, giving their attention to the young man in green scrubs.

Dixie wiped her tears away. "I'm Dixie Bradley."

The nurse smiled at Dixie as he introduced himself. "Mrs. Bradley, I'm Jake Phillips. I wanted you to know that we're taking your son up to his room now. You're welcome to come with us or you can meet us up there. He'll be in Room 257."

Reaching out his hand to shake Jake's, Alex introduced himself. "I'm Alex Bradley."

Turning back to Hailey and Josh, Dixie asked hopefully, "Do y'all want to come with us?"

Hailey smiled at her mother. "Yes, we want to come."

Jake had been patiently standing by, waiting. "Shall we go?" he asked.

"Yes," Dixie said, taking Alex and Hailey's hands.

Layne spoke up as Alex and Dixie started to walk away. "Betty Jo, Nona, and I thought we'd go to your house to get your phones, purse, and other stuff you might need. Don and Monty can get y'all some lunch and bring it back."

"Thanks!" Dixie said. "I don't know what we'd ever do without our friends."

Chapter Twenty-four

D ixie was concerned that Jason had slept through the whole trip to his room. Jake assured her it was normal for someone in Jason's condition to go into a deep sleep for long periods at a time. As Dixie helped Jake get Jason settled in his room, she asked, "Why do you think Doctor Patterson put Jason in a regular room instead of intensive care?" Dixie was concerned about Jason being in a regular room. She believed that after all he'd been through he needed to be in intensive care where they would watch him more closely.

"I assure you that we will be closely monitoring your son, Mrs. Bradley," Jake said. "All the nurses and doctors in this area have been specially trained to handle patients who have suffered from an opioid or heroin overdose. We're also set up for medical detoxification."

"He's in good hands, Mom," Hailey assured her. "I've only heard good things about the work done in this area."

Jake connected Jason to a heart monitor. "We'll be monitoring his heart and his oxygen levels around the clock. We started an IV down in the ER, making sure he's getting the fluids he needs to stay hydrated and also to wash whatever drugs he's taken out of his system. We may need to order dialysis to continue that process. Once we get the toxicology screening back, we'll know if that will need to be done."

Dixie watched and listened carefully to all that Jake did and said. "When do you think he'll wake up?" she asked as Jake turned to leave.

Dixie was surprised when she heard Jason's weak voice. "Now." Looking around the room at his family, he began to cry. "I'm so sorry. I never meant for this to happen. I never meant for any of you to even know."

"I'm sorry we didn't see what was going on," Dixie said as she sat down next to him on his bed. "I should have picked up on it."

Jason's sudden bitter laugh shocked her. "Are you kidding me, Mom? I've always been good at keeping you from seeing who I truly am. I'm a master at deception."

"That's the truth," Hailey said as she punched his arm. "You did a good job of deceiving all of us, brother."

Walking over to stand at the foot of Jason's bed, Alex said, "I want to know how you became addicted to drugs, Son."

Jason avoided looking into his father's eyes, He began to fidget with his sheet.

Seeing her son struggle with Alex's question, Dixie intervened. "I think we've all been through enough today. Why don't we save that question for another time?"

Jason looked up at his father and said in a soft voice, "I can tell you how it began, Dad."

Alex nodded, encouraging him to continue.

"The doctor prescribed Oxycodone for me after my ACL surgery in," Jason said.

Dixie flashed back to when he'd complained about his pain after surgery and how she'd actually thought that it was a blessing when they'd given him a pill to take away that pain. She hadn't asked the doctor for any information about it. She wondered how different things would be if she'd insisted Jason be given aspirin instead and learn to deal with the pain that would have eventually gone away. Would they be in this room right now with their son who had almost died from an overdose?

Dixie shook the thought out of her head as she leaned over to hug

Jason. There was so much she wanted to say to him, but she knew in her heart this was not the right time. There would be a time later when they could all say the things that needed to be said. Right now, he only needed to know one thing to be true. She whispered in his ear, "I love you." That was enough for now.

"There's something else I have to tell you."

"I'm sure it can wait until you're rested, Jason," Dixie said, smiling down at him.

"No, Mom, this can't wait."

"Okay, what is it that you have to tell us now?"

Jason swallowed hard. "I've been stealing things from the house, things I thought you wouldn't notice, like Grandpa's pocket watch and money clip, and pawning them. And that's not all. Mom, I stole a check out of your checkbook, wrote it out for fifteen hundred dollars, forged your name on it, and cashed it to pay my drug dealer."

Stunned, Dixie stared at Jason, her son, whom she'd always believed she knew. She stepped away from his bed. She didn't know how many more revelations she could handle in one day.

"Excuse me."

They all turned to see a short, rather heavy young man with shockingly red hair standing just inside the door of Jason's room.

"I'm Doctor Kelly," the man announced with a heavy Irish brogue. "I'll be the one tending to Mr. Bradley for the time being."

Alex reached out to shake the doctor's hand as he introduced himself. "Doctor Kelly, I'm Alex Bradley, Jason's father. This is Jason's mother, his sister, and his brother-in-law."

"Since you're the one who's lying in this bed," Doctor Kelly said as he walked up to Jason's bed, "I take it you're the Mr. Bradley with the drug problem."

"Yes, sir," Jason managed to say.

Looking down at Jason, Doctor Kelly spoke frankly. "I don't need to tell you that you're one lucky man to even be alive. With the amount of drugs in your system, by all rights, your parents should be preparing a funeral for you right this minute. I can promise you this. But you're not going to be feeling so lucky for very long. In fact, you're probably going to wish you'd been left on the bathroom floor to die."

Silent tears began to run down Dixie's cheeks as she listened to the harsh way the doctor was talking to Jason. She knew that everything he was telling Jason was true, but it was hard for her to see how much his words were hurting her son. She wanted to stop the doctor, but knew that she shouldn't. Jason needed to hear his words, and so did she.

Doctor Kelly continued. "The drugs are being flushed out of your system. You aren't feeling your best right now, but you need to know that you're going to feel much worse in just a short time. The time has come to make some decisions right now, this minute, about your future. It's not up to your mother, your father, your sister, or your brother-in-law to decide. It's your decision alone."

Doctor Kelly paused for a minute as he continued to stare down at Jason before he asked, "What are you going to do, Jason?"

With tears in his eyes, Jason looked up at Doctor Kelly. "I want to live."

"Then," Doctor Kelly said as he patted Jason's arm, "let's get you started on living."

Aaron glanced at his watch as he got in his car. With all that was going on, he hadn't realized the time. He took his cell phone out of his pocket and saw that he had missed several calls from Jenny along with two voice mails from her. He knew she had to be wondering where he was considering he wasn't scheduled to work today. He decided not to take the time to listen to the voice mails and instead speed-dialed her number.

"Where in the world have you been?"

Aaron gave Jenny an abbreviated version of what had happened since the night before when he dropped her and Emma off at her house.

"I can't believe we didn't have a clue all of that was happening last night. I'll give Blair a call to see how she's doing. Do you think I need to go to the hospital to see if I can help out in any way?"

"I think they may need more later at the hospital," Aaron said. "I'll let you know if I find out anything new."

"Do you think we'll still have the dinner tonight at your Mom's with the whole family?" Jenny asked. "With all that's happened, she may want to cancel."

"You'll have to ask Mom about that. I gotta go," Aaron said as he ended the call.

Aaron knew that Jenny was looking forward to the dinner tonight. She wanted Emma to get to know his family a little better in a more casual setting. Since Emma was leaving in the morning, tonight would be their only chance. He knew she and Jenny would be disappointed if his mother canceled, but he couldn't worry about that right now.

As Aaron turned into the Kerry County Sheriff's Department, he saw Deputy Miles standing outside the door. "I hope you haven't been waiting for me all this time," Aaron said as he approached the deputy.

"No, I was heading out to get in my car when I saw you coming. It looks like a Mr. Jimmy Kwok was an eyewitness to robbery that took place last night on Phoenix Street. You want to ride along?"

"Sure." Aaron followed the deputy to his car.

As Aaron got in the car, he asked, "What's this evidence the sheriff was telling me you've found?"

"With Mrs. Coby coming up on them like she did, we were hoping we might get some fingerprints since they had thrown them off their usual routine, but we didn't have any luck with that."

"I can't think how my sister's interrupting the robbery would make them take off their gloves and use their bare hands," Aaron said more to himself than to the deputy.

"However, even though they didn't leave any fingerprints, after thoroughly searching the area, we found something of interest that they did leave behind."

Aaron looked over at the deputy, eager for him to continue.

"A hat."

"A hat?"

"Yep, we found a hat from the Apalachicola Florida_Seafood Festival in the driveway."

After thinking about the deputy's discovery for a minute, Aaron asked, "Are you sure it's not Zeke's hat or someone else's hat who's been there in the past few days? Were you aware that Zeke is a deep-sea fisherman and he goes to Florida several times a year to fish?"

The pleased look on the deputy's face disappeared.

Shaking his head, Aaron said, "Don't tell me you haven't checked with Zeke to see if the hat could be his."

The deputy remained silent.

Aaron sighed. "After we meet with this 'eyewitness' you say you have, we need to talk with Zeke about this hat you have in evidence."

They rode in silence until they arrived at Jimmy Kwok's address. He lived across the street from where the ATV had been reported stolen the previous night. As they got out of the car, a short, bald man came walking out of the house toward them. Aaron allowed Deputy Miles to take the lead.

"Good morning, sir. I'm Deputy Miles and this is Deputy Weaver. We're from the Kerry Sheriff's Office. Are you Mr. Kwok?"

The man nodded as he held out his hand to the deputies. "Yes, sir."

After the deputies shook Mr. Kwok's hand, Deputy Miles took his notebook and pen from his shirt pocket. "I know you gave a statement to the officer last night, but I'd appreciate it if you would tell me what you saw last night."

As Mr. Kwok began to tell Deputy Miles what he'd witnessed last night, Aaron took some mental notes. Mr. Kwok appeared to be in his late sixties. He was of average height with a protruding middle section that Aaron concluded was from drinking a great amount of beer since it was just afternoon and he'd greeted them with a beer in hand. He most likely took pride in his well-kept yard and devoted a lot of his time to keeping it well maintained. Since he spent so much time in his yard, he probably knew most of what went on with his neighbors and in his neighborhood. He came to the conclusion that Mr. Kwok would make a good eyewitness.

"I ain't never seen a truck like that one around here," Mr. Kwok was saying. "It looked like one of them you-haul-it trucks you use when you're movin', but it didn't make no sense to me that it'd be pulled up in Mr. Daniel's driveway at nine o'clock at night since I knowed they ain't movin' nowhere. Especially since I seen Mr. Daniel and his wife Miss Betsy leave around six. I watched it for a bit. I didn't want anybody to think I was being nosey, but when it done pulled out, somethin' tole me that I needed to write down what I seen 'case I forget it. I tend to do that from time to time. Here's what I seen parked right over there." Mr. Kwok handed Deputy Miles the description of the truck he'd written down—big 2004 or 2006 white Ford truck with box on back and over-cab with nothing on sides.

Aaron had been listening to what Mr. Kwok was saying, but hadn't been paying close attention until he heard two names he recognized. When Mr. Kwok paused to take in a breath, Aaron took the opportunity to ask, "Are you talking about Daniel and Betsy Tucker?"

"Yes, sir. They was the ones was robbed."

Aaron realized he hadn't checked who'd been the victims of robberies last night, but was finding it highly suspicious that the Tuckers and his sister were guests at his engagement party last night and they'd both been victims of the same crime. He walked over to the patrol car where he called dispatch to get the names of the other two robberies that had taken place last night. As he jotted down each name, he felt a cold chill go through him. Every one of the victims of last night's robberies had attended his engagement party. This was no coincidence. Someone, somewhere, had used his engagement party guest list to target who would be away from their homes during that time.

When he finished taking Mr. Kwok's statement, Deputy Miles joined Aaron in the patrol car. "His description of the vehicle matches the one Mrs. Coby gave us last night," Deputy Miles reported.

"That's good, but we've got something bigger than just a description of the truck, Miles," Aaron said. "It looks like whoever planned out the robberies for last night used the guest list from my engagement party to target their victims."

"Do you think it was someone who was actually at the party with you who could have given out the list?" Deputy Miles asked.

"That's what I'm thinking."

As Deputy Miles sped away from the Kwok house, Aaron said, "We need to get back to the sheriff's office to put all the evidence we've got together. We may be making some arrests before the day is over."

Dixie had learned more about opiates, overdoses, and detoxification in a few hours than she'd known in her whole life. She'd been clueless about how easily someone could become addicted to painkillers. She'd been one of the millions who believed that when a doctor prescribed a painkiller, it was a good thing. She'd had no idea that that very prescription could become your worst nightmare. Of course, she'd heard on the news that there was a drug problem in America, but she'd just never imagined her own son would be a victim.

Doctor Kelly had been brutally forthright with all that Jason would be experiencing in the next hours, days, and possibly weeks with the medical detoxification treatment: nausea, vomiting, diarrhea, fever, stomach cramps, sweats, anxiety, depression, etc. He would be given decreasing doses of methadone to avoid the more severe effects of detoxification. The doctor strongly urged the family to stay away during this time for Jason's sake as well as their own. This was something that Jason needed to go through on his own. The doctor assured Dixie that he would be with Jason throughout the ordeal.

Dixie liked Doctor Kelly the minute he'd walked into Jason's room. She truly felt that he'd been sent to them as one of God's many blessings. It also helped that Hailey had complete trust in him after extensively researching his credentials and speaking to several of the hospital staff about him.

Hailey and Josh had taken Alex home so he could get his truck, while Dixie stayed with Jason until he fell asleep.

Dixie was totally exhausted. She felt like she'd been at the hospital for days. When she stepped off the elevator after leaving Jason's room at four o'clock that afternoon, she was shocked to find Layne, Nona, and Betty Jo waiting for her. She fell into their waiting arms.

"I can't believe y'all are still here," Dixie said.

Layne embraced Dixie. "We wouldn't want to be anywhere else."

"With Jason being in the drug treatment section of the hospital, they wouldn't even let us up there to give you your phone and all," Nona shook her head in disbelief. "We couldn't just drop off your stuff at the front desk and then leave you here alone."

"Thank you." Dixie began to cry.

Betty Jo patted her on the back. "You go right ahead and cry all you want. That's what we're here for."

All the emotions that Dixie had held in check since she'd found Jason on his bathroom floor came pouring out as Layne, Nona, and Betty Jo cried with her.

When Dixie's tears finally came to a halt and she could speak, she asked, "So, what happened to that lunch y'all promised us?"

"We ate it!" Layne said, laughing.

"It was good too," Betty Jo said as she joined in with Layne.

Soon, they were all laughing. As Dixie looked at her friends through tears of laughter, she thanked God for the blessings each one of them had brought to her life.

"Why don't we take you out for a late lunch or early supper or whatever you want to call it?" Nona said after the laughter had died down.

Dixie sighed. "I can't tell you how good that sounds. I'm starving!"

"Should we ask the men folk to join us?" Betty Jo asked.

"Let's do," Nona said. "They have to eat too. I know I don't feel like cooking tonight."

Betty Jo looked at her. "What about Mr. James? Won't you have to cook something for him?"

Nona smiled. "Thanks for thinking of Daddy, but I've already made arrangements for Miss Althea to stay with him."

Betty Jo turned to Dixie. "Where do you want to go?"

"Well, if I remember correctly," Dixie said, "our plan for today was to eat at the Rustic Bistro. Let's go there."

Betty Jo took out her cell phone. "I'll let Don know the plans and he can let the others know. I'm hoping he's still with Monty and Alex. He'll only have to get in touch with Mark."

"Oh, no!" Layne cried out, slapping her cheeks with her hands. "I'm not sure I can go out to eat with y'all!"

"Why not?" Betty Jo asked.

"I've invited Jenny and her sister to have supper with our whole family tonight," Layne said. "I know that Jenny was looking forward to her sister getting to know us. But with everything that's happened, I'm thinking maybe I should cancel."

"It's okay, Layne. Don't cancel," Dixie said. "It's important that you have this supper for your family. You don't need to worry about me. You go ahead and take care of your family."

"Thanks," Layne said as she hugged Dixie. "I need to get home and start cooking or I'll have a hungry family to contend with. I'll let y'all know how it goes."

Layne picked up her purse and started toward the door, but suddenly stopped, turned around, and with her head down walked back to the group. "I forgot," she said. "I don't have my car here. I need one of you to take me home."

They all laughed.

Jason felt as if he'd been beaten with a baseball bat, run over by a truck, and left to die. As he looked around at his hospital room, that's exactly what he wanted to do– die. He wondered why his mother had even bothered rushing in to save his life. If there was one thing he was sure of this very minute, it was that his life wasn't worth saving. He'd been living on borrowed time for years. Now, all he wanted was for his life to be over. He knew for certain that when his family learned about all he'd done to feed his addiction, they'd wish him dead as well.

Looking up at the IVs that were attached to his arm, pumping yet another drug into his worthless body, Jason made a decision he should have made years ago. His life needed to end. If he could turn the drip going in his arm into a stream, he would overdose. Then he could be at peace at last. He sat up to study the apparatus that was controlling his dosage of methadone to see how he could increase it when a pain shot through his body like a bolt of lightning, throwing him back against the bed.

Jason felt the air leave his lungs by the sudden force. He gasped for air, but try as he might he couldn't fill his lungs. It felt as if an enormous force was pushing down on his chest, crushing his heart and lungs. Jason was aware of the high pitch of an alarm sounding. He could hear hurried footsteps followed by concerned voices coming into his room and surrounding him. Panic and fear filled his mind.

Suddenly, Jason understood what was happening to him. This was how his life was going to end. He closed his eyes, welcoming the death he knew was coming. Slowly, the sounds in the room began to fade away as the panic and fear left him almost as quickly as they had come. Just as he was giving in to the sweet release of life leaving his body, an unexpected thought entered Jason's mind. He knew it was more than a mere thought; it was his heart's desire.

I want to live.

Jason knew it had been a very long time since his desire was to live—not to simply exist, not to die—but to live. He didn't know if it was too late for him, but he knew who held dominion over life and death and would listen to his plea.

Jason's thoughts screamed his prayer.

God, I beg you for my life.

Jason couldn't name the sensation that flooded over and through him. But he knew with all certainty in that instant that he would live. God was granting him life with peace, not the peace of a life without problems, but the peace that comes from the knowledge that God is ever present.

Jason took in the first breath of his renewed life.

Chapter Twenty-five

Aaron and Deputy Miles went straight to Mark's office. Before either had a chance to sit down, Mark said, "What do you have for me?"

Deputy Miles took his notebook out of his front pocket, referring to it as he reported the details to Mark. "Mr. Kwok's description of the truck he saw parked in the Tuckers' driveway last night corroborated Mrs. Coby's description. It appears they were loading the vehicles onto a white 2004-2005 Ford moving truck sans any distinguishable markings."

The deputy paused as he looked up from his notebook, allowing Mark a chance to make a comment. Mark motioned for him to continue. "A hat was discovered at the Coby house on the driveway. It could be one of the hats that Mrs. Coby described the perpetrators wearing."

"The hat 'could be'?" Mark leaned up to ask. "You don't know?"

Aaron spoke up. "It's a hat with an Apalachicola Florida Seafood Festival logo, but whether it belongs to the perpetrator or not hasn't been established."

Mark sat back. After a minute of considering the information he'd been given, he looked at Aaron and asked, "Is that all?"

"No," Aaron said, shaking his head, "that's not all."

He sat down across from his father. "Something occurred to me while we were at Mr. Kwok's house. I hadn't read any of the reports from the robberies last night, but when Mr. Kwok mentioned that it was the Tuckers across from his house who had been robbed, I realized he was talking about Betsy and Daniel Tucker."

Aaron paused to see if his father had made the same connection he'd made to those who'd been robbed. When he said nothing, Aaron continued, "I thought it was suspicious that two people who were robbed, or almost robbed, last night had been attending my engagement party. So I called dispatch to get the names of the other victims and found they'd all been at the party last night."

"All four of the owners who were robbed last night were at your party?" Mark asked in disbelief as he leaned over his desk to look directly at Aaron.

"All four," Aaron confirmed. "Which means that someone who had direct access to the guest list either set up the robberies himself or gave the names to the guilty party."

"That's the logical conclusion," Mark said. "It's highly improbable those places that were robbed last night could have been chosen at random."

"I'm going to find out who had access to the guest list," Aaron said as he got up to leave. "I'll let you know what I find out."

"I'll find out more about the hat," Deputy Miles said, following Aaron out the door.

After talking to Aaron and Deputy Miles, Mark was feeling optimistic that they were getting closer to putting an end to these robberies. He was about to call Layne to check on how Jason was doing when his office phone rang.

"Sheriff Weaver," Mark said into his phone.

"Sheriff Weaver?" the person on the other end asked.

Mark tried to keep the irritation he was feeling from his voice. "Speaking."

"This is Sheriff Denard up in Rabun County. I took a chance that I might catch you in on a Sunday afternoon." Sheriff Denard spoke with a slow Southern drawl.

Mark smiled, remembering Sheriff Denard from a conference he'd attended a few years ago. He remembered him as a man who closely resembled the stereotyped Southern "Good Ol' Boy" sheriff that many cartoonists drew. "What can I do for you, Sheriff Denard?" he asked.

"Well, I believe that I'm the one who can do a great deal for you, Sheriff Weaver," Sheriff Denard said with a short laugh.

Mark waited for the sheriff to continue.

"I seem to recall that you sent out a notice to be on the lookout for several stolen ATVs and such."

The sheriff had Mark's full attention. "Yes, sir, I did."

"Well, Sheriff, it appears that a few of those ATVs have made their way up here to Rabun County."

Mark had sent out the notice two weeks ago and had almost given up hope that any of the vehicles would be found. He'd assumed they'd been stripped down and sold for parts. He could hardly keep the excitement out of his voice as he asked, "One of the ATVs itself or parts from an ATV?"

"I'm standing here looking at three of those ATVs right now," Sheriff Denard said slowly.

Mark said with a chuckle, "Sheriff Denard, you have just made my day."

"Well, Sheriff, I believe I can make your week when I tell you that I have the gentleman along with a young lady in custody who happened to be delivering those vehicles to one of our less reputable business owners."

Mark was surprised to hear there was a woman who had been apprehended. This would be the biggest break yet in putting an end to this robbery spree that was terrorizing the town. "You have made my week, Sheriff. How did you catch them?"

"The two in custody made the mistaken assumption that we don't check expired license plates in Rabun County. We've also taken into custody the vehicle they were using to transport the ATVs."

"Is it by chance a white 2003 or 2004 Ford moving van?"

"Bingo!" Sheriff Denard exclaimed.

"Can you give me the names of the two you've taken into custody?" Mark took out his pen.

"Let me see here," the sheriff said. "We have a Jack Coley and an Angie McKelvey."

"Angie McKelvey?" The name sounded familiar to Mark, but he wasn't sure why.

"Yes, that's the name. Do you know her?"

Mark hesitated. "I'm not sure."

"I'll be sending some deputies up your way as soon as I can to take custody of the two you've got locked up as well as the truck," Mark said. "I can't thank you enough, Sheriff Denard."

"Glad I could help."

Mark smiled as he hung up the phone. He realized that it'd been a long time since he'd had this feeling that things were falling into place.

As soon as Nona dropped her off at her house, Layne was searching the freezer for the two pans of her special homemade lasagna that she was sure she'd put in there a couple of weeks ago. She always liked to have a couple frozen just in case she needed one to take to a friend or when the kids decided to come for supper. She hoped she hadn't already used one. She'd need both pans to feed everyone who was supposed to come for supper tonight. She breathed a sigh of relief when she found the two pans stacked on top of one another toward the back of the freezer.

Layne carried the pans into the house and turned on the oven to preheat. She checked the clock. She was going to have just enough time for the lasagna to cook. While the oven preheated, she looked in the refrigerator hoping she had the makings of a salad. Luckily, she had all she needed. As she put the lasagna in the oven to bake for ninety minutes, she realized she didn't have garlic bread. Who served lasagna without garlic bread?

Layne got her cell phone out of her purse to call Blair. If Blair didn't have garlic bread, at least she could pick it up on her way over. The phone went straight to voice mail. She decided not to leave a message. With all that Blair had gone through last night, Layne decided it was a bad idea to ask her to do anything extra. That left Nathan or Heather to get the bread. She decided to call Nathan's cell.

"Hi, Mom," Nathan said.

"I need garlic bread for tonight's supper. Do y'all have any there at the house?"

Layne thought the call might have been dropped since it was taking a long time for Nathan to answer her question. "Nathan?"

"Sorry, Mom," Nathan said, "I was thrown off by your question. I thought you were calling about Nana."

"Nana?"

"Yes, you do remember that she's at our house, don't you?"

Layne was speechless. How could she have forgotten that her mother was at Heather's house? She had told Heather she would be over there first thing this morning to get her, but with all that had happened it had slipped her mind.

"Oh, Nathan," Layne said, "I am so sorry. Has she driven y'all crazy?"

The relationship between Layne's mother and Heather hadn't always been the most pleasant. Layne's mother had reached the age where she said what was on her mind, and sometimes that came across as too brutally honest for Heather's sensitive nature. Which meant that Nathan had probably spent his day refereeing.

"No," Nathan said with a laugh, "it's actually been one of the best visits we've ever had with Nana. She and Grayson have had a great time together. I think this is the first time he's had Nana to himself without the other grandchildren."

Layne was relieved to hear this news. "Thank heavens. I can come get her right now if you want me to."

Nathan took a minute before answering. "No, we'd really like for her to stay. We'll bring her when we come for supper."

"Could you also bring some garlic bread?" Layne asked.

"Sure thing," Nathan said.

Will wonders never cease! Layne thought to herself as she hung up.

Finally, her mother got to have a good day with Nathan's family.

By the time Dixie and Alex had finished their supper with Nona, Monty, Betty Jo, and Don at the Rustic Bistro, she was exhausted. She was grateful to her friends for taking them to supper, but all she wanted to do now was go home, get her pajamas on, get into bed, and crawl under the covers. But, even though she wanted to fall into a deep sleep, she knew she'd never be able to sleep without first going back to the hospital to check on Jason. Doctor Kelly had strongly urged her to stay away as Jason began going through his medical detoxification. He warned her that it would be hard to stand by and watch her son go through what he described as agony. However, her instincts told her that she needed to be with him.

Dixie turned to Alex who was sitting beside her. "Alex, I want to go back to the hospital," she said in a soft voice.

Alex was talking with Monty about some work he needed to be done in his kitchen and hadn't heard her. He continued with his conversation.

Nona, who was sitting on the other side of Dixie, took hold of her hand and asked, "Are you sure?"

Dixie's eyes filled with tears. "Yes, I'm sure."

Gently squeezing Dixie's hand, Nona said, "I'll take you."

"Thank you."

Standing up, Dixie put her hand on Alex's shoulder and leaned down to kiss him. "Alex, I have to go to the hospital. I can't just leave him there alone."

"Oh, Dixie, I don't think you should."

"I know, but I have to."

Alex looked down at the floor. "I don't think I can."

"I know, and it's okay." Dixie kissed his cheek.

"I'll go with her," Nona said as she came up beside Dixie.

Betty Jo held out her keys. "Well, y'all can't leave me behind. I'll drive."

With Nona on one side of Dixie and Betty Jo on the other, the three of them left together.

It took Betty Jo less than ten minutes to get to the hospital. Dixie was surprised when she turned into the visitors' parking area. Looking over at Betty Jo, she said, "You don't need to park. You can just drop me off at the entrance."

"I'm not going to do any such thing," Betty Jo said as she pulled her car into an empty parking place.

"Did you really think we'd just drop you off and leave?" Nona asked.

Laughing, Dixie turned around in her seat to look at Nona. "Truthfully, I'm not sure what I was thinking. I just don't want y'all to be bored out of your minds sitting in the waiting room while I go up to see Jason. I could call Alex to come get me when I'm ready to go home."

"We're sitting and waiting for you," Nona said as she got out of the car.

Dixie turned to Betty Jo hoping she could convince her that the smart thing to do was to leave her, but found that Betty Jo was already out of the car. She hurried out of the car to catch up with the two of them. "Y'all are stubborn, you know that."

"And you wouldn't want us any other way," Betty Jo said as she put her arm in Dixie's.

"I guess not," Dixie admitted with a chuckle.

Dixie left Nona and Betty Jo at the front entrance as she headed to the elevators. She wasn't sure she was going to be allowed to see Jason, but in her heart, she knew she needed to try. She got off the elevator on Jason's floor and turned left to go to his room. She thought it was odd that there was no one at the nurses' station, then decided they were all busy with patients. She was heading towards Jason's room when she heard what sounded like an argument. As she got closer to the room, she realized that the commotion was coming from his room. Dixie slowly pushed open the door and peered in. Jason's face was red with anger. He was shouting at Jake, who was talking to him in a controlled voice trying to get him to calm down.

When Jason caught sight of Dixie standing in the door, he called out, "Mom, I've got to talk to him now! He needs to know this!"

Hurrying to his bedside, Dixie asked, "Who, Jason? Who do you need to talk to?"

"Mark! I have to tell Mark!"

Clearly exasperated, Jake looked at Dixie. "He's been saying over and over that he has to talk to Mark. But he won't tell me who this 'Mark' is."

Dixie could see how agitated Jason was at Jake for not understanding. Taking Jason's hand in hers, Dixie asked, "Do you want to talk to Mark Weaver?"

Grabbing her hands, Jason said with relief, "Yes."

"Okay," Dixie said, still holding onto Jason. "I'll get Mark."

In a weak voice, Jason said, "Thank you." He sank back onto his pillow and closed his eyes.

Turning to Jake, Dixie explained. "He wants to talk to Mark Weaver, the sheriff. He must have something important to tell him."

"I had no idea who he was talking about, and the more I questioned him, the more irritated with me he got." Jake sighed. "I feel bad that I didn't make the connection."

"You shouldn't feel bad about that. There was no way that you could have known that Mark, the sheriff, is one of our dearest friends."

"I'm just glad you showed up when you did and knew who it was he wanted me to call." Jake looked over at Jason. "You can see how much he's calmed down."

Dixie nodded her head as she crossed her arms in front of her. "I just wonder what he wants to talk to Mark about."

Chapter Twenty-six

Layne was just taking the lasagna out of the oven when her family began to arrive. Mark had called earlier to tell her they were making progress on the robbery investigation and he would be late, but assured her that he'd make sure Aaron left in plenty of time to pick up Jenny and Emma. Since Nathan, Blair, and Aaron had grown up with their father often late for supper, Layne knew this would be nothing out of the ordinary. Soon, the house was filled with the noise and love of a family coming together.

Layne was putting Nathan's garlic bread in the oven when Aaron came in the kitchen. She gave him a hug and said, "I really like Emma."

"Yeah, me too."

Layne could tell by the way Aaron was walking around the kitchen that he had something on his mind he wanted to talk to her about. Taking off her oven mitts, she sat down at the kitchen island and watched him pace for a few more minutes before she said, "Okay, that's enough. Out with it."

Aaron stopped his pacing and gave her one of his innocent looks. "What?" he asked.

"Come on," Layne said. "I can tell when something's bothering you. Go ahead and ask."

Aaron pulled out the bar stool next to hers and sat down. "I'm not sure this is the time to be talking about this, but something's come up in our investigation into this robbery spree that's bothering me. It turns out that the four people who were robbed last night, or almost robbed, were at the engagement party. Which makes me think that whoever is targeting the victims had access to the guest list or were actually at the party."

Layne put her hand to her throat. "You really think they're connected?"

Running his hand through his hair, he said, "It's just too much of a coincidence that all four victims last night were at the party."

Layne considered this for a minute. "So what is it you want from me?"

"The guest list."

Slapping him on the knee, she said with a smile, "That I can get for you."

Layne got up and went to her desk that Alex had built for her and that fit perfectly into the corner of her kitchen. She went through the papers that were stacked in a neat pile. When she found what she was looking for, she walked back to Aaron and handed it to him. "Here's the list of those we invited. Dixie will have an updated list of those who accepted or declined."

"Thanks, Mom," Aaron said, taking the list. "This will help."

"Glad I could help," Layne said.

Aaron gave her a kiss on the cheek. As he was walking out of the kitchen he said, "By the way, I think your bread is burning."

Layne looked over to see smoke coming out of the oven.

"Oh, no! Not again!" She grabbed her oven mitts. When she opened the oven door, the smoke set off the ear-piercing scream of the smoke alarm. She couldn't even begin to count the times in her life that she'd burned bread. It had been something that her kids had teased her about since they were toddlers when along with their father they would shout, "Mom's burned the bread again!" Many times she'd simply scrape off what she could of the burned part and serve the bread anyway. Unfortunately, this bread was too far gone to try that trick.

"Oh, Mom!" Blair said as she ran in the kitchen with Nathan, Heather, Jenny, and Emma close behind. "Don't tell me you burned the bread again!"

"I sure did," Layne said, exasperated with herself. She didn't know whether to laugh or cry. Seeing the looks on the faces around her she decided laughter was the way to go.

"I can't believe it!" Emma cried out, holding her stomach as she leaned over laughing.

"What?" Layne managed to ask between bouts of laughter.

"It's a sign!"

"Of what?"

Sitting down on one of the stools at the kitchen island, Emma took several deep breaths. Looking at Layne as she wiped away the tears of laughter running down her cheeks, she said, "That you're meant to be Jenny's other mother. Our mother burned the rolls, the biscuits, the corn bread. Any bread she put in the oven came out scorched or burned to a crisp."

"Oh, Emma," Layne said reaching out to hug her. "I've never been happier to have burned a pan of bread in my life!"

Mark decided it was too late in the day to send deputies up to Rabun County to collect the two Sheriff Denard had locked up and the truck that'd been impounded. It could wait until morning. Right now, all he wanted to do was go home to be with his family. He had just turned off his office lights and was locking the door when his office phone rang. If he'd left a minute earlier, he could have made it out and wouldn't have to deal with whoever was calling.

Taking a deep breath, he turned back around and picked up the receiver. "Sheriff Weaver."

"Mark, this is Dixie."

"Dixie," Mark said, "is everything alright?"

"As alright as it can be right now," Dixie said. "Mark, Jason insists that he needs to see you. He says he has something important he needs to tell you. Can you come to the hospital?"

"I'm on my way," he said as he hung up the phone.

As Mark drove to the hospital he wondered if Jason's insistence on seeing him had anything to do with his overdose or if it was something else. He was headed to the information desk to find Jason's room number when he heard someone call his name.

"Mark?"

Mark was surprised to see Betty Jo and Nona walking toward him from the waiting room.

Before he could say anything, Nona asked, "What are you doing here?"

"I got a call from Dixie that Jason wants to talk to me." Mark said.

"I'm sure you're anxious to get up there to hear what he has to say," Nona said. "He's in Room 257."

"Thanks."

It didn't take Mark long to get to the second-floor nurses' station. When he reached the door to Jason's room, he paused for a moment then knocked lightly on the door.

"Come in."

Mark took a deep breath as he pushed open the door. It took a minute for his eyes to adjust to the dim light of the room. He'd expected to see Dixie with Jason since she'd been the one to call, but he found Jason sitting up in bed, alone in the room.

"Thanks for coming, "Jason said in a low voice. "I asked Mom to call you because I have something I need to tell you and I didn't want to wait."

Mark sat down in the chair next to Jason's bed. "I'm listening."

"I've done some things in my life that I knew were wrong," Jason began, biting his lower lip, "but this is by far the worst. God's honest truth is that I never thought something like this could happen to me."

"What are you trying to tell me, Jason?"

"I'm a drug addict."

Jason lifted his head to look directly at Mark. "That's the first time I've ever said that out loud to anyone. I've been trying to hide my addiction for a long time. I'm finally ready to face the consequences of what my drug addiction has done to those who have loved me."

"I'm proud of you, Jason. I'm sure that was a hard thing for you to admit." Mark placed his hand on Jason's arm.

"I'm ready to pay the price for all I've done. I'm well aware that it's not going to be easy on me or my family." Jason paused before adding, "Or my friends.

He took a deep breath before continuing. "My drug dealer's name is Eddy." He leaned over to open the drawer of his bedside table. He took out a small sheet of paper and handed it to Mark. "I've written down his address for you. I've never asked him his last name, so I can't help you with that."

Mark took the paper from Jason. "The same Eddy I met last night at Aaron's party?"

"The very one."

Mark glared at Jason for a long minute. "I have to tell you, Jason, that I find it hard to believe you had the audacity to invite your drug dealer to Aaron's engagement party. I can't imagine what would have motivated you to make such an invitation."

"I could put the blame on someone else or give you excuses, but I know I was wrong to allow him to come. But none of that will change anything. I'm sorry for my poor judgment." Jason ran his fingers through his hair. "But I know that won't help much either. The truth of the matter is that I have a great deal to apologize for."

Mark said with a sigh, "I'm not the one you need to apologize to, Jason."

"Actually, you are," Jason said, turning back to Mark. "I did something else that I'm asking you to forgive." He took a deep breath. "I gave Eddy some names of people who were going to be at the party and away from their homes for the evening. It's Eddy's gang of thieves who've been stealing vehicles around Kerry."

In one swift move, Mark stood, kicking his chair across the room. He leaned over Jason until his face was only inches away. He punched his fists into Jason's pillow on either side of his head. With an anger that was rising from deep within, he said through clenched teeth, "You're telling me you purposefully had Blair's house targeted? How could you?"

"I don't know."

Mark had been fighting the strong urge to hit Jason, punch him right in the face. But now, as he stared down into Jason's eyes, he could see his regret along with something else he hadn't expected to see–shame.

"I'm sorry, Jason," Mark said softly as he sat down on the side of Jason's bed. "I was wrong to react like that. It's just, when I think of what you did that put Blair in danger…"

"You have nothing to apologize for. I'm the one in the wrong. I've wronged my family. I've wronged my friends."

Taking another deep breath before continuing, Jason said, "I've been on the wrong side of the law. That's why I asked for you to come see me tonight. I'm ready to face the consequences of all I've done wrong."

Mark stood up. When he'd entered Jason's room, he hadn't been sure if he was entering as a friend or the sheriff. Now he knew he'd entered as both. His first reaction had been that of a friend who'd been wronged. Now it was time for him to be the sheriff.

Looking down at Jason, both friend Mark and Sheriff Mark Weaver said, "I'll follow up on this address you've given me. I'll send a deputy over in a few days when your head is clearer to read you your rights and take your statement." Then patting Jason's shoulder, he added, "We'll go from there."

Mark turned away from Jason and walked out the door without looking back.

Mark was on the phone to Aaron as a soon as he left Jason's room, He was frustrated when his call went to voice mail. He left a brief message asking Aaron to call him as soon as possible. His mind was consumed with trying to process everything that Jason had just shared with him. He couldn't imagine what had motivated Jason to purposefully target Blair and Zeke's house. He couldn't keep the "what ifs" out of his mind about what could have happened to his only daughter last night all because of Jason. He knew he needed to let that go and concentrate on locking this Eddy guy up for a very long time.

"Mark, "Dixie said in surprise, "I thought you'd still be up with

Jason."

"We finished."

"And?"

Mark hadn't expected to see Dixie standing there when the elevator doors opened. Mark slowly shook his head. "I'm not going to tell you what Jason told me, Dixie. It's confidential. If he wants you to know, I'll leave it to him to tell you."

"Okay."

"See you later, then," Mark said as he walked away.

"Are you okay?" Nona asked as she came up behind Dixie.

Dixie turned at the sound of her voice. "I'm fine."

"Ready to go home?" Betty Jo asked.

"I am," Dixie declared. "Jason's in good hands. I need to trust the people in charge, and trust my son to stick with the program."

"So, you won't be coming back up to the hospital first thing in the morning to check on things?" Betty Jo asked.

Dixie sighed, "All I can say is that I'm going to try my very best to stay away and not hover over Jason."

Nona put her arm around Dixie and led her out of the hospital. "That's all you can do is try."

"Well, we're here to help anytime you need it," Betty Jo said taking Dixie's other arm.

"That's what I'm counting on," Dixie said.

<h1 style="text-align:center">Chapter Twenty-seven</h1>

Mark was on his way back to his office when Aaron returned his call. Mark quickly filled him in on all he'd learned through his conversations with Sheriff Denard and Jason.

"I've got a call in to Judge Evans for a search warrant for drugs, ATVs, golf carts, lawn mowers, and various motorized vehicles for the house and property located at the address Jason provided," Mark said.

"I want to be in on that search," Aaron said. "We're about finished with supper here at Mom's. I'll take Jenny and Emma home and be on my way."

"I'll meet you at my office," Mark said.

Mark had the warrant in hand before Aaron arrived. He had called in three of his deputies to help with the search. He'd also called in the Georgia State Patrol for backup. If everything worked out like he hoped it would, this could be the end the robbery spree in Kerry, Georgia. An added bonus would be putting another drug dealer out of business. It could very well be a winning night for the Kerry County Sheriff's Department.

Before strapping on his bulletproof vest, Mark gathered his law enforcement officers in the training room to review their plan.

"We've obtained reliable information that a man by the name of Eddy Ventors has been selling drugs from the address you were given. Ventors has also been named as a person of interest in our ongoing robbery investigation.

"We will take a silent approach to the property with lights off. We don't want to give them any warning that we're coming. The element of surprise should work best for us." Mark looked around the room. "Everyone clear?"

"Yes, sir," the officers responded.

"Let's get 'em!"

Mark rode with Aaron. They met up with two Georgia State Patrolmen a mile from their destination. Mark sent Aaron, along with the two patrolmen, to cover the side and back to catch anyone trying to escape. With warrant in hand, Mark and Deputy Snyder quietly walked up on the porch. With their hands on their guns, they took a stand on each side of the door. Mark pounded on the front door and yelled, "Kerry County Sheriff's Department! Open up!"

Mark listened for a response. When none came, he pounded harder and called out louder, "Kerry County Sheriff's Department! Open up!"

Mark heard shouting coming from the back of the house. Next, he heard Aaron shout over the radio, "Runners!"

Deputy Snyder nodded to the deputy with the battering ram to break down the door. When the door was torn from its frame, Mark and Deputy Synder went in the house with guns drawn. They were almost knocked down by two men who came barreling down the stairs at the front of the house.

Pointing his gun at the men, Deputy Synder yelled, "Freeze!"

Both men stopped. With his gun still pointed at the two men, the deputy ordered, "Kiss the floor, gentlemen!"

While Deputy Snyder zip-tied their hands behind their back, Mark and the two other deputies proceeded to clear the rooms. Although they didn't find anyone else in the house, they found a room filled with boxes of what he would later learn were various dosages of oxycodone, hydrocodone, morphine, and fentanyl. After clearing the house, Mark sent the two deputies out the back door to aid Aaron in his pursuit of the runners.

As Mark headed to the front room to help Deputy Synder, he radioed Aaron, "What's your status?"

"Two wrapped up on the ground," Aaron reported back. "You gotta see what's back here!"

Mark checked with Deputy Snyder to make sure he had everything under control before heading out back to meet up with Aaron. At first, he couldn't believe what he was seeing when the beam from his flashlight swept across the yard filled with ATVs, golf carts, and lawn mowers– many more than had been stolen from Kerry residents alone.

Mark was shaking his head as Aaron walked over to him. "I think we discovered the mother lode of missing off-road vehicles. We're going to need to call in reinforcements just to inventory all of it."

Mark smiled.

As Betty Jo turned into her driveway, Dixie could see that Alex had all the lights outside and inside turned on. She took it as a welcoming sign. She'd always hated to come home to a dark house.

"Do you want me to walk you to the house?" Nona asked from the front seat as Dixie got out.

"I think I can make it," Dixie said with a smile. As she closed the car door, she added, "Thank you both for all you've done for us today."

Betty Jo and Nona waved as they drove out of the driveway.

Dixie looked up at the house as memories of the events from that morning came flooding back to her. It seemed like it had been days ago since she'd found Jason on the bathroom floor. She didn't know if she'd ever be able to walk in that bathroom ever again. She wondered if she could talk Alex and Josh into doing a complete remodel on it. She slowly started walking toward the house, when she caught sight of Alex standing in the door waiting for her.

"Dixie? Everything alright?" he called out.

"Fine," Dixie said with a wave of her hand.

When she reached the door, Alex took her in his arms. Dixie had thought she was doing fine until that moment, when all her emotions came pouring out of her. Alex held her, gently rocking her back and forth as she wept.

When Dixie's tears stopped, Alex helped her to the sofa where they sat huddled together.

Dixie sniffed. "Oh, Alex, how do we get through this?"

Resting his chin on her head, Alex said, "I've been thinking about that all evening, Dixie, and I think I know what we have to do."

Dixie pushed away and looked up at him. "You do?"

Pulling her back into his arms, Alex said, "This drug addiction thing is much bigger than you and me."

Dixie nodded in agreement.

"We have to turn it over to the Big Man."

"'The Big Man'?"

"You know, God."

Alex had never been one to talk about God. Dixie knew her husband had a deep faith in God, but he'd never been comfortable talking about his beliefs. It had never been easy for him to share or witness about his faith, not even to her or their children. She knew it had taken tremendous courage for him to say what he'd just said to her.

Dixie gave him a squeeze. "You're so right. I know that's what we need to do. But the problem I always seem to have is that when I turn something over to God, I find myself taking it back again."

Alex kissed her forehead. "That's where prayer and trust come in. Together, I think we can do this."

In all their years of married life, they had never prayed together for anything except to bless their food before a meal. Would he truly be willing to pray with her now? Dixie pulled away from Alex and sat up to look into his eyes. She wanted to see the truth in his eyes when she asked her question. "Are you saying that you truly want us to pray together?"

Alex didn't hesitate. "I do, and I think we should start right now."

Taking Dixie's hands in his, Alex bowed his head. "Holy Father, we thank you for the blessing of our son's life. We thank you for giving Jason a second chance for a better life free of addiction. We ask for Your guidance in how both his mother and I can help him overcome his dependence on drugs. We place our son into Your loving care. Amen."

"Amen."

Raising her head, Dixie kissed Alex on the cheek. "Thank you. That was the perfect prayer," she said.

Alex stretched out his arms and yawned. "I don't know about you, but I'm so bone tired I can barely keep my eyes open."

"I'm right with you." Dixie yawned in agreement. "I think we both need a good night's sleep, and now that we've put Jason in God's hands, maybe we can get it."

"You go on to bed," Alex said, turning away from Dixie. "I'll get the lights and make sure the doors are locked."

After changing into her pajamas and completing her nightly routine, Dixie dropped down on her bed. Putting her head in her hands, her thoughts turned to the wide range of emotions she'd experienced since leaving her bed that morning. She remembered the death of her parents and Scarlett as the worst days of her life, but they wouldn't have compared to how horrible a day it would have been if she'd lost her own child. She shuddered as the thought crossed her mind that this day could have been Jason's last.

Dixie knew it wouldn't do her or Jason any good to dwell on what could have been. Instead, she resolved to keep her mind on the blessing from God that Jason had been given another chance at life. As she pulled back the covers and got into bed, she realized that for the first time since she'd found Jason on the bathroom floor, she was feeling hopeful. She closed her eyes and was soon sound asleep.

Nona had Betty Jo drop her off at the front door instead of making her drive all the way around to the back door. As she looked up at her father's house—now her house as well—she noticed that a lamp in the front living room had been left on. She wondered if Miss Althea had left it on for her so she wouldn't have to enter a dark house. She'd called

Miss Althea earlier when she realized she'd be late getting home to arrange for her to stay the night so her father wouldn't be left alone.

Nona unlocked the front door and walked into the dimly lit living room. As she was returning her keys to her purse, she jumped at the sound of her name.

"Nona."

"Daddy!" Putting her hand to her heart, Nona said, "You scared me to death!" She could see her father more clearly now in his pajamas, slippers, and robe.

"I didn't mean to scare you." Her father chuckled. "I thought you'd see me sitting here when you came in the door. That's why I sat in the chair by the lamp."

"I guess I'm not as observant as I should be," Nona said as she took the chair next to her father's. "What are you doing up this late?"

He gave her a questioning look. "Where else would I be when my little girl is out late at night?"

"Oh, Daddy," Nona said. "I'm not such a little girl anymore, and you don't need to wait up for me."

She looked closer at her father. Was he living in the past or was he here with her in the present?

She breathed a sigh of relief when he said, "I know, but sometimes a father enjoys waiting up for his daughter who believes she is grown."

"Well, I'm glad you did, "Nona said, getting up from her chair, "but it's late, and I think we both need to get to bed."

"Would you do me the favor of sitting with me for a bit?" He patted her chair. "I've got something I want to talk to you about."

Nona did as her father asked and sat back down, wondering what could be so important it couldn't wait until morning.

"I don't want you to be upset by what I have to tell you," her father began. "Bill stopped by this evening to tell me he's leaving town."

Even the sound of Bill's name filled Nona with trepidation. Trying to remain calm, she said with only the slightest hint of irritation in her voice, "I knew he was leaving town to go to Grace's big event."

"There's something else." Reaching out to take Nona's hand in his, her father continued his explanation, "Bill is moving. He's accepted a part-time position as an instructor of finance at Georgia State. He's sold his house and is taking up residence in some upscale apartment complex in Atlanta."

Nona was stunned. She wasn't exactly sure how to process the information her father had just given her. A part of her wanted to jump up and down with joy, but another part of her felt sad, although she wasn't quite sure why. After a bit more consideration, she decided that for now, she was going to take this as good news.

"Good for Bill," she said. "Now, can we go to bed?"

Chapter Twenty-eight

*D*ixie woke Monday morning to the sound of rain pounding on her window. She leaned up on her elbow to check the time on her alarm clock and was surprised to see that it was a little after nine. She couldn't remember the last time she'd slept this late. Even more surprising to her was how well she'd slept, without any disturbing dreams, even after the day she'd had. She wondered what Jason's night had been like.

Concerns for her son filled her mind. *Had he slept? Had he been sick? Was he hurting? Had he asked for her?* When she'd talked to him last night, he'd made it clear that she should stay away while he was going through detoxification. It made sense to her mind that he had to go through this on his own, but not to her heart.

Dixie knew it would be a long day ahead of her if she allowed her mind to be filled with worries about Jason. She decided the best thing she could do for herself was to get up out of bed and get busy. She got up, showered, and dressed. When she opened her bedroom door, she caught a whiff of bacon. She hurried down the hall wondering who could be in her kitchen frying bacon.

She found Alex standing at the stove with a towel slung over his shoulder. Smiling, he greeted Dixie as she entered the kitchen. "Good morning. I was beginning to wonder if you were going to sleep all day. How about some breakfast?"

"Alex?"

Dixie stared at her husband in disbelief. In all their years of marriage, Dixie couldn't recall a time when she'd found him standing at the stove frying bacon or anything other than blueberry pancakes.

"How do you want your eggs?" Alex asked as if he fixed her eggs every morning.

Dixie walked over to the stove wanting to see for herself that Alex was actually frying bacon. She put her hand on his shoulder. "Alex, are you seriously fixing breakfast for me?"

"Yes, ma'am," Alex said, leaning over to give her a kiss on the top of her head.

Dixie threw up her hands and backed away. "What's really happening here? First you want to pray together, and now you're fixing breakfast for me. Are you really my husband?"

Taking the frying pan off the burner and wiping his hands on the towel, Alex slowly turned to Dixie. "To tell you the truth, Dixie, I'm not sure I am the same man I was before yesterday morning."

"What do you mean?"

"I think what I saw happen with you and Jason has opened my eyes to how precious our lives together are."

Alex paused a moment, collecting his thoughts. Dixie waited for him to continue.

"I've taken so much for granted, and I don't want to do that anymore. I want to show you how much I love you."

Dixie went to Alex and wrapped her arms around his waist. "I know you love me, Alex." Looking up into his face, she said, I love you too."

They held one another for several minutes until Alex broke the silence with a question. "Would you teach me how to fry an egg?"

"You betcha!" Dixie said with a laugh.

They laughed and talked as they prepared and ate their breakfast together.

As they sat at the kitchen island drinking their second cup of coffee,

Dixie asked, "What are your plans for the day?"

Alex set down his coffee cup and looked at Dixie thoughtfully. "I know this is going to be a hard day for you and you're going to be worrying about Jason all day. So, I was thinking that maybe we'd get out of the house and maybe even head over to Savannah to see a movie or something."

"You're going to spend the day with me instead of going to work?" Dixie asked doubtfully. She couldn't remember the last time the two of them had spent a weekday together.

"I'm sure they can get along without me at work for one day."

By eleven they were in the car headed to Savannah for a day together.

Dixie opened her eyes and glanced around the room. For a minute, she couldn't think where she was. When she heard Alex's snoring beside her, she remembered that she'd spent the night in his bedroom. She wasn't sure what time it was, but knew it was early. She thought about going back to sleep, but knew she wouldn't be able to with his snoring. She didn't want to wake Alex, so as quietly as she could, she slowly got out of his bed and tiptoed out of the room.

Dixie tried going back to sleep in her room, but it wasn't working. Instead of wasting her time tossing and turning, she decided a cup of coffee was what she needed. She put on her jogging pants and sweatshirt and slippers before heading down to hall to the kitchen. As she waited for the coffeemaker to fill her cup, she noticed the sun was just peeking over the horizon. It looked like today would be one filled with sunshine, a welcome change from the dreary weather of the day before.

Despite Monday's rainy and gloomy weather, Dixie had to admit that it had been a good day. Alex had spent the day with her as promised. He'd even taken her to a movie. It'd been years since they'd gone to a movie theater together. Alex had done his best to keep her mind from what Jason was going through. Even though she pretended for his sake that it was working, she'd managed to check in with Jake to see how Jason was doing. She knew Jake was trying his best to be positive, but she could tell that things were not going well for her son. Jake kept telling her that it had to get worse before it could get better, but that was little comfort to her.

Once again, worried thoughts about Jason began to fill Dixie's mind. *Will he be able to beat his drug addiction? What will we do if he can't? What will we do if he starts taking drugs again? What if he overdoses again? Will he serve time in jail for the information he gave Eddy?*

Dixie knew that she and Alex had put Jason in God's hands. Why was it that she was finding it hard to completely trust God? Why did she keep taking him out of God's hands and putting him back into hers?

With coffee-filled cup in hand, Dixie opened the back door to get a better look at the sunrise. She decided the best view would be from the patio table beside the pool. The rain from the day before had made the air crisp and clean. She breathed in deeply as she sat down.

As Dixie watched the sun slowly rise higher in the sky, she noticed how beautiful the flowers she'd planted along the edge of the patio were. *They don't worry or fret.*

As a child, Dixie had memorized verses with God's promises from the Bible. Brother Richard called them "Heart Verses." One sprang to her mind now.

Peace I leave with you; my peace I give you. I do not give to you as the world gives. Do not let your hearts be troubled and do not be afraid. John 14:27

Dixie knew beyond a shadow of a doubt that God had sent that verse to her mind. Was God sending her a message telling her to stop worrying, to be at peace? She stood up and walked to the edge of the patio to look at her flowers– petunias, geraniums, begonias, dahlias.

She stopped when she noticed a flower that should not be growing in the heat of the Georgia summer. It was a flower that grew in the sweet coolness of spring, yet there it was, standing tall, waving in the soft breeze like a blue flag. Tears began to fill her eyes as she bent down to take a closer look. God had sent her a blue iris, the symbol of peace.

As Dixie looked from the iris to the rising sun, she felt at peace. She knew her problems and Jason's problems hadn't magically disappeared, but she knew without a doubt that God was with her, always. With that knowledge, she could face anything. She stayed on the patio until the sun had risen high in the sky.

Three Weeks Later

Dixie hurried up the back stairs of the Dream Bean Coffee Shop to the Skinny Dippers_meeting. She hated that she was running late, but she had a good reason for her tardiness. She'd gone by the NextStep Center on the way to her meeting to drop off the art supplies Jason had requested through his counselor. Jason was moving from phase one in his drug rehabilitation to phase two, which meant he could begin a hobby. He'd decided to rekindle his artistic talents. He still wasn't allowed visitors, but hopefully that would happen in a few weeks when he moved on to phase three. Dixie was hopeful that he'd continue to move forward with his rehabilitation and not backslide.

Doreen was wrapping up of one of her semi-motivational talks when Dixie entered the room. She'd decided to skip the weigh-in today since she was pretty sure she'd gained a pound or two. Lately, she'd been "cooking up a storm" as Hailey called it. Dixie was well aware that along with "cooking up a storm," she'd also been "eating up a storm."

Layne motioned for Dixie to come sit beside her. Dixie carefully made her way to take the seat between Layne and Betty Jo. She was surprised to see Nona sitting on the other side of Layne. Nona was rarely on time to these meetings.

As soon as the meeting was over, the four of them went back down the stairs to the Dream Bean. They sat down in their regular booth, and when Alice came up to get their order, they gave her their regular order.

As soon as Alice left Nona asked, "Did y'all see this morning's headline?" Taking the *Kerry Dispatch and News* from her bag and putting on her glasses, she read, "Sheriff Breaks Up Ring of Thieves."

Looking over her glasses at Layne, Nona dramatically announced, "Looks like we have the wife of a celebrity with us today!"

Betty Jo and Dixie began to clap.

"Thank you," Layne said with a laugh, "but none of it would have been possible without Jason's help."

"Helping catch the 'ring of thieves' was just a lucky happenstance," Dixie corrected Layne. "I believe Jason's assistance was with the drug bust that was the headline two days ago."

Turning serious, Layne asked, "How's Jason doing?"

"I'm happy to announce that Jason's moved from phase one to phase two in his rehabilitation, which is progress."

"That's great news," Layne said.

"Well, it's all thanks to Mark and Nathan that he's even in rehabilitation at the NextStep Center," Dixie said. "If they hadn't convinced District Attorney Menard to let him turn state's evidence and allow him to serve his time there instead of jail, there's no telling how he would be right now."

"I'm just glad everything has worked out as well as it has," Layne said.

"Well, I've got more news," Nona said.

The three of them looked to Nona, waiting for her to continue.

Smiling, Nona said, "William Robert Harris is no longer a resident of Kerry, Georgia."

"Good riddance!" Betty Jo said with relief.

"When did this happen?" Layne asked.

Nona thought for a minute. "If my information is reliable, it happened this past Saturday."

"And where is your information coming from?" Dixie asked.

"Mr. Michael Montgomery," Nona announced.

"Monty!" All three cried out together.

Nona said with a sly grin, "It turns out Monty has been keeping an eye on Bill since that day I found him at Dad's house."

"I'm glad to know that," Betty Jo said. "It shows he really cares about you."

They stopped talking as Alice brought their order to the table.

After taking a sip of her coffee, Betty Jo said, "I haven't had the opportunity to tell y'all my good news." She set her cup on the table. "It looks like Ethan and his family will be back in Georgia by the end of the summer."

"Oh, that is good news," Dixie said.

"I know you're excited about that," Nona said, smiling at Betty Jo.

"I am. I'll have a chance to really get to know Kelli, Matthew, and little Chase."

"Grandchildren are such a joy," Dixie said.

"Yes," Layne agreed, "but the best part is that when they're misbehaving or driving you crazy, you can send them home to their parents."

They all laughed.

"I wonder if I'll ever have any grandchildren," Nona sighed, "or if I do, will Grace ever let me be a part of their lives."

"Oh, Nona," Dixie said, shaking her head, "that would be a nightmare to not know your grandchildren."

Nona looked at Dixie. "Speaking of nightmares. Have you had any lately?"

"Funny you should ask," Dixie said with a nervous laugh. "I haven't had any 'nightmares' lately, but I did have an unusual dream a couple of nights ago. But…I don't know if I can even tell y'all about it. It was so corny."

"Come on," Betty Jo said, "we want to hear it."

Layne piped up, "You know how much we like corny."

Smiling at her friends, Dixie said, "Okay, you asked for it. Y'all remember how I told you about that Bible verse coming to me and the iris appearing?"

The other three nodded at her.

Dixie looked down at the table as she began to recall the details of her dream. "In my dream, I was standing at the back of our church's chapel. It was filled with people from my past and present. Suddenly, I heard a voice singing softly. I couldn't quite make out the words, so I began walking down the center aisle, searching for where the singing was coming from. As I got closer to the front of the chapel, I could see a young boy standing in the choir loft singing. The boy smiled down at me as he motioned for me to come closer. The closer I got to him, the more I understood the words of his song. The boy reached out his hand to me. When I took his hand, the words he'd been singing became clear in my mind.

When peace like a river attendeth my way.

When sorrows like sea billows roll.

Whatever my lot, thou hast taught me to say,

'It is well. It is well, with my soul.'

"When I turned around to look back at everyone sitting in the chapel, I found that it was no longer a chapel filled with people. Now it was a garden filled with irises waving back and forth like flags caught up in a soft breeze."

Dixie paused. "That, my friends, was my dream." She chuckled. "I told you it was corny."

No one spoke for several minutes.

"Oh, Dixie," Layne said, wiping her eyes, "that was anything but corny. I felt like I was right there with you when you turned around and saw those irises."

In a voice filled with emotion, Betty Jo said, "That was a dream sent from God, Dixie."

"God wants you to be at peace," Nona said as she put her hand over Dixie's.

Betty Jo and Layne put their hands on top of Nona's. "And so do we."

Smiling at her friends, Dixie put her other hand on top of theirs, knowing without a doubt that her life was one truly blessed with God's peace.

About the Author

Carol Cannon lives near the small town of Hawkinsville, Georgia, with her husband David in the log home that they, along with their three children, built. She is a member of the Hawkinsville First Methodist Church where she teaches Sunday School, sings in the choir, and directs the children's choir. She was a teacher for thirty years in nearby Perry, Georgia. Once she retired from teaching, she took up her lifelong dream of becoming an author.

Since the three most important factors in Carol's life have been God, family, and friends, it was only fitting that those would be the subjects she would choose to write about. Her first series of books is about four vibrant, retired, Southern women–Layne, Nona, Dixie, and Betty Jo– who have been friends for more years than they can remember. Their friendship, along with their faith in God, gives them the strength and courage they need to make it through life's trials.

Peace is Carol's third book in her Kerry Series. She released her first book in the series, ***Forgiveness***. Then followed with second book, ***Hope***. A fourth book, ***Joy***, will complete the series.

Carol's books are available for purchase through Christian bookstores and online as an eBook or paperback. Carol would appreciate an honest review of this book